Unmasked

The Revealed Series – Book 1

Alice Raine

Published by Accent Press Ltd 2015

ISBN 9781786150974

Acknowledgements

I'd like to dedicate this new series to all the readers out there – without you this journey that I have been on simply would not have happened. The response I have had to my first series, The Untwisted Series, has been completely overwhelming, so thank you all for reading, reviewing, getting in touch and supporting me.

Huge thanks also, and always, to Accent Press, my fabulous publishers and all the staff who work there, in particular Alexandra Davies, my ever patient editor, and Hazel Cushion, Stephanie Williams and Beth Jones who work tirelessly to get my books put together, marketed and noticed.

As part of the planning process for this book I decided to invite my Facebook followers to help pick one of the character names, it was a great way to interact with readers, and made for a very fun few days. In the end the name Caitlin was chosen, and was picked by the following readers: Alison Carroll, Debbie Battley, Meghan Hurley and Clare Grant, so thanks for reading, girls, and for taking part in the competition.

I shall leave you now to venture into this new world that I have created, I hope you enjoy this second series as much as I have enjoyed writing it.

Alice x

Chapter One

Allie
One week before Christmas

Sarah owed me for this. *Big time.* I still couldn't flipping believe I was driving out here in the countryside, way up into the hills, when the weather looked as menacing as it did. It might only be two in the afternoon, but the thick, grey clouds that scudded in several hours ago had progressively thickened, and now the sky had darkened to the point where I had my headlights on and it was definitely threatening to rain … or snow, if my car thermometer was any indicator. I was no meteorologist, but even I knew that it would only take another degree drop to become perfect snow weather. I sighed heavily, now seriously regretting answering my friend's call this morning.

All this just a week before Christmas, too, I thought miserably. Shaking my head, my gloved hands clutched the steering wheel tighter in irritation, the shiny wool sliding annoyingly over the plastic wheel and only serving to up my agitation levels. I should be doing my last-minute present shopping, or sharing a mulled wine at the Christmas market now, not covering a cleaning shift for Sarah at some godforsaken house in the middle of godforsaken nowhere.

To be honest, the only reason I *was* doing this at all was because Sarah was one of my best friends, and I knew how desperate she was for her new business not to flop right from the outset. What with walking out of her last job after she was repeatedly hit on by her sleazy boss – who she later found out was not only a slime ball, but a *married* slime ball – then recently setting herself up as an independent housekeeper to support herself and her three-year-old son, Scott, I knew she needed every penny she could get. She certainly couldn't afford to lose her newest cleaning job for missing a shift, and having personally witnessed the blotchy, snot-covered state of her face this morning, I could vouch that she was in no state to be working.

So here I was. Allie Shaw to the rescue. Wrapped up in a cocoon of scarves, hats, and gloves and driving to the arse end of nowhere to cover a three-hour cleaning shift. Add to that the fact it was bloody freezing and I really did look like a prize idiot. Huffing out a moody breath at my stupidity I cranked the heater up until it started to groan its complaint, suddenly whining and sounding decidedly like it was going to die at any moment. Wincing at the high-pitched noise coming from the vents, I turned it down a fraction and sent a silent prayer for its survival to whoever might be listening. Today was maddening enough as it was – I didn't need to add "freezing my arse off in my icebox of a car" to my list of complaints.

The heater in the car blew my long hair all over the place until I was actually struggling to see through the swirling mass of blonde strands. Cursing under my breath, I haphazardly tried to brush it out of my eyes while still keeping my gaze on the road and one gloved hand on the wheel. Which was actually a lot harder than it sounds, because my gloves had no grip at all, and on top of that, I'd been neglecting to get my hair cut, so it was far longer than usual and seemed to have a mind of its own today. It was *too* long, according to my nagging mother, who for some reason thinks that anyone over the age of twenty shouldn't have hair below their shoulders. God only knows her logic behind that thought.

Glancing in the rear-view mirror to check the traffic, I saw my dishevelled reflection and rolled my eyes with an accepting sigh. I looked like I'd been dragged through a hedge backwards, sideways, *and* upside down. My wayward hair resembled an aged scarecrow, and my cheeks were ruddy and flushed from the buffeting warmth of the heater, making me look half drunk. All in all, it wasn't the best look I've ever rocked.

Heaving out a huge breath I checked the sky with a squint and frowned. If possible, it looked even greyer and more ominous than it had five minutes ago – definitely not a good sign.

As my satnav barked an order to turn off onto a small lane, I slowed to navigate the narrower road and thought back to what Sarah had told me about the job. Apparently the client was working away at the moment and was due back on Christmas Eve. He'd requested a clean of the house and for some food to be prepared and left in the freezer, which sounded simple enough. To be honest, just the thought of it made me nervous – I was a school teacher, for goodness sake. I kept my flat tidy and cooked passable meals, but I wasn't sure I was up to Sarah's standards, and was mostly just hoping that I could blag my way into convincing the client that their house had been cleaned by a professional. The client's only stipulation was that there was to be no turkey in the food. Perhaps he was a Christmas hater, I thought with a smirk. Bah, humbug to that!

It had all sounded relatively easy when Sarah had begged me between thick, wet coughs this morning, but that was before the weather had changed for the worse. Oh well. My satnav showed me I was just two miles away, so I'd get in, whip round with the hoover, make a pasta dish and a casserole, and get the hell out of there before the weather really set in.

Finally pulling up to the property, I sat in my car for several seconds, gazing in open-mouthed wonder at the gigantic house that lay behind the metal gates in front of me. It was enormous, basically a mansion, and beautiful, with wooden shutters on the windows, weather-softened grey bricks, and ivy-covered columns by the front door. After a second or two, my wonderment was ceased rather abruptly by the horrible realisation that my idea of a 'quick hoover' might take a little longer than I first anticipated. *Bugger it.* Grimacing at the gargantuan task waiting for me, I used the code Sarah had scrawled on a piece of paper to activate the front security gate, then pulled up the curved gravel driveway and to the impressive looking double doors.

It seemed a bit of a crime to park my decrepit Fiat Punto outside such a beautiful house – a Ferrari would have been more appropriate, but also rather outside of my price range. Sarah had told me that the owner was quite fussy about his house and grounds, and liked everyone to use the allocated parking bays to the side of the drive, but after a brief glance at the four neatly marked tarmac spaces, I rebelliously ignored them and pulled onto the gravel right outside the front doors. Well, the owner was away, so no-one would know that I'd broken his silly rule, and if it saved me thirty seconds of being out in this freezing weather then it was worth it.

Before I exited the car I sorted through the big bunch of keys Sarah had given me to find the one with an elastic band around it. This was the key for the front door, and the elastic band was Sarah's low-cost method of distinguishing it from the multitude of other keys. I couldn't possibly imagine how one house could require so many different locks, or understand why Sarah would need a copy of all of the keys, but I certainly felt quite like a prison guard with this handful. Finally armed with my entry method, I switched off my ignition, leapt out of the car and into the seemingly sub-zero weather, and dashed toward the house praying that the heating was on.

Mercifully, as I burst through the door and into the hallway, it was decidedly warmer inside than out. Thank goodness for that. Closing the door with a relieved breath, I leant back on it and raised my eyebrows in appreciation. This place was gorgeous. For some reason I had expected modern fixtures and fittings – perhaps because Sarah had said the owner was fussy about his property – but instead it was a perfect country house, complete with beautiful wooden floors, a curved staircase, mismatched (but lovely) furniture, and soft rugs as far as the eye could see. I loved it immediately.

Sarah hadn't mentioned the client's name when I'd gone to get the keys from her this morning, she'd just referred to him as 'he', but as I pushed off the door and began to walk through the beautiful space I found myself wondering about what type of person – or people – might live here. Just because Sarah said 'he' didn't necessarily mean that he lived alone, did it? It might just mean that she only dealt with the man of the house. Was he single or married? Young or old? One thing was abundantly clear though – the owner clearly wasn't short of a few quid.

Glancing around again, I decided on an older male, probably a little overweight and living alone, because although the house was incredibly cosy considering its vast size, there weren't many mementos or personal touches like photographs. There was, however, a floor to ceiling wine rack, full to the brim with excess bottles sitting by the side of it. The owner obviously liked a drink, hence my guess at the slightly overweight part.

I'm not a snooper as such, but if it hadn't been threatening to snow I would certainly have been tempted to poke about a little and play my own version of *Through the Keyhole*. As it looked like I might be on a deadline, though, I shelved my curiosity and decided to try to save time by putting the pasta on to cook while I hoovered.

Guessing that the kitchen would be at the end of the hallway, I proved myself right when I found myself coming to a standstill as I crossed the threshold into the vast space. Wow. This kitchen was *a-maz-ing*. Completely different from the traditional entrance hallway, it was a modern example of glass, marble, and sparkling steel. Spanning the entire back of the house it was completely immaculate and fitted with some impressive floor to ceiling windows which looked out onto a wooden deck, huge, neat lawn that stretched into a seemingly endless forest beyond.

The marble surfaces were mostly clear, but a gleaming pasta machine, bread maker, and fancy juicer caught my eye in one corner. My eyebrows rose at the high-tech gadgets – these people liked to cook as well as drink. My gaze was drawn to a coffee machine like no other. At least I think it was a coffee maker. With all its dials, knobs, and handles it looked more like a spaceship, but the familiar bag of beans sat on the top seemed to confirm my speculation. The house owners were people after my own heart, because I absolutely *loved* a good cup of coffee.

As tempted as I was to linger and enviously admire the various gadgets lying around, I cast another worried glance out of the window and saw the clouds were now even lower, a sight that soon had me searching to find the food cupboards.

To my surprise, the cupboards were full, indicating that somebody had shopped this week – maybe these people had a housekeeper as well as a cleaner. How very upper-class – because the fridge was also full of fresh food. Grabbing a large knife, I set about quickly and haphazardly chopping some vegetables I found to make a casserole, hoping that the client wasn't as picky about the size of his vegetable dice as he was about his parking arrangements.

As the pasta was also cooking, I hastily went in search of the cleaning cupboard Sarah had said was located under the stairs. Dragging a high-tech Dyson from the cupboard, I turned my iPod on and set about hoovering the luxuriously furnished lounge.

With Mika blaring in my headphones and me tunelessly singing along, the time started to pass quite quickly and I began to meticulously work my way from one end to the other. The owners of this place really did have remarkable taste, because this room was once again different from the previous two, somehow managing to effortlessly combine traditional features like the stunning inglenook fireplace with a modern flat screen television, curved leather sofa, and an enormous DVD rack. From the vast array of movies on the shelves, they clearly liked to watch films, and did so in considerable comfort. The couch curved elegantly across the room, ending at a well-stocked drinks cabinet topped with a selection of sparkling glasses, decanters, and even a bowl full of packaged snacks. Pursing my lips appreciatively, I nodded my approval. Mind you, there wasn't really anything *not* to like. How the other half lived, I thought with a wry smile.

I was midway through my mammoth vacuuming session and singing along with Mika when the hoover suddenly cut off. Assuming I had pulled the cable from the wall in my exuberance, I spun around to remedy it before letting out an ear-piercing shriek and leaping backwards, clutching at my chest as my heart suddenly beat frantically against my ribs.

The hoover hadn't pulled itself from the wall. No, as I followed the trail of the cable it led me instead to the hand of a very large man, his arms folded and an incredibly angry expression on his face. Swallowing loudly, I briefly scrunched my eyes closed to make sure I wasn't imagining him, but he was still there when I opened them again. And from the deep frown on his brow, he was still angry. Even through the shock of his sudden appearance, this man was undeniably handsome; a shock of dark hair sat in a ruffled mess on his head, his jaw was defined and lightly stubbled, his lips were drawn into a tight line of disapproval but were infinitely tempting, and his dark eyes, although irate, seemed to somehow draw me in to the point where I felt the urge to step closer. Thankfully, I didn't, instead forcefully making my legs stay still.

On top of all of that, it suddenly permeated my consciousness that he was only semi-clothed. He was wearing nothing but a pair of navy pyjama bottoms. Jesus. My eyes flicked over his body and I think my heart stopped for a few seconds before taking off again at such a rate that it was now booming in my chest like some badly played bongo drums.

Crikey, what a sight – so good, in fact, that it really should be illegal. His legs were long, the thin cotton clinging to muscles hidden beneath, and the waistband hanging deliciously low on his hips, so it exposed a 'v' of muscles that led to goodness knows what splendidness below. Everything looked narrow and tight and … well, inspiring all sorts of delicious thrusting naughtiness to spring to mind.

He was, quite simply, glorious.

My mouth suddenly felt as parched as a dry riverbed. Licking my lips, my eyes lingered on his well-muscled abdomen far longer than necessary, but I couldn't seem to pull my gaze away as I gulped desperately and absently reached to tug my earbuds out. I didn't even know him, but the urge to step forwards and run my tongue up the centre of his chest was almost overpowering.

His appearance had definitely sent me into an instant tail spin, there was no doubt about that.

'You're not Sarah,' the man stated grouchily, completely bursting my lovely erotic bubble of pleasurable chest licking and hip thrusting. Of all the words I'd briefly imagined coming from his beautiful lips, those were not the ones I'd hoped for. Although exactly what I *had* hoped for, I wasn't sure – his mere presence seemed to have completely thrown me. His bluntness, however, did bring me somewhat back to earth and raised my hackles, so instead of asking the obvious question of who he was – the house owner, I hoped – I instead opted for a sarcastic response.

'Good observation. You must be a genius,' I said dryly, rather glad that I didn't sound as shaken as I felt. God, my heart was pounding so hard that I could feel my ribs vibrating. My reply caused his dark eyes to narrow in annoyance as he began to roll his lovely lips until they formed a tight line of disapproval. Hmm … there was something about that intense, broody look that made my knees feel a little weaker, and to my surprise I felt a low ache of arousal settle in my belly.

Crikey. This was all very much unexpected.

I had expected to clean, cook, and scarper, but now I was faced with a hulking great pile of hot, angry male, who for some inexplicable reason was turning me on more than I had been in a long time.

I hadn't dated for a while. A *long* while. I'd been too busy with work to even notice men – being a newly qualified teacher does that to you – but apparently right now, in a strange house with an equally strange and irritable man, was the moment that my libido decided to kick back in. Just flipping typical.

'Look, I've been up for the last forty-eight hours, I don't need your sarcasm,' he informed me in a low, gritty tone, which was so incredibly masculine that it caused goosebumps to rise on my arms and did absolutely nothing to help my lust decrease. Jeez. I *really* needed to get a grip.

'You're in my bloody house, who the hell are you?' Ah, so he *was* the home owner. That was a marginal relief. As my eyes greedily skimmed over him again I decided I needed to rewrite my earlier speculation about what the owner would be like, because this guy was clearly neither old nor fat. Young, hot, and trim would be more accurate. I'd guess he was older than my twenty-six years though, probably mid-thirties, but not "ancient" old like I'd expected. For some ridiculous reason I nearly found myself telling him about my earlier assumptions, but my inability to reel in my skittering emotions indicated that perhaps now was not the time to push this guy with my runaway mouth.

Keeping it short and sweet, I tried to soften him with a small smile, but his face remained folded in a deep frown, his lips drawn into a thin line and his expression completely unchanged, as if my effort had no effect whatsoever. 'Sarah's ill, I'm covering for her. I'm Allie.'

Nodding once, he raised a hand and rubbed it through his short, dark hair, leaving it ruffled and messy and pulling my gaze to the tightness of his bicep as he moved his arm. Gosh, he was so well built it would almost be criminal *not* to look. From the lovely taut bulge in his arm, this guy must work out on a daily basis – either that or there were some seriously good genes in his bloodline.

'Well, *Allie*.' He pronounced my name sarcastically, as if it were a strange and irritating foreign language, which immediately irked me. 'As I just said, I've been up for the last two days and I really need to sleep, so leave the bloody hoovering and just have a tidy up instead.' The random attraction I *was* feeling was somewhat doused by that remark – he spoke as if I had turned the hoover on deliberately to wake him. What a grouchy, gorgeous bastard.

I might be suffering from an unnervingly serious case of lust toward this man, but I wasn't one to lie down and let people walk all over me, and his condescending tone had my annoyance quickly building. Narrowing my eyes at him, I straightened my spine to look as tall as I could. Not that it took me anywhere near his impressive height, but at least it made me feel a bit better. 'You weren't even supposed to be here today, so don't have a go at me for trying to do what I've been asked,' I replied tightly.

My snarky reply caused a brief flash of surprise to cross his face before he resumed that bloody frown. As hard as I tried to ignore it, I noticed that he was doing that lip rolling thing again too, and in response I found myself slowly licking my tongue across my own lips. Realising what I was doing, I quickly whipped my tongue back into my mouth and slammed my jaw shut so hard that my teeth made a cracking noise that caused me to wince. What the heck was I doing? This guy was acting like a stuck-up idiot and I was here appreciating his good looks? Regardless of his handsomeness, I seriously needed to get a grip!

'Yeah, well, I'm back early and I need to sleep and eat, so just make some food and leave it in the fridge.' As well as being stuck up he apparently lacked manners too, so I raised my eyebrows at his rudeness like I did with the children in my class when I expected them to consider their wording. '… *Please*,' he added wearily, and I nearly smiled at this small concession from his foul tempered behaviour. Watching him watching me, I briefly thought that perhaps he looked familiar, but couldn't place where I would know him from. Shrugging it off, I decided it was probably just his good looks that were continuing to confuse me, because even if he was a moody bastard there was no denying that he was definitely a very attractive moody bastard.

With his minimal clothing there was no disguising the raw appeal of his well-muscled body either – the light covering of hair on his chest looked soft, filling me with an urge to touch it, and the angles of his stubble-covered chin were appealing and something I always found particularly sexy. All in all, it was a rather nice view. Apart from the frown, of course, but seeing what a mess I already was, it was probably safest that I didn't see him smile. It would no doubt be devastatingly good.

In the space of two minutes in this man's company I felt like I was well on my way to losing my mind, so drawing in a shaky breath I tried to clear my head before looking back at him. To my annoyance I found him watching my appraisal of his body with apparent amusement. It wasn't exactly a smile, but he had a smug quirk to his lips that made me realise with horror that my staring – and no doubt goofy expression – must have made it pretty obvious what I was thinking.

Damn my traitorous body, damn this bloody job, and damn this man.

Annoyed at my own lack of control I refused to show him that I was bothered by his presence, even though I clearly was, so I turned in the direction of the kitchen without so much as a backward glance at him. 'Fine, I'll make you some food and leave,' I muttered.

As I strode back to the kitchen I realised that I had unconsciously crossed my arms over my chest – clearly as well as being horny I was also a little bit defensive from my run-in with the nameless, and shirtless, handsome stranger.

Chapter Two
Allie

As soon as my feet hit the tiled kitchen floor I became a human tornado, speeding through my jobs with focus and barely even pausing to draw breath. My haste was partly fuelled by the angry, lusty feeling that he had sparked in me, and partly because I was keen to escape before it started to rain. Or as I had predicted earlier – snow. Whatever it was I was running from, man or weather, I wanted to get the heck away from this house as quickly as possible.

Unfortunately, I had been so distracted by thoughts of the handsome bastard that I'd left the pasta for so long that it was less 'al dente' and more 'a sticky mess at the bottom of the pan' and had to start all over again.

When the food was finally complete I pushed my hair from my face and looked up to see thick, fluffy flakes beginning to fall outside the window. Snow? Damn it, I hated when I proved myself right. Cursing under my breath, I angrily shoved lids on the Tupperware containers and slid them in the fridge, grabbed my bag, and started to shrug my jacket on as I dashed through the house for my car. If I was lucky, I could escape the twisty country lanes and get to the main roads before the snow got too bad.

There was no sign of Mr Misery Guts as I made it towards the front door, which was mostly a relief, but did also trigger a brief flicker of disappointment that I wouldn't get a last look at his godliness. I was definitely going to ask Sarah about him, though. I couldn't believe she hadn't mentioned what a hottie he was, and knowing Sarah's love of a fine male specimen there was no way he could have escaped her notice.

However, thoughts of sinfully sexy pyjama bottoms were abruptly pushed from my mind when I yanked the front door open and to my dismay found a flurry of white snow falling all around me. *Shit!* The flakes were already falling far quicker than I had imagined, and judging by the eerily silent white landscape, it had been doing so for quite a while. I'd been chopping vegetables by floor to ceiling windows – how had I not seen it start?

Annoyed at myself for not noticing the snow earlier, I practically ripped the door off my car as I opened it, threw my bag onto the passenger seat, and slid inside. Shoving the key into the ignition I turned it, praying that it would start. Wincing as it pathetically coughed and turned over several times I finally heard the rumble of the engine kicking to life and blew out a relieved breath. Thank God for that. I'm not sure I'd ever been more relieved about anything in my entire life.

Ramming it into first gear before the engine could change its mind, I went to pull away when my front wheels immediately started to spin uselessly below me, the mixture of snow and gravel combining to become slippery and useless under my tyres. Lightening my touch on the accelerator, I muttered a small plea under my breath and tried again. And again.

Attempting to coax my car forwards with soft, gentle encouragement I even stroked the steering wheel in my desperation to persuade it to move, but nothing was working, and after five more minutes and several additional failed attempts, the only progress I had made was a marginal skid to the right. Scowling at the dashboard, all thoughts of gentle coaxing went up in smoke as I instead began to hurl abuse at it. 'Bloody bugger it!' I yelled, banging my hand on the steering wheel several times.

Pausing in my tantrum, I calmed my panted breaths and stared miserably ahead of me at the tarmacked parking spaces a few meters away. The snow was thinner there because of the tree cover above, and this sight did nothing to brighten my mood, because there was no doubt that if I'd parked there like I was supposed to, I would have managed to get a good enough start to make it down the driveway. Thinking of the gravel beneath me, it suddenly occurred to me that all my wheel spinning had probably done a bit of damage to Mr Mean and Moody's treasured driveway. Oops. Hopefully he was sound asleep by now and I would be able to escape before he noticed my property destruction. Briefly chewing on a fingernail, I realised that I probably should have felt a bit guiltier at this realisation, but I was far too busy feeling sorry for myself about being stuck in the middle of nowhere to dwell on it.

Jumping from the car, I slammed the door as hard as I could and vented some of my frustrations through yelling a further stream of fiery expletives at my useless hunk of junk. My mouth was worse than a sailor as I dredged up every single swear word I'd ever encountered and flung it at my poor unsuspecting Fiat. I was seriously tempted to kick the car, but thankfully, common sense told me that I would only end up damaging myself more than it, so I instead hurled another tirade of abuse and abruptly stopped as my shoulders slumped in defeat and my head hung low.

Calming myself for a few seconds I watched as my breath steamed in the cold air. I sighed heavily and shook my head. I knew I should have had the tires changed at the last service, but the mechanic had told me they still had a bit of life in them yet. It seems he was wrong.

Not willing to let the weather beat me without a proper fight, I spent a good ten minutes getting cold and soaking wet as I tried to build ramps in front of the tyres from larger, nearby pebbles, hoping that they might help me get some grip, but the snow was falling so quickly that they were covered and useless by the time I climbed into the car to try. Bugger.

What should I do? Chewing nervously on the inside of my lower lip, I glanced back at the house and grimaced so hard that my eyes scrunched up. No matter how stuck I was, there was *no way* I was asking *him* for help. The miserable git could wallow in his cosy warm bed and catch up on his sleep for all I cared. I'd be just fine out here.

Turning purposefully towards the rear of my car I popped open the boot and rooted around in the multitude of junk. With a pleased yelp I produced my sleeping bag and thermal survival blanket. Thank God I'd been too lazy to clean out my car since my camping trip in September. This sleeping bag was warm, not arctic standard perhaps, but definitely thick enough to help me out today. I'd just nestle down and wait it out. It couldn't snow forever, could it? Shaking my head, I rolled my eyes at my own stupidity. Of course it couldn't, it would probably just be a short flurry. I'd be fine snuggled in my sleeping bag and then as soon as I saw it start to clear I'd make another attempt at moving the car.

With my plan sorted I settled down into the driver's side again and wrapped myself up as best I could in preparation for a rough few hours ahead. I usually really liked snow, but only if I were safely tucked up in a nice warm house looking out at the pretty sparkly crystals. Sitting in it was *not* on my favourites list, mostly because I bloody hated being cold. On the plus side, at least I had a fairly full petrol tank, so I could keep my car running to keep my decrepit heater turned on.

Unfortunately, my optimism about my "warm sleeping bag" was soon quashed, because after ten minutes I had pretty much lost all feeling in my toes. After fifteen I was shivering uncontrollably, and by twenty minutes my wet, gloved fingers were stinging so much they felt like they'd been bitten by a thousand wasps. I was also starting to feel a bit claustrophobic because the snow had covered my windows and windscreen so much it felt like I was sitting in a giant ice cube. Or a not so giant ice cube – my Fiat wasn't exactly large.

Huffing out a frustrated breath that steamed the air, I suddenly yelped loudly as someone knocked on my car window, sending snow cascading to the ground and clearing the glass so I could see out of my icy cocoon.

As I looked out through the frosted glass I saw the owner of the house stood there in a snow jacket, waterproof trousers, and snow boots, looking annoying warm and dry and holding a mug of something which was sending tempting plumes of steam into the air. Even clothed, he still looked magnificent. He now came across all outdoorsy and competent, which stupidly seemed to appeal to my inner fragile female who was apparently clamouring to be rescued by him.

Grumbling my annoyance at my complete inability to rein in my thoughts, I grouchily looked up at his face again. The brightness of the falling snow seemed to make his dark hair look almost black, and his eyes stood out like charcoal against the white. Frustratingly, I still couldn't tell if his eyes were brown or dark blue, but yet again they seemed to be trying to pull me in, so I hastily dragged my gaze away, looking anywhere and everywhere except his eyes. No doubt he was amused by my neurotic behaviour, because there seemed to be a smile threatening to break on his lips for a second or two, but he never let it fully emerge. It was almost as if he wouldn't allow it.

Disliking him even more now that he was dry and warm, I reluctantly forced my frigid fingers to draw the window down a few inches.

'What's the problem?' he asked conversationally, as if it wasn't screamingly obvious what the issue was. If I could have felt my legs, I swear to God I would have jumped out of the car and kicked him. *Hard*.

As stupid as his question was, I found myself answering anyway, politeness winning out over grouchiness. 'The snow is heavier than I thought and my car can't handle it. I just keep skidding. I'm going to wait it out, I'm sure it'll pass soon enough.' Although judging from the colour of the clouds, that might be wishful thinking on my part.

Watching as he sipped his drink, I felt my mouth begin to water with the almost desperate need to taste whatever was in that cup. God, the things I would do to get my hands on that drink right now. Narrowing my eyes as I looked at his wide stance I felt my heart leap in my chest again. Forget the drink – the things I would do to get my hands on *him* right now. I bet he was really toasty beneath all those layers of clothing.

Mmm. Solid, warm skin and hard, protective muscles … he could no doubt heat up my chilled body in just a few minutes. It vaguely crossed my lust-filled mind to tell him that the best survival technique was to get naked and share body heat, but thankfully sanity prevailed and I held back. The mere thought of sharing some skin–on–skin action with this man sent a shiver running through my body that had nothing to do with my chilled bones. I then had to firmly shake my head to try and clear my wandering thoughts. This man was dangerous for me. I just couldn't control the way my body responded to him, it was crazy.

'If you had parked in the proper parking space you probably would have been fine,' he commented, mildly casting a glance across the driveway to his bloody perfect flipping parking spots which were still mostly untouched by the snow. 'The tarmac would have provided a far better grip. As it is, you've dug trenches in my otherwise perfect driveway with your wheel spins and now you're stuck.' My mouth briefly hung open. Smug, irritating, self-righteous bastard. But I couldn't say anything because he was right, and basically saying exactly what I'd been thinking just a few minutes earlier. My hands clenched into balls in my lap – I *really* hated that he was right. I also felt slightly guilty about the damage I had no doubt done to his precious driveway, but in my current state I didn't feel like apologising so I simply chose to ignore him and rolled my lips shut while I stared defiantly at my fisted hands instead.

'You can't stay out here, you'll freeze. Come inside,' he told me, in a presumptuous tone that rubbed me up the wrong way but simultaneously made me feel all pathetically melty inside too.

Sneering at my pitiful hormones, I dug my icy body deeper into my rubbish sleeping bag and turned away from him to avoid the temptation of further ogling. Seeing as I seemed to have a strange sort of attraction to this equally strange man I was decidedly unwilling to go back inside with him. God knows what I'd do or say if I had to spend any more time alone with him. He made my insides feel warm and gooey when my brain was telling me that he was a rude, pompous prick. It was an unfamiliar imbalance that I didn't like at all, so I decided to play it safe and stay away. 'I'm fine here, thank you.' Although I still really wanted him to offer me whatever was in that cup.

'Have it your way,' he murmured, then took another teasing sip of his drink, briefly licking his lips and humming in appreciation before turning and walking back to the house, leaving me staring at his broad, retreating back in disbelief.

What a bastard! I was completely stunned. He was actually going to leave me out here in the cold. Although I reluctantly had to admit that that was exactly what I'd told him I wanted. He wasn't supposed to listen to me! He was supposed to talk some sense into me with that lovely, raspy voice of his. Huffing out an irritable breath I flopped back in my seat with a scowl. So he was a chauvinist pig *and* ill-mannered? My treacherous mind was midway through trying to remember his good points, like his muscular build and startlingly handsome face, when the door to my car was wrenched open and I was suddenly dragged from my sleeping bag as I found my world rapidly turning upside down.

What the heck? It took me a second or two to actually realise that he had tossed me over his shoulder like a rag doll, and once my new reality had sunk in, I literally couldn't believe it. Talk about being man handled. Gripping him at the waist to balance myself I took a brief second to note just how toned he felt under his clothing before I grasped what I was doing and instead began to pummel him with my fists while yelling at him to put me down.

Ignoring me completely, he kicked my car door shut and strode into the house as if I weighed nothing, disregarding my kicking, yelling, and flailing as if I weren't even there. Pausing inside the hall he kicked his boots off, climbed the stairs, and paced down several long, brightly lit corridors, all the while swinging me precariously on his shoulder.

As furious as I was, I couldn't help but notice just how good he smelt – the down jacket underneath my cheek smelt faintly of wood smoke, but there was also a spicy, manly scent to him which seeped into my senses. It was just typical that as well as being blessed with the body of a model and the face of a god that he would smell divine as well.

There was the sound of a door opening and then, with no warning at all, I found myself being tumbled forwards and deposited roughly onto my feet, where I swayed slightly until he reached to steady me. Blinking several times to clear my dazed vision, I saw I was now stood by the side of a large bed in a very big bedroom. Blimey, half my house would fit in here.

I probably should have been concerned that this nameless stranger had basically abducted me from my car and now had me holed up in his bedroom, but being carried so far had made my head dizzy and legs wobbly and it didn't really occur to me that I should be nervous.

I'm not sure if it were the result of my upside down trip up the stairs, or just the effect that touching him had had on me, but my knees suddenly gave way and I plonked down onto the soft bed as I gazed up at him in shock and tried to process what the hell just happened.

'I'm not having your frozen corpse on my conscience. This is my spare room – dry off, warm up, and when it's safe to leave, you can. *Not* before. No more ridiculous stubbornness, and no more unnecessary risks. Understand?' He was actually rather imposing, I realised, as I took in his huge frame and steely eyes again. God, he was really tall. His tone and wide-legged stance didn't really leave any room for refusal, not unless I wanted to get into a slanging match with him which I would no doubt lose. Besides, this warm, dry bedroom was an infinitely better option than my freezing cold car, so, being sensible for once in my life, I licked my lips and nodded cautiously.

'I'll turn your car off and lock it. The water supply is fine because my pipes have frost protection so shower if you like, there are clean towels in the en-suite. I've left a hot drink for you,' he informed me briskly, indicating to the bedside table where I now noticed a mug was sitting. Unable to look away from him for long, I left the drink untouched and turned my gaze back, predictably finding his eyes still on me.

He assessed me for several long moments, as that strange tension seemed to fill the space between us again just like it had when we first met. It felt like static electricity was bouncing between us as the hairs on my arms went into overdrive and stood to attention. Considering how he'd insulted and practically manhandled me earlier, I was still undeniably attracted to this man, and as a result I was now finding it quite hard to breathe as he just stood there, all tall and foreboding and staring at me in silence.

Surely it wasn't normal for two people to just stare at each other like this? The stupid thing was, I simply couldn't seem to drag my eyes away from him. It certainly seemed to break most of the rules of how to act in polite company, but then again, he wasn't looking away either, so at least it wasn't just me who seemed affected by the situation. And I really was affected. My heart was fluttering, I felt shaky, warm, and even a bit sick from the tumbling of my stomach. It was like I'd lost all control over my own body.

He was magnificent. A prime example of masculinity if ever I had seen one. But then he broke me from my wandering thoughts by making a sudden strange, dismissive grunt, spinning on his heel, and leaving. My eyebrows practically rose into my hairline. Charming. He didn't said another word, just left me sat on the bed blinking at the now-closed door.

What a man. What a turn of events. And I still didn't know his bloody name!

Chapter Three
Sean

Striding from the spare room, I immediately made my way to my own bedroom just a few short, stomped steps away from where I'd left Allie. Slamming the door behind me I winced as it rattled on its hinges and stopped in the middle of the room, tipping my head back as I drew in a long, deep breath to try and clear my mind. There was something about that woman that had immediately gotten under my skin, and I didn't like it one bit. Some unexpected, unknown frisson had occurred inside of me the moment I'd laid eyes on her in the lounge, drawing me to her even though she was a complete stranger, and it hadn't lessened at all in the time that had passed since her arrival.

In different circumstances, if a random woman had turned up inside my house I would have immediately been on the phone to my security team to get her removed from the property, but I had requested a clean of the house, so her story of covering for Sarah seemed believable enough. Unusually though, this girl genuinely didn't seem to know who I was. It was actually quite refreshing, and perhaps one of the reasons I was finding her so fascinating.

And the staring just now – what the fuck had that been about? I ran a hand jerkily through my hair, almost pulling out a handful in aggravation. We must have watched each other in complete silence for more than five minutes, which was not only odd, but really fucking unnerving. I hadn't felt a reaction to a woman like this for years, if ever, and to make it more peculiar I didn't even know anything about her. It was distinctly unsettling, and not a feeling that I particularly relished. Had she felt the connection too? Did I even want to know? No, actually, I did not need a romantic attachment, especially not with someone that had sparked such a visceral response in me. That would just be asking for trouble, and I was already way too busy at the moment to invite trouble into my life.

Raising both hands, I rubbed them over my face to try and clear the fog that seemed to have descended on my sanity since the arrival of that woman in my home. Grunting irritably, I rolled my neck and briefly closed my eyes. God, I was tired. I'd literally had about three hours sleep in the last two days, but now that I knew that there was someone else in my house – *her*, a woman that I seemed to be inexplicably pulled toward – I couldn't get my mind to move beyond the fact that she was in my spare bedroom just a few paces away. Was she in bed to warm up? Perhaps naked under the sheets, the cool material laying over her skin and tucked around her? Or maybe she was washing that long hair of hers in the shower?

Fuck. With my mind on overdrive and full of temptingly teasing images I just knew that sleep was going to be near impossible.

Jerkily walking to the window, I began drawing the curtains shut when I eyed her rust bucket of a car currently collecting snow outside my house. I couldn't believe she drove that thing. It was almost offensive to look at it, dumped haphazardly by my front door. Shaking my head, I blew out an irritated breath, almost sure that my driveway would be ruined where she'd repeatedly spun her bloody wheels. Tugging the curtains closed to hide the infuriating sight I walked to my bed and began peeling off my clothes.

Chucking my jacket, jumper, and T-shirt carelessly onto the chair I grimaced as I kicked off my snow trousers and jeans and looked down at the huge erection jutting out hopefully in the warmth of the room. Fuck it. I'd been in this state pretty much since I'd seen her downstairs. In fact, if she hadn't turned and left to go and cook earlier, she would have seen the arrival of my arousal for herself, because my thin pyjama bottoms certainly hadn't managed to conceal it a great deal when it had first sprung to attention. My cock seemed just as affected by this woman as my mind was. The only saving grace was that at least with my jeans and snow trousers on she wouldn't have been aware of my rock hard excitement. At least I hoped she wouldn't have noticed.

Hissing air between my teeth, I watched as my cock jerked about optimistically, looking enflamed and needy. Sighing heavily, I shook my head. The bloody thing seemed to have a mind of its own sometimes. Sleep was going to be impossible, so I turned and made my way into my en-suite instead. I always felt drowsier post-orgasm, so perhaps I'd been able to sleep if I worked off the tension.

Turning on the shower, I cranked up the temperature and stepped under the warming jets with a groan of satisfaction as the hot water hit my tired muscles. After briefly pausing to allow the spray to run over my body I placed my left hand on the tiled wall and leant forwards a little so I could look down at myself. Using my right hand to loosely grip the base of my throbbing shaft, I groaned as the weight settled in my palm, jerking against my hand. Closing my fist I drew my hand up to the top of my cock and let out a hiss at just how solid it was. Fuck, I couldn't remember the last time I'd been this turned on.

My eyes rolled shut for a second as I absorbed the feeling, before opening them to watch as I repeated the movement, this time a little faster. I was careful not to go too quick, because the way I felt, it wouldn't take long for me to come, and I at least wanted to enjoy this for a minute or so before I blew my load.

With the next pump, I watched under heavy-lidded eyes as a drop of pre-come emerged from the tip. I ran my thumb across it, groaning at the sensation across the sensitive slit. With visions of that beautiful girl now rooted in my head, I began to move my hand quicker, tightening my hold until I was pumping like a man possessed. Christ, that felt so good.

Not as good as it would feel if her hands were wrapped around me, though.. Or perhaps her sarcastic little mouth. Oh God. A long, throaty groan left my lips. What I wouldn't give to have her kneeling in front of me right now, taking me deep in her mouth as she worked me to climax with her hot tongue.

My body shuddered at the thought, coming with such explosive force that the first pulse of come hit the shower wall in front of me. Keeping my hand moving, my orgasm continued for an absolute age, each pump of my wrist causing another hot spurt to slide out until both the wall and my fist were covered, my cock was half hard, and my head hung in exhaustion.

Panting like I'd run a marathon, I rinsed my hands and rested them on the shower wall as I tipped my head back and let the jets wash over my face and tumble down my body. If I could sleep now, then hopefully the snow would be gone when I woke and that woman could leave. Wincing, I realised that I really should use her name instead of "her" or "that woman". *Allie*. Once the snow had cleared, *Allie* could leave.

Grinning down at my satisfied cock, I smiled smugly. That had been a monster orgasm. If coming with that much volatility didn't help me get to sleep, then nothing would.

Chapter Four
Allie

I hadn't meant to fall asleep.

But now, as I blinked blearily and began to come back to consciousness, it was quite obvious that I had. My senses zeroed in on a steady ticking noise coming from somewhere in the room, which was strange because I didn't have a clock in my bedroom. Not a proper ticking clock, anyway. I had a bedside radio alarm, but that was digital, and the only noise I ever heard from it was the annoying alarm telling me to wake up. Frowning in confusion, I rubbed at my sticky eyes before trying to make sense of where the heck I was.

Looking around, I saw the source of the ticking – a small, wooden clock on top of a chest of drawers, both of which looked to be antique, and completely unfamiliar. My clothes were heaped on and around the radiator, no change from the norm there, because I was habitually messy. But that was not my radiator, and this was definitely not my room.

Where on earth was I?

My eyes moved to the bedside table and the large mug sat beside me, several dribbles of chocolate dried on its side, and that's when I finally woke up properly and remembered.

The job for Sarah, the sudden snow which had rendered my car useless, and Mr Magnificent and Moody.

Of course. Picturing him again in all his glory, I fell back on my pillows with a load groan. I was in his house because he had dragged me here, muttering things about not having my death on his conscience. Not that I should really complain; he'd provided me with the most delicious hot chocolate I'd ever tasted and a bed so comfy that I'd gone out like a light. My plan had just been to warm myself up under the covers while my clothes dried, but obviously tiredness had overtaken my senses because as I glanced at the window, it definitely seemed to be light outside.

Looking back at the clock in confusion I saw that it read eight o'clock. Eight p.m., or eight a.m.? I hadn't slept the entire night, had I? It had been late afternoon by the time I'd finished the cooking and run to my car, so surely I'd just slept for two hours. Although if that were the case, I would have expected it to be dark outside. In a sudden panic, I quickly climbed from the cosy covers and ran to the window, hoping for two things: firstly, that it was still the same day, and secondly, that the snow would have melted.

Both of my hopes were dashed the second I pulled back the plush curtain. It was definitely light, which indicated that it was morning, and unfortunately, the snow was still falling outside the window and lying in thick blankets around the garden. It was so dense that apart from the occasional dark tree branch here and there, I could barely see any colour other than white. Grimacing, I ran my hands through my hair in aggravation. What was this, a new ice age? I couldn't remember a winter in England where it had snowed like this.

Considering I'd just spent the night in a strange house, in a strange bed, I must have slept incredibly well, because apart from my dismay at being trapped, I actually felt rather good. Physically speaking, anyway. Mentally, I was dreading having to see the house owner again, and deal with the strange attraction he had sparked in me. Even briefly considering it made my stomach jitter nervously. Sighing heavily, I dressed in yesterday's clothes, which due to my lack of proper unfolding last night, were still damp, and then prepared to head downstairs.

Pulling open my bedroom door, I tentatively stuck my head into the corridor and glanced around the unfamiliar space. Seeing as I'd been draped upside down over a firm shoulder during my 'tour' of the house yesterday, I had no idea which way to go, but as I looked around, the sight of my handbag and laptop case leant next to the door caught my attention. Raising my eyebrows, I moved them into my room and quickly checked the contents. All was still as I'd left it, so presumably

Mr House Owner had merely grabbed them from my car to stop them getting frozen, which for someone with a seemingly permanent scowl, was really rather thoughtful.

Heading back out of my room I looked both ways and still had no clue which way to go, because the corridor stretched out in both directions, seeming to turn corners at either end. Bugger. Pulling in a nervous breath I contemplated what to do, but then smiled. That gulp of air had given me the answer I needed, because I had gotten a definite whiff of brewing coffee coming from my left side. Turning in the direction of the delicious aroma, I followed the hallway, turned a corner, and discovered a wide landing and the large, curved staircase I recognised from yesterday.

Thank goodness for caffeine – not only did it start my days with a buzz, but it had now saved me from getting lost in the huge house's maze-like corridors. Smiling to myself, I began to trot down the stairs, feeling far more positive about my day. I might be snowed in somewhere in the English hills with a godlike (but miserable) man, but from the smell of it there was at least some decent coffee in the house, so all was right with the world.

Entering the kitchen, I drew to a stop when I found the mystery man sat at the counter with a mug of coffee in one hand and his gaze focused on an iPad. I had expected the kitchen to be empty, and his presence had completely thrown me. Again. He didn't look over at me, so I took a quick moment to assess him; he was wearing a pair of grey trousers, army type with pockets on the sides of the thighs, and a beige woollen jumper. Simple clothes, but he somehow made them look almost indecently good. For some reason, as my gaze trailed down his body I ended up focused on his feet. They were bare, and surely cold given the weather outside, but I just couldn't help but stare at them. I didn't have a foot fetish or anything, but impossibly they were just as perfect as the rest of him. Was anything lacking about this man?

Beyond my control my brain and body were most definitely reacting to him again, and I'd only been in the flipping room for less than a minute. Even without any caffeine in my system my awareness had already sprung to seemingly impossible levels as my heart quickened, skin heated, and nerves tingled. What was this crazy reaction he seemed to cause? I'd never felt anything like it before, and it was completely beyond my comprehension that a man could affect me so instantaneously. But this man did. And I *still* didn't know his name. I made a conscious decision to ask him this morning once I was feeling braver.

Drawing myself to my full height, I pulled in a calming breath and mentally set my plan: ignore his gorgeousness and act nonchalant. Not that it had worked yesterday, but still, it was worth a shot.

'Morning,' I murmured, already feeling awkward, decidedly out of place, and not nonchalant at all.

Finally turning his head, his steely eyes grazed over my appearance and seemed to linger on my lips for way longer than necessary, which, for some reason, made me instinctively lick them. His eyes narrowed, and then blinking twice, he raised his gaze, his eyes now hooded and unreadable.

'Apparently the snow has set in for at least a week,' he murmured, his eyes snapping away as he stared out of the huge windows. So no 'good morning' or niceties then, just ploughing in with the bad news. And what bad news it was. My face fell, along with my heart.

'A week?' I squeaked, 'I can't be stuck here, it's Christmas soon! Can't you drive me out?' Besides the fact that Christmas was my favourite time of year and my mum would kill me if I missed it, the thought of being stuck here all week trying to battle my crazy responses was almost enough to send me into a fit of hysterical tears.

'It isn't exactly my dream situation either,' he replied bluntly, draining his mug and standing up to put it in the sink. 'You better make yourself at home, because there's no way any car is getting though these country lanes for a while, sweetheart.' I was about to complain about his casual endearment, which had sounded far nicer to my ears that it should have, and was really way too informal given our

30

situation, but he suddenly struck me silent by striding across the room and encroaching right into my personal space.

And I mean *right* into my space. God, he was really, *really* close. So close, in fact, that if I jutted my head forwards ever so slightly I'd be able to rub my chin on his chest.

What was he doing this close? I might be attracted to him, but it certainly didn't seem to be reciprocated by him – he'd been nothing but irritable and brusque with me since we'd met, so suddenly placing himself this close to me didn't make any sense at all. The only benefit to this new positioning was that I finally got to see what colour his dark eyes were – a navy blue with a slightly lighter centre and just a few flecks of green and hazel around the pupil.

He was now so far inside my personal space that I could smell his aftershave. It was the same slightly smoky, spicy scent I'd smelt on his coat yesterday and it reminded me of the great outdoors, which I suppose was about right for a man like this. With his broad shoulders and large build, he looked nothing if not capable. My breath caught in my throat as I inhaled another lungful of lovely maleness, the scent making my stomach clench. God, breathing in his delicious smell was *not* a good idea.

Tilting my head back I looked up warily into his face, but instead of initiating conversation, he simply stood there and silently scrutinised me, his dark eyes latching onto mine and sucking me in again.

This really wasn't ideal at all. My body was in overdrive again – I was aroused every time I laid eyes on this guy, and now it looked like I was going to have to endure this for an entire week.

Seemingly incapable of moving away, I simply stood there and sent up a silent prayer that he wasn't going to start a staring thing like he had last night. His eyes remained blank, but I saw just the tiniest flicker at the corner of his lips that seemed to indicate that he knew exactly what devastating things his close proximity did to my composure, but then, breaking the moment, he lifted a hand and fingered the damp material of my jumper.

Now he had broken the eye contact I felt like I could breathe again, but that was about the only function I was managing. To be honest, this was all getting a bit much; my body seemed totally out of my control when he was around, and despite my brain screaming at me to do something, *anything*, I did nothing.

As if my throat could take no more tension, a loud swallow forced its way down as one of his knuckles accidently brushed across my stomach as he continued to run the hem of my jumper between his fingers. A gasp flew from my lips as my skin tingled in the wake of his brief touch and I mentally kicked myself for the slip. Self-consciously flicking my gaze to his, our eyes met again, and for the briefest of seconds I could have sworn I saw a flash of mutual attraction reflected in his irises before he looked away again.

'This won't keep out the chill,' he muttered. Letting out a weary sigh, he shook his head and stepped back, breaking the spell he'd cast upon me so suddenly that I almost slumped forwards from the loss of the intense connection. 'I'll leave out some clothes you can borrow. Layer up; this is a big house and it gets cold.' With that, he cast me one final look and abruptly left the kitchen.

Behind his departing figure I immediately sagged onto the nearest work surface with a huge sigh. Turning my burning cheek onto the cool marble, my eyes fluttered shut as I tried to calm my raging heartbeat and equally as enflamed lust. I was so overheated I felt like I was going to melt, and vaguely considered the option of opening the back door and throwing myself into the snow to cool down. Mind you, that would no doubt lead to the house owner thinking he'd have to "save" me again by throwing me over his shoulder and dragging me back inside, then I'd just be back at square one, except with soaking wet clothes.

Pushing myself upright I blew out a long breath and turned towards the coffee maker, intent on clearing my head with a nice burst of caffeine. Thankfully, I didn't have to attempt to negotiate with all the buttons and handles on the space age machine because there was a large jug steaming away on a hot plate at one end. Opening several cupboards, I finally found the cups and selected the largest mug I could see as I pondered my feelings and poured from the heated coffee jug.

What the heck was happening to me? He was a virtual stranger, but I found myself absurdly drawn to him. It wasn't for his personality, that was for sure, but the way I had caught his eyes on me twice this morning had been unnerving in a ridiculously exciting way.

Rolling my eyes, I decided that I'd been single way too long if I was hankering after a man as miserable as this one, I thought, lifting the mug to my lips with a smile.

An appreciative moan slipped from my throat, and this time it had nothing to do with a domineering, sexy mansion owner, and everything to do with the delicious contents in my mug. That had to be the best coffee I'd ever tasted. Curious as to where it came from, I opened a few more cabinets before finding a bag of coffee beans carefully folded and sealed with a clip. Reading the label I smiled to myself: Columbian Fairtrade. No wonder I liked it – Columbian was my favourite because of its nutty and almost sweet flavour. Taking another sip, I licked my lips approvingly and topped it up.

As I carefully placed the coffee jug back I decided to put my strange attraction down to nothing more than some sort of chemistry between us. I'd heard tales of instantaneous lust and attraction so strong that people did crazy things, but I'd never actually experienced it myself. It looked like I was getting a first-hand taste of it now though, that was for sure. Shaking my head in mild frustration I stared out at the snow-covered garden and shivered as I relived the sensations this man had awoken in me. Chemistry. That's all it was. Really, *really* potent chemistry. But it would wear off. Especially if I avoided him, which after this morning's stomach stroking encounter, I certainly planned to do.

Realising just how hungry I was after skipping dinner last night, I grabbed a banana and went back to the coffee cupboard where I'd spotted some cereal bars. My stash complete, I headed from the kitchen, careful to avoid the door to the lounge that the mystery man had taken.

Making my way back to my bedroom I set myself a plan to hide out as much as possible. It was warm, cosy, had a large, full bookcase to keep me busy, and best of all, it seemed the perfect way to avoid any more run-ins with the owner and his annoyingly magnetic muscles.

Outside the door I saw a pile of clothes, and after feeling mildly surprised that he'd followed through on his promise so quickly, I picked it up to take it inside. Giving the pile a quick sort through, it all seemed to be male, which presumably meant that no female ever stayed here – a thought that pleased me far more than it should have done, and one that I shoved to the back of my mind with a scowl. It didn't matter if he had a girlfriend, wife, or even a flipping harem of women hanging on his every word, his relationship status really should be none of my concern.

Piling the clothes on the dresser I stubbornly stayed in my own damp attire for the time being as I grabbed my handbag and pulled out my phone to dial my mum. The signal was low, but it rang, which was a relief as it meant the snow wasn't completely blocking phone signal. The answerphone kicked in, so with a slightly sad sigh I left a message explaining the situation and telling her where I was before promising to call back soon.

I really wanted to hear another human voice – other than the raspy, sexy one that I could find somewhere in this house, of course – so I called Sarah. After all, she was the reason I was in this mess in the first place, the least she could do was fill me in on who the heck this guy was – and explain why she hadn't informed me that the shift I was covering for her was at the home of a demi-god.

Once again I got a ringing tone, but disappointingly, after eight rings her phone also went to answerphone. Where *was* everyone? Surely they were all at home and snowed in like me? Or was the weather only bad up here in the hills? Huffing in frustration, I left a brief message wishing her a speedy recovery and telling her to call me as soon as she could, and hung up. Damn it, I'd really wanted to pump her for information on my unintended host.

Looking miserably at my phone, I fiddled with it for a second or two before deciding that I still had the urge to talk to someone other than myself. Scrolling through my numbers for my other best friend Caitlin Byrne – or Cait, as she preferred – I smiled at what she would make of the guy I was staying with. She was super shy, so would no doubt be even more of a wreck around him than I was.

Cait, Sarah, and I had known each other since high school. We'd lost touch and gone our separate ways during college, but then bizarrely all ended up on the same teacher training course in Manchester. It wasn't long before we were an inseparable trio again, and after making the effort to keep in contact we had stayed firm best friends ever since.

Sarah's teaching career was short-lived when she got pregnant during the last year of the course. It was unplanned, and unwanted by the father, who promptly buggered off never to be heard from again, thus proving my theory that he had been a horrid human being all along. Refusing to be gotten down, Sarah had worked hard since then at several jobs, before recently setting up the housekeeping business, which was now going rather well.

As for Cait and I, as well as the three years of teacher training together, we had managed to get our first teaching jobs at the same school in Buxton, but had both quickly realised that perhaps the profession wasn't quite what we'd expected. Too much unnecessary paperwork for a start, not to mention the political crud that got in the way of actually enjoying the time in the classroom with the children. While I had stuck it out, Cait had barely managed to last the first year before quitting and heading off to travel around the world. Her departure had been spurred by the pressures of the job, but she had also been keen to escape from her then-boyfriend, Greg, a complete shitbag of a man who deserved to be behind bars for what he'd put Cait through during their time together.

To be honest, when I thought about my few experiences with the opposite sex, I had been rather lucky compared to my two best friends.

What had started off as a three-month expedition of self-discovery and healing for Cait had expanded somewhat, and it had now been three years since she'd left the UK. As far as I could tell from our regular phone calls and occasional flying visits home, she had no intention of returning long-term either. While travelling, she had discovered that her talent for art could actually pay the bills, and so she'd starting working in various places she stayed; she'd built props for the Sydney Opera House, helped to redecorate a monkey sanctuary in Borneo, and was currently teaching outdoor art lessons to orphans in Vietnam.

Pressing the call button I sat impatiently, picking at the hem of my jumper as I listened to the call attempting to go through. Since Cait had been in the Far East, our phone chats had been less often, as we were frequently let down by the unreliable connections. Today, however, after several clicks and a beep, I heard the ringing tone and smiled happily.

The phone rang for quite some time, and I was just about to hang up when it connected and I heard Cait's voice. 'Allie! Hi! Hang on a second, OK?' This was followed by several loud noises and a constant pattering sound which almost sounded like a river or stream rushing in the background. Was she swimming? Surely not with her phone? There was another bang, and then several squelching noises before Cait came back on the line. 'Hi! Sorry about that.'

She sounded breathless, which added to my overall confusion and had me frowning as I spoke. 'What on earth are you doing?'

'Trying to escape the rain!' she laughed. 'We're getting a late monsoon storm. I was up with the kids at the orphanage when it started so I had to run back to my hut before the ground got too swamped. You wouldn't believe it, it's absolutely falling down.' I could still hear the pattering noise, which I now knew was rain drops, and I smiled, knowing that Cait – Mrs Great Outdoors – would be loving these experiences. 'Phew. OK, I'm at the hut and I've got my muddy boots off. So, how are you?'

Wasn't that just the question. Rolling my eyes, I flopped back on the bed and stared at the ceiling. I was snowed in, stranded in a mansion, horny beyond belief, and magnetically attracted to a stranger. That was a pretty succinct evaluation of my current situation, wasn't it? Opting for a slightly less telling answer, I gave a huffed sigh and explained about the snow and being trapped in the house in the hills.

'Wow. It must really be snowing then,' Cait murmured. I could hear the sound of a door closing in the background, and then a happy sigh as Cait presumably sat down in the dry of her hut.

'It is.' I sounded gloomy, but I couldn't help it, especially not when I pulled the curtain back and saw just how heavily the snow was still coming down. 'Bloody Sarah owes me for this,' I muttered, dropping the curtain and practically throwing myself on the bed.

The sound of Cait chuckling down the line marginally relaxed me as I threw my free hand up over my head and began absently fiddling with a lock of hair. 'Did you say the owner is there though?' she enquired, which promptly erased my relaxed feeling and made me scrunch up my face as images of him in his pyjama-clad magnificence filled my mind again.

'He is,' I answered vaguely.

'Well at least you're not on your own then.' Cait was looking on the positive side, but the more time I spent here, the harder I was finding it to remain upbeat. I knew my slumping mood was largely due to an annoyance over my inability to control myself around the mystery owner, but as boring as it would be, this enforced stay would actually be easier if I were here on my own. Then I wouldn't keep succumbing to these strange lusty sensations every time I was within fifteen feet of him.

'What's he like?'

'Stunning.' My hand flew to my mouth as I realised I'd said that out loud. Oops. I'd meant to keep my description a little low key, perhaps something along the line of "fairly attractive, but brutishly moody", but apparently my brain was

37

having none of those pansy descriptions and just blurted out exactly what it was thinking.

Cait giggled loudly on the other end of the line, and I couldn't help but smile too. I missed her so much. 'Well, that was certainly a concise description. Is he stunning and married, or stunning and single?'

Pulling in a deep breath, I pondered the question, and realised that I knew basically nothing about him – apart from the fact that he was grouchy, had the face of a model, a body to die for, superb taste in coffee, and was quite pernickety about his parking spaces. But I knew nothing of importance about him. Rolling my eyes, I rubbed a hand over my face – I didn't even know his name.

'No idea, but I'd describe him as way out of my league.' He was after all, basically a *GQ* model, and I was a lowly school teacher. 'I don't know his name,' I admitted. 'To be honest, I feel a bit in the way being here, so I'm doing my best to avoid him.'

'Hmmm.' Cait sounded thoughtful, but then suddenly there was a loud clattering down the line and she gave a small yelp, making me sit up in concern. 'Cait? *Cait?* Are you OK?'

'Bugger!' There was a further more muffled crash and then I heard a laugh down the line, which relaxed my panicked state slightly. 'My bloody drain pipe just fell off the roof. God, that made me jump!' she giggled. 'I better go. Sorry to cut you short, Allie, but if I don't get that thing back on quickly, my roof will be leaking like a colander in minutes.'

Disappointed at the briefness of our call, I nodded in understanding. 'No problem. Be careful, OK?'

'I will, don't worry. I've done it before, I just need to wrestle with the clips a bit.'

'OK, and remember, it's not long until April when we actually get to see each other!' I reminded her, my words making my earlier smile spring back onto my face. April – the date I would be officially ending my career as a teacher to live off my savings (mostly some recent inheritance I'd received from a great-aunt) and make a go at writing full-time. I wrote vampire fiction in my spare time, and had recently had a little interest from a publisher, which prompted me into giving it a proper go. April was also when Cait and I had agreed to meet in LA to do a little travelling together. I couldn't wait.

'Actually, I might be home in the next few weeks if you're around?' she said, making my eyebrows nearly pop from the top of my head in excited surprise.

'God, yes! Why?'

'I'm going to be flying on to my next stop of America, so it seems logical to break up the journey in the UK for a week or so and see my family for a late Christmas. I'm not sure of a date yet, though, need to book my flights.'

'OK, fantastic. Well, I'll be here whenever,' I murmured with a smile. 'Let me know dates as soon as you can. Bye.'

And with that I heard Cait give a slightly distracted farewell as her attention turned to the job of fixing her roof.

Hanging up, I popped my phone on the bedside table, feeling much better after my chat. I was so lucky to have a best friend like her, and I couldn't believe I might actually get to see her soon. That overseas call from my mobile had probably cost a small fortune, but it had certainly raised my spirits, so in my mind, it was worth every penny.

There was only so long that my stomach could survive on one banana and two oat bars, so later that evening I cautiously made my way downstairs in search of some dinner. Flinching at the squeak from the kitchen door as I pushed it open, I poked my head inside and warily checked for any sign of human life like some kind of pathetically unskilled spy. What I would have done if the house owner had been inside, I have no idea, because I would have looked like a complete and utter idiot sneaking around, but thankfully, I didn't have to deal with that because the kitchen was blissfully empty.

Stepping in, I relaxed my tense shoulders and looked around, once again appreciating just how gorgeous these fittings were. With the beautifully traditional features in the other rooms and this stylistic kitchen, it was almost my dream house, really. Not that I was dreaming about living here, almost the opposite, in fact – I'd spent the best part of the day imagining escaping so I could spend Christmas with my family. Although if I managed to sleep tonight and not dream about the owner, it would be a miracle, because he was a whole other story that I couldn't seem to get out of my head for more than five minutes at a time.

Sighing, I began my search for food when a note on the counter caught my eye. Walking over, I looked closer at the piece of A4 paper, which had a hastily drawn arrow on the top pointing towards the stove top and what appeared to be the chicken casserole I had made yesterday. Judging by the steam coming from the top, it had been recently re-heated. Grinning broadly and almost laughing out loud to myself, I read the note, written in large, edgy capital letters: "You made it, you may as well get to enjoy it too." I was compelled to trace his handwriting, and I reached out a hand using the tip of my finger to follow his words letter by letter.

Snapping out of my trance I dropped my hand and looked at the casserole again with a happy shrug. It certainly saved me cooking, which could only be a good thing. Smiling, I grabbed a bowl and ladled some out before smiling appreciatively. It smelt pretty great, if I did say so myself. Carrying the bowl back to my room I decided on dinner in bed with a book and an early night. Maybe when I woke up tomorrow the snow would be gone. That was what I was pinning my hopes on, anyway.

Chapter Five
Sean

When my security team had insisted on cameras in my house I'd been highly unimpressed by the idea, thinking it a complete invasion of privacy, but now, finally, they were actually coming to some use. Only I could access the footage, and they only covered the downstairs areas (one of my stipulations so I could retain just a sliver of my much valued privacy), but it meant I had caught the brief interaction between Allie and myself in the kitchen yesterday morning on film. Adjusting myself in my office chair I stretched out my long legs and scrolled back through the footage to find the start of the section again before pressing play.

I must have replayed this snippet of film fifty times now. In fact, I practically had it memorised; the sleepy mussed state of her hair when she entered the room, the way she seemed to tense and flush when she first saw me, the slight widening of her eyes as I stepped close to her body, and finally, the thrust of her breasts as she gasped when I accidentally touched her stomach.

Clenching my teeth as I watched the screen, I could remember exactly how soft her skin had been and my fingers tingled at the memory, desperate to acquaint themselves with her body properly. She wasn't the only one who had been affected by that moment – I'd felt it too, the chemistry between us that was so strong it was almost palpable. Predictably it had also given me an instant erection, which was why I'd left the room so hastily. That, and my reluctance to start anything with her. With my workload about to get crazily busy in the next few months, it was hardly perfect timing – and besides, I seemed to feel things for her that would surely only lead to trouble in the long run.

Groaning, I pushed back in my chair and adjusted my groin. I was rock hard. *Again*. I had been on and off since she'd arrived in my life two days ago. It was the most intense connection I'd ever felt with a woman and we'd barely even interacted. In fact, I'd deliberately been quick at breakfast today to avoid another run-in like yesterday. From the electricity I'd felt between us then, I'd place money on the fact that we would be dynamite in bed. Best not to dwell on that thought for too long though; I'd had enough issues with my cock running wild since she'd arrived.

Pursing my lips, I spat out a harsh, indecisive sigh. If the connection I'd felt was an indicator of how good it could be between us, then perhaps I should pursue it? Pursue her. *Allie*.

It was a slightly strange name, and probably short for something, but what? Alison? Alexandra? Alana? Thinking about her name seemed to make it all the more real and I gave up pursing my lips to chew on the bottom one instead as I wondered if I could really do this. Do her. Or perhaps even something more.

It had been years since the accident that had put me off relationships … maybe it was time to get back in the game. I exhaled a long breath and rubbed my chin thoughtfully as I continued to watch the screen. The part I couldn't understand was her reaction after I'd left. I was almost sure Allie felt the same magnetic attraction as I did, but once I'd left the kitchen she'd practically folded over the counter in apparent relief. Had I completely misread the chemistry between us? Did she actually loathe every minute of being here? Perhaps she was scared of me?

Leaning forwards, I moved the cursor so I could open up a different set of footage. This time it was of the kitchen last night, when Allie had found the casserole and note that I'd left for her. Now two of my three screens were filled with images of her and I felt a smile tug at the corners of my lips. She was so pretty. And her hair – I was obsessed with her hair. It was so long it almost reached her arse, and the colour was a perfect sun-lightened gold. As perverted as it sounded, my dreams last night had mostly centred on me wrapping the soft strands around my fist as I bent her over any available surface and took her from behind.

On the screen, I watched in amusement as Allie cautiously entered the kitchen, her posture tense and eyes darting around as she looked for something – presumably me – before she relaxed and strolled in. From this camera angle I could see her face perfectly as she saw and approached the dish of food. I then watched in fascination as she traced my handwriting, her finger following every letter almost reverently.

Swallowing hard, I blinked, trying not to read too much into her action. The smile that lit her face was my favourite part, and right on cue, there it was; her lips curling at the edges and eyes sparkling. Her pretty face transformed into something utterly beautiful. *She* was beautiful. We had hardly spent any time together, but I hadn't seen her smile often, and I felt almost upset that I had been denied them. She probably hadn't smiled because I'd been such a miserable bastard around her.

Looking at my desk and the monitors filled with her face, I suddenly flushed. God, I was basically a stalker. A touch of guilt entered my brain before I quickly pushed it aside. She was in *my* house, and the security footage was mine, so technically I was allowed to look at it. That's what I'd keep telling myself, anyway.

Suddenly picking up movement on the screen to my left, my eyes widened as I turned to the real time feed and saw the woman currently residing in my thoughts make her way towards the stairs. Shit. I needed more time to think about this. I wasn't ready to see her again, but seeing as she had two mugs in her hands – *two* – she was either very thirsty, or she was on her way to my office with a drink for me. Fuck.

Briefly forgetting about my tangled emotions, I quickly flew into action, closing down programs and hastily switching to less incriminating images on my screens, because if she saw this stuff, Allie would no doubt freak out and do something ridiculously dangerous again, like try to walk home – blizzard be damned.

Chapter Six
Allie

Cowardice was never something I would attribute to myself, so after getting sick of hiding away in my room, I gave up that afternoon and headed back downstairs to stretch my legs and get a cup of tea. As much as I liked – loved – coffee, I usually tried to limit myself to only drinking it in the mornings, as it had a tendency to give me the jitters if I drank it past lunch. The house had been silent as a tomb all day, so I could only assume that Mr Conversational had also been hiding somewhere. Perhaps he worked from home, or had a home cinema hidden away that he was using to kill some time. I had no idea, but he was certainly never around in the main rooms when I was.

As reluctant as I was about interacting with him again, I had used my hours of solitude to come to the conclusion that it might be wise to try and build some bridges if I was going to be here for a few days, so as well as my tea I made him a coffee – he didn't strike me as a tea man – and set off in search of him.

It took a while because this house really was massive, but eventually on the third floor I saw a light around the crack of a door and made my way towards it. Once I got closer I saw that the door wasn't entirely shut, so with a small knock of my elbow to alert him of my presence, I bravely pushed the door open and found myself entering a home office. Wow, there were more computer monitors, printers, and projector screens in here than my local electrical store. This space appeared to be just as tricked out with gadgets as his kitchen, if not more so. Seems like my assumptions about him being a home worker were correct.

The room appeared to be far fuller than the rest of the house, with some pictures, certificates, and other personal items on shelves to my right, but I ignored them, my eyes instead being instantly drawn to the house owner again. As his handsomeness filtered through my senses it hit me full in the face again, and briefly struck me speechless. God, his looks really hadn't dulled in the time since I'd seen him.

While squirreled away in my room earlier, I'd actually persuaded myself that I'd exaggerated his appeal, but boy, how very wrong I'd been. I'd never responded to a man like this before and as my traitorous body buzzed with energy I grumpily decided that it should be illegal for any guy to be this good looking. He was wrapped up in a large beige jumper today, but no item of clothing could hide his impressive build, no matter how bulky the wool.

Getting a grip on myself, I drew in a shaky breath and smiled politely, stepping forward as I held the mug up. 'I thought you might like a coffee.'

Briefly narrowing his eyes and assessing me cautiously, the man finally nodded his thanks and reached out to take it. As he clasped the beverage, our fingers briefly touched, causing the hairs on my arm to stand up as that same strange electricity shot between us, just like it had when he'd touched my stomach yesterday. A gasp disturbed the silence, but I was fairly sure it came from him, which was a very interesting development. I was still half-holding the bloody coffee mug, but I seemed frozen to the spot and unable to move away as he suddenly began to run his fingers over my hand.

Oh God. He was caressing me – on purpose, this time – and I was doing nothing whatsoever to stop him. Stroking his thumb over my knuckles, he smiled, an expression which was almost as breath-taking as the tingling sparks shooting over my skin.

'You have very soft hands for a cleaner.' His bizarre observation brought me back to the present as I laughed softly and shook my head.

'I'm not a cleaner, I'm a schoolteacher. Sarah's my best friend, she runs the cleaning business and needed someone to cover this shift. Seeing as I was on school holidays I got lumbered with it.'

Perhaps it was my phrasing, or the fact that I was getting too chatty, but the God – uh, I mean man – stared at me intently for a few more seconds, the smile fading from his lips before he practically snatched the mug from me and turned his attention back to his laptop and the bank of screens on his desk, all traces of friendliness vanished.

'Thanks,' he murmured sullenly, not a hint of genuine appreciation in his tone. He really was a grumpy bastard, wasn't he?

As I trailed towards the door it became obvious why he was wearing the jumper; his office was freezing. A small shiver shook my body, so I pulled mine closer around me and decided to head to my room to read in bed and warm up. It wasn't exactly like there was anything else to do, was there?

'Allie, stop. Come over here,' he whispered behind me just as I had reached the door. It was more a statement than a request, and beyond all logical reasoning I found myself turning back into the room and instinctively walking towards him.

Once I got closer I felt awkward about how easily I had bent to his will, and didn't quite know what to do with myself, so I leaned my hips on his desk, hugely aware of the way he was watching my every move with those intense blue eyes of his.

Several silent seconds passed with no actions, and in the absence of conversation I crossed my arms for something to distract me from the charged static that seemed to hang around us. The sexual tension was like treacle – at least that's how it seemed to me, anyway. God knows what he thought, because apart from a brief stroke of my hand just now, he'd given away nothing since I'd met him except moodiness.

'Do you know who I am?' he asked quietly, causing me to blush instantly. How embarrassing; I'd spent two nights in his house and hadn't even bothered to find out his name. But then again, what kind of host was he to allow me to stay and not introduce himself properly? A grouchy, miserable host, that's what, I thought with a barely supressed snort.

'No, Sarah didn't mention your name,' I mumbled, to which he merely nodded thoughtfully at my response. 'You look vaguely familiar, but I can't place where from,' I added, voicing my own earlier thoughts. 'Have we met before?'

A frown creased my brows as I considered him again. He definitely looked a fair few years older than me, but perhaps I went to school with him? Maybe he was one of the college guys I'd been pathetically gazing at in the canteen with hormonal longing back in my teenage days of braces and bunches.

'No. We've not met before.' His response was immediate and his tone so brusque it ended the conversation right there. Deep down, I already knew that if we had crossed paths before I would have remembered someone this attractive. I had a feeling that even after just these few days, he wouldn't be an easy man for me to forget, either.

After his question I had expected him to share his name, so I was caught completely off-guard when he instead swivelled his chair, took a firm grip on my hips, and guided me sideways so I was leaning back on the desk directly in front of him.

Good Lord, I was practically nestled between his spread thighs. In fact, if he just shifted forwards a few centimetres then my knees would be getting incredibly friendly with his groin.

A small gasp of shock escaped my lips, partly from his unexpected actions but also from the fire that leapt across my skin where his hands still lightly rested on my hips. Even through my jeans, it felt as if his touch was searing my skin and I instantly found my hands clinging to the edge of the desk until my knuckles ached.

'W … what are you doing?' I whispered raggedly, my breathing short and sharp from his sudden contact – not to mention the close proximity. I was too shocked to want to know the answer, but also too intrigued to consider moving away.

In one fluid movement, he stood up and stepped even closer to me then, using one of his thighs to part my knees, he positioned himself right in between my legs, well and truly within my personal space so that our bodies were just millimetres apart.

Talk about up close and personal.

I gulped loudly, so loudly that I saw the corner of his mouth tweak in a smug smile, looking positively satisfied with my physical response to him. What a smooth mover. Not to mention arrogant. 'You were shivering, gorgeous girl, I thought I'd warm you up,' he murmured, before one of his hands rose and slid into my hair as his lips descended on mine, crushing my mouth as he held me immobile with a gentle grip by my nape.

Gorgeous girl. His bizarre turn of phrase rang in my head as my lips parted and a lusty moan escaped my throat. Rational thought told me I shouldn't respond to his kiss; I'd only just met him and I didn't even know his name, but I simply couldn't help myself. For whatever reason – be it chemistry, magnetism, or just plain old lust – this man attracted me like no other I'd ever met, and my body's response was immediate as I joined in his kiss and reached up to wrap my arms around his shoulders, where I dug into his jumper and pulled him closer.

My heated reaction seemed to please him because I heard a growl of approval shortly before the hand on my hip slid around behind me to grasp my bum. His grip was hard, almost firm enough to hurt, but the possessiveness in his touch was actually quite thrilling. In seconds, he had pulled me forward until the heaviness of his growing erection was pressing against my stomach, causing both of us to let out heated moans of pleasure into each other's mouths.

This man was an incredible kisser. Actually, forget that, this man was incredible, *full stop*. Everything about him screamed experience, and after just a few seconds of his touch he had my whole body alight with arousal. I literally couldn't get enough and arched myself against him, feeling totally alive for the first time in years. He seemed to ignite my body, and my desperate, almost primal response surprised even myself, as I keenly allowed his hands to explore before reciprocating with curious exploratory touches of my own.

Before I even realised what was happening, he had gripped the hem of my jumper and T-shirt and pulled them over my head to expose my lacy bra. 'Bloody clothes are still damp. For the love of God, woman, stop being stubborn and wear the ones I gave you,' he muttered hotly before tossing the garment aside. 'Understand?' He was aroused, pressed between my legs, and striping me of my clothing and he actually expected me to converse with him? Really?

I only managed a husky, 'OK,' which thankfully seemed to satisfy him.

Letting out a groan, his head dipped to explore one of my nipples through the fabric of my bra, causing me to let out a high keening noise. God, was that me? It sounded more like a distressed piglet, which made me blush with embarrassment and hastily close my lips. I really wasn't myself around this man – it was like he had consumed the normal me within seconds and left behind a wild shell of my old self. My embarrassment was soon forgotten, when seconds later he used his tongue to skim and lick at my needy flesh through the lace, an act that was so erotic that my head began to swim with lust.

The nipple getting his attention tightened almost painfully and I wiggled in his embrace to try and press it more firmly into his mouth. His response was immediate, as he used his teeth to tug on the bud, pulling it and causing me to let out a garbled moan and grip at his muscular shoulders for support. Quite frankly, I was so aroused by this point that he could rip the bra clean off with his teeth and I wouldn't care.

After driving me almost insane with need, his hot mouth diverted its attention to my other breast, trailing wet kisses across my chest and leaving goose pimples in his wake as I shivered and trembled with need below his mouth. His free hand traced a path down across my flat abdomen, sending tremors of pleasure radiating across my now overheated skin. His hand gently began to push inside the waistband of my jeans, and then seconds later I let out another cry of pleasure as his fingers trailed through the hair there and then made their first contact with my swollen clit.

I couldn't believe I was doing this. It was completely out of character for me, but as soon as his fingers found my sensitive clitoris and began their slick, wondrous circling I knew I couldn't stop. I didn't want to stop. This just felt right, not to mention really, *really* good. He might be a miserable, nameless bastard, but he certainly knew how to flick my buttons, and right now the sensations ripping through my body were too all-consuming to care about anything else.

Raising his lips to claim mine in another furious kiss, his tongue lashed and lapped as his dextrous fingers went to work on the buttons of my jeans. Doing my best not to be entirely consumed by him, I kissed him back with everything I had, my fingers now clutching at the soft, silky hair at the nape of his neck until I was practically pulling it out in a frenzy. My jeans were undone in a flash, before he pushed his hand back inside my underwear and ran a finger firmly down the slit of skin between my legs. He caught my moan of pleasure with his lips, swallowing it in a deep kiss, his tongue exploring my mouth as his free arm tightened around me possessively and dragged me even closer.

'You're so fucking wet for me, Allie,' he murmured hotly in my ear, but there was no point getting embarrassed about it, or trying to deny it, because it was true – and the crazy thing was, his dirty words just seemed to cause even more wetness between my legs.

Pasting a trail of kisses across my collarbone, he began to rise away from me, and my body instantly missed his heat as he stared down at me.

'Take off your jeans,' he instructed quietly, as he stepped back and removed his jumper and shirt in one fluid tug to reveal that beautiful chest again. A happy sigh left my lips as I soaked up the perfection stood before me. His hair was ruffled from its journey through his clothing, his face intent and flushed, and his chest was just … simply the most tempting thing I had ever seen in my life – muscular, but not overly so, with that covering of soft, dark hair I wanted to run my hands across.

Stalling in my need to touch him, I didn't hesitate to follow his lead as my trembling hands managed to push the material of my jeans down my legs before I kicked them off and they lay on top of his discarded shirt on the floor.

He gave an approving nod and stepped toward me again as he used his jean clad thigh to wedge himself back between my legs. Pressing his chest to mine, he lowered his mouth to the crook of my neck, where he began kissing and nipping at the sensitive skin, and of course, like the virtual slave to him that I was, I tilted my head to give him better access. This was heavenly. Sliding an arm around his neck, I trailed my nails across the solid warmth of his back muscles appreciatively as I let out another strange lusty noise that sounded so alien to me, but seemed to occur with increasingly regularity when this man was around.

Intent on kissing him, I decided to drag his head up to mine, but as my hands threaded into his hair he straightened up with a purposeful look in his eye that swiftly stopped me in my tracks. Slowly reaching up, he linked his fingers through mine, then pulled our joined hands down until they were pressed on the desk just behind me. Placing one short, swift kiss on my lips he then unlinked his hands from mine and placed them on my hips, pushing me backwards so I was sitting more fully on the edge of the desk, then opened my thighs before lowering to kneel in front of me. There was no time to feel embarrassed about what he was about to do, because no sooner had I realised his intentions that he had parted my knees with his large hands and promptly buried his face between my legs.

OK, so there was no hesitancy or gentle introductions; he had literally dived between my legs and begun exploring with his mouth as I gasped and writhed under his passionate touch. My head rolled backwards as the warmth of his breath touched my sensitive flesh through the thin material of my panties before I felt his tongue returning to tease me, this time pushing against my opening with strong, warm movements.

'I have to taste you properly,' he muttered, sounding irritated by the presence of my underwear. Sliding his hands up the inside of my thighs he pushed my legs even further apart, and then with one deft flick of his thumb this magnetic man had pushed aside my knickers and preceded to run his tongue the entire length of my slit. The stretched position of my hips was immediately forgotten as I squeezed my eyes shut from the pleasure, lolled my head, and clenched my lips closed to try and avoid any more embarrassing noises escaping.

My hands desperately thrashed further behind me to prop up my sagging body as he used his tongue to lap and tease my opening, and then he worked his way higher, circling my sensitive clitoris and causing me to push myself forwards to increase the pressure. His murmur of approval caused ripples of desire to rush across my skin and then, with no warning, he gripped my hips and plunged his tongue inside me.

This time there was no hiding the yelp of pleasure that escaped my lips as his thumb circled my clit and he thrust his tongue inside me again and again, sending me spiralling towards a dizzying peak so quickly that I could barely keep up. Shifting his position slightly, he moved his tongue to my throbbing clit before thrusting two fingers deep inside me, causing my hips to buck as I cried out below him. This man certainly didn't lack confidence or ability, that was for sure. Giving me no time to adjust to his thick digits he started a rapid, hard rhythm, curving his fingers so they immediately managed to zero in on my G-spot.

This man not only looked like a god and was built like one too, but he was now proving that his skills at pleasing women were also off the charts.

The combination of tongue, fingers, and his complete control was too much for me to deal with and after just seconds of attention, a tightly coiled spring inside me burst, causing me to spasm against his mouth as wave after wave of pleasure swept over me. My head thrashed around and I clenched around his unrelenting fingers as he continued to thrust them into me, scissoring and twisting them to draw out my climax until I was almost sobbing from the intensity of it all.

Blimey. I was completed sated, and my head, body, and heart were spinning. I'd never climaxed with such intensity before and the knowledge that a complete stranger had been the one to do it made me blush to my core. Not to mention the volume of the noises I'd been making – what was that about? I was usually relatively quiet in bed, so to yell, cry, and groan like an animal was so unlike me. Mind you, it hadn't seemed to bother him. In fact, every time I'd moaned or mewled he had upped his efforts even more, so perhaps being a bit vocal had its benefits.

I felt utterly exhausted in a wholly pleasurable way, and was considering if it would be acceptable to lie back on his desk to rest, when he stood up and leant into my field of vision, his handsome, angular features sending another small shudder of desire through my body. Seeing my sleepy eyes, my mysterious stranger slowly shook his head as a wicked expression emerged on his painfully handsome face.

'I'm not finished with you yet,' he promised, as he looped his fingers into the waistband of my knickers and swiftly pulled them off my body.

I was now completely naked and half lying on the desk of an almost total stranger. A flicker of shame began to permeate my consciousness, but I immediately forgot the concern as my gaze was drawn to him locating and pulling his zipper down, before stripping off his trousers with swift, precise movements, leaving him stood in just a pair of tight black boxers. Tight black boxers with a very large bulge protruding at the front. *Holy shit.* I could see so much lovely taut skin and softly defined muscles that I barely knew where to look first. He was just hotness personified.

My eyes widened and I definitely got an area to focus on in the next second, because he dispensed his boxers and it became abundantly clear what the cotton had been hiding – this guy's large build clearly extended to all areas of his anatomy. And I mean *all* areas. Not only were his thighs broad and muscled, but there was a rather magnificently proportioned manhood nestled between them. Blimey. I think I was actually hyperventilating, my breaths sounding all raspy and breathy as I sat there eagerly awaiting his next move. His eyes were hooded when they briefly flicked to mine as he pulled his wallet from his jeans pocket, dumped the trousers on the floor again, and flicked through it to retrieve a condom.

Donning the protection, he tossed his wallet aside, leaned over me so I was well and truly caged in by him, and laced a hand through my hair, bringing his lips down to mine. As soon as our mouths collided, the fire within me re-ignited, sending fresh heat coursing between my legs and warming the skin of my entire body. Nudging his hips between my legs he tilted me back so I was fully lying on the desk, and then palmed his arousal and positioned it at my opening. As I felt the heat of his erection rub against me I let out a long, breathy gasp, the feeling of his solid tip so amazing that I nearly came from the anticipation of how it would feel buried within me. My expectation was then replaced by the real thing as he began to edge himself inside me.

Mr Sex God was barely halfway in when he paused, his rough breath hot against my face as he cupped my chin and leant over me with a deep frown, 'Are you a virgin?' he questioned, his tone gritty and strained from holding himself back, but his thumb displaying the complete opposite as it gently stroked my cheek.

Embarrassment flooded through me and my face flushed. 'No ... but it's been a while ....' This was the complete truth. I was far from a virgin, having had several partners before, but I'd been so engrossed in work over the past few years that my love life had taken a serious backseat. In fact, the only vaguely masculine thing to have graced my bed in the last four years was my vibrator. 'I'm OK, it doesn't hurt.' Which was a marginal untruth, because he was definitely stretching me, but I was so turned on that there was no way I was going to ask him to stop.

Nodding, he placed a brief kiss on my jaw. 'You're so fucking tight,' he groaned.

That's because you are so big, I thought, but I was completely beyond coherence by this point. As he edged himself in another inch and paused again, I noticed a sheen of sweat building on his brow and began to wonder if I was *too* tight, so tight that he found it uncomfortable. But as he suddenly pushed himself fully inside me with a lusty growl, I suspected not. 'God, you feel so good …' he muttered against my neck, his hot breath tickling my skin and adding to the eroticism of the act.

Pulling out slowly, I was expecting a similar, slow thrust back in, but he instead gripped my hips, and after staring at me for a second or two, hammered forwards in one almost brutal thrust until he was buried to the hilt.

'*Ohmyfuckinggod*!' My gargled words came out in one strangled cry as my body desperately struggled to stretch and accommodate his considerable size and the speed with which he had just impaled me. Thankfully, after a second or so where I had expected to feel pain, I realised that I was more than adequately lubricated from his mouth and my orgasm.

'Are you OK?' he asked on a growl. Was I? He was flipping huge, and my body already felt full, stretching in places so deep inside me that I didn't even know they existed. Panting, I clutched his shoulders, my nails digging deep as I squeezed my eyes shut and tried to relax my straining muscles around his twitching cock.

'Allie? Christ, woman, you're killing me. Are you OK?' he barked, his voice so roughened that I pried my eyes open to find a sheen of sweat on his brow and his jaw tense from the strain of holding himself back as his eyes burnt into me.

Wiggling my hips slightly to accommodate him, I felt my slight discomfort gradually seeping away as the pleasure of his intrusion began to overwhelm me, making my entire being feel lax. Managing to relax the grip of my fingers on his back I stroked his cheek, swallowed hard, and then nodded.

'Yes. God, you feel amazing.' Giving a curt nod, he then began to move inside me, thankfully slightly slower than last time, allowing my body to fully accept him until *I* was the one trying for harder movements by raising my hips into each thrust to increase the speed and depth of his penetration.

Suddenly our breathy, lusty bubble was burst as we were disturbed by a shrill ringing to our right. The mystery man glared across at the ringing phone, banged one of his fists on the desk beside me in irritation, and looked into my eyes intently. His breath was coming just as hard and fast as mine, but instead of continuing, he shook his head as if clearing his mind and pulled out of me so quickly that I winced at the sudden loss. 'Get dressed. I've been expecting this call, I need to take it.'

With that, he simply stepped back, flicking the condom into a nearby bin as he went, pulled his jeans over his still hard cock, and without even another glance, turned his back to me and picked up the phone.

Lying there on the desk, still stark naked and spread-legged, I stared at the wide expanse of muscled back in complete shock. How flipping rude was that? Not to mention confusing. He'd seemed so into it until his phone rang that I'd almost describe his lovemaking as generous. The way he'd paused while I adjusted to him had been incredibly thoughtful, poles apart from his grouchy behaviour around the house that I'd witnessed so far. But as soon as the phone had rung he'd snapped straight to back to being shut off again.

Who was on the phone? Was it his girlfriend? Or a wife calling to check up on him? I was flummoxed and still struggling to understand what on earth had just happened, but seeing as he was clearly waiting for me to leave the room, I snapped my legs closed, grabbed my clothes, and left without looking back, hurrying to the privacy of the guest room flushed with shame and perilously close to tears.

Slamming the door, I flung my clothes on the floor and headed straight to the en-suite. I was so desperate to clean away the feeling of smut still lingering on my skin that I flicked the taps on and stumbled straight into the tumbling water without even bothering to wait for it to warm up sufficiently. Immersing myself under the lukewarm water, I grabbed a bar of soap and began to scrub furiously at my body in an attempt to clean off any traces of that man that might remain on my skin, all the while cursing myself under my breath. Having sex on a desk with a man I barely knew – what the hell had I been thinking?

Cleaning between my legs with a frown, I shook my head at my stupidity. Any pleasure I'd had from his talented fingers and my amazing climax had now been tarnished by his appallingly rude behaviour, and I rubbed at my poor abused skin extra hard to try and cleanse myself of the guilt that our encounter had left on me.

Shaking my head, I climbed from the shower and wrapped myself in a large towel, pulling it tightly around my body like a protective shell. Tucking my chin into my chest, I stood for several minutes, dripping and fuming. How could I have allowed myself to be drawn in like that? I was usually sensible where it came to sex, but that bloody man and the lure he had over me was completely unfathomable.

Glancing up through the open bathroom door I could see it was still snowing heavily, and felt myself crumble inside. So it looked like I'd be stuck at least another day, then. I wasn't sure I could cope with another twenty-four minutes in the company of Mr Half-Fuck-You-Crazy-And-Then-Demand-You-Leave let alone twenty-four hours.

Grimacing at my predicament, I realised that I was being overly optimistic if I expected this snow to clear up in a day – it was at least three feet deep in places and still falling. Things could get really awkward between us if we didn't clear the air soon, and wasn't that just an understatement. We'd just had sex – albeit unfinished sex – on his desk before he had unceremoniously chucked me out – it didn't get much more awkward than that.

Sighing heavily, I began rubbing my damp hair and decided to try and be mature about it. We were both consenting adults, and it was just sex, after all. Admittedly, rather mind-blowingly good sex, but still, just sex. Once he was off the phone I would talk to him, try and smooth things out so we could get over this strange connection between us and move to being civil for the next few days while I was stuck here. Nodding my head decisively, I piled my hair up inside a small towel and wandered into the bedroom to dress.

Plus, it would probably be advisable to find out the name of the man who I had just given free rein over my body to, I acknowledged with a self-derisory scowl.

Over the next twenty minutes, I wasted time by brushing and trying to towel dry my hair more thoroughly. I knew I was secretly just trying to delay the inevitable meeting, but my hair *did* need drying, so I began searching in the drawers and wardrobe in the hopes of finding a hairdryer. After five minutes I concluded there wasn't one, so the towel would have to do. With the length of my hair, it would take an age to dry. In fact, I'd probably be going to bed with it still wet.

I hung my dirty and still slightly damp clothes over the radiator and followed through on his earlier order by sorting through the pile of garments that the house owner had left for me. As pissed off as I was with him, I couldn't help but smile at these options – they were all enormous. But at least they were dry and warm.

Holding up a pale grey T-shirt, I lined it up with my shoulders and saw in the mirror that it practically came to my knees. Sighing, I pulled it over my head and accepted the fact that I was going to look like I was wearing a flipping tent until I'd washed my own clothes. As I pushed my head through the soft cotton I was immediately surrounded by his heady, spicy scent, and the sudden smell caused me to sigh and push the material to my nose for another, deeper, inhale. Drawing in a long breath I smiled as I briefly drowned in his fragrance. He might be a nameless, miserable sex god, but wow, did he smell good. Predictably, my mind immediately wandered back to our liaison on his desk ... he kissed rather well too, not to mention the other skills he had with that tongue of his ...

Argh! I must stop thinking about him like that. I shoved my hands irritably through the arm holes of the T-shirt and set about digging through my handbag for my face cream, before letting out a squeal of delight as I saw a pair of yoga leggings in there. I'd shoved them in just in case I got sweaty when cleaning and wanted to change for the drive home, but I was so thankful for them now. Judging from the size of the gargantuan T-shirt, the tracksuit bottoms he'd left out would be useless. They'd probably come up to my armpits.

Luckily, I also carried two spare pairs of knickers in my bag in case of feminine emergencies, so I pulled on a fresh pair and donned my leggings. No spare bra, unfortunately, but I wasn't averse to wearing my bra for a few days in a row and at least it was still dry. Selecting a navy blue fleece jumper, I pulled it on, giggled at how long the sleeves were, and rolled them each up several times so my hands poked out the bottom.

The last items I selected were a thick pair of warm, woollen walking socks. Pulling them on I smiled at how big they were; they would be perfect as impromptu slippers, but once again as I tried to roll them into some usable size I was reminded of other areas of his anatomy that had also been rather large. And hot. And *hard* …

Grunting in irritation at my inability to focus on anything other than the man lurking somewhere in this house, I jumped up and walked towards the dressing table to put my watch back on. A glance in the mirror showed that I looked like a complete ragamuffin, so thinking on my feet I grabbed yesterday's snow-dampened clothes and headed to the kitchen intent on washing them. I wasn't brave enough to ask the owner if I could use his washing machine – I hadn't even seen one since I'd arrived – but once I was in the kitchen I found some hand soap under the sink and washed my knickers, jeans, and jumper before wringing them out and putting them on the radiator in my room. This time I was careful to unfold and spread them properly so hopefully they'd be dry by tomorrow. That way at least I could look normal again, even if my roiling emotions felt about as far from normal as possible.

Pushing my damp hair back from my face, I stood in the centre of my bedroom and gave myself a brief pep talk before taking a deep breath for bravery and leaving my room to go to his office. I'd much rather be doing this looking a bit better than I currently did, but I suppose circumstances wouldn't allow me to wait until my own clothes were wearable again.

On arriving, I once again I found the door half open, and through the gap I could see him at his desk, his frown in place and his eyes latched onto the screens. This time I didn't dare just enter, instead knocking tentatively and waiting on the threshold, almost too scared to go any closer in case I became sucked in by the strange magnetism between us again.

He obviously heard me because he jumped slightly when I knocked, but then barely even bothered to lift his head from whatever hugely important task he was doing.

'I'm really busy, what do you need?' he snapped, causing me to flinch from the discernible lack of warmth in his voice. My heart sunk. He might be a stranger, but I obviously felt something towards him. From his cold reaction, however, what we had shared earlier had obviously meant nothing to him other than a quick fuck. I'd probably just been a small distraction from his busy day. What a depressing thought.

Doggedly trying to ignore the pounding of my heart and rapidly wilting confidence, I decided to at least persevere with my mission. 'I … uh … I was hoping you'd tell me your name.'

At my enquiry, he glanced up and met my eye, and for the tiniest of seconds it seemed like his gaze softened as he observed me. His eyes trailed over my appearance, eyebrows flickering as if he were deep in thought as he took in my peculiar clothing and wet hair, but he didn't laugh or smile as I'd expected. Instead, he licked his lips and simply continued to stare at me. 'Sean,' he said quietly. *Sean*. Finally he had a name.

His jaw briefly slackened, as if he were about to say more, but after blinking several times in silence, his shoulders stiffened and he turned back to his computer with a shuttered expression. It was obvious I'd been dismissed, but stupidly I felt frozen to the spot, my feet rigidly refusing to move, and after several seconds he glanced across again, his dark eyes intense.

'Anything else?' he asked icily. This time there was definitely no softening of his expression, just the cold pangs of dismissal, and I literally wanted to melt into the floor and disappear into the folds of his stupidly big clothes.

'No. Nothing, forget it.' I turned away, feeling like a used toy, dirty and unwanted and furious with myself when I felt the sting of tears building behind my eyes. Wanting to put as much distance between us as possible, I strode away and decided to go back to yesterday's plan of avoiding him until the weather lifted and I could leave.

It wasn't cowardice, just common sense. Besides, the house was certainly big enough, and he seemed to cocoon himself in his office all day anyway, so it shouldn't be hard to keep out of his way. I might go stir crazy in the process, but it was better than the alternative of spending one more minute in his company.

Absently wandering the house, I found myself in the lounge and padded across the plush carpet to the huge windows at the rear. As I watched the snowflakes continue to fall in thick swathes I felt a few of my hidden tears finally leak from my eyes and a stab of melancholy hit me squarely in the chest. It was partly from loneliness and depression; after all, it was nearly Christmas and I was still stuck here, but mostly my tears were those of shame. How could I have let myself be used like that? By a man as foul tempered as he was? This really did prove the old saying that looks aren't everything, because Sean certainly had the handsome gene by the bucket load, but from what I'd seen, there was absolutely nothing nice inside him to back it up at all.

As the snowflakes grew thicker still, I felt my stomach drop with them until I felt well and truly sorry for myself. Leaning my back against the wall, I slid down until I was hunched in a tiny ball, with my arms wrapped around my knees protectively. Swiping at my cheeks I tried to clear the tears that were now falling, glad that Sean couldn't see me and know that he'd made me cry. He'd probably get a kick out of knowing he'd upset me. Pulling in a deep breath, I let it out in a long, calming flow as I stared at the white garden. This may turn out to be a long, tough few days and the worst Christmas of my life, I thought with a heavy sigh.

Once I'd allowed myself a few minutes to vent my misery I engaged my usual positive mind-set and distracted myself from my predicament by spending the next hour cooking a beef curry. I might be stuck in the hills and feeling distinctly sorry for myself, but I may as well eat nice food.

As much as I wanted to pretend he wasn't around, I couldn't help myself in the end and I cooked enough dinner for Sean as well. Considering his callous behaviour before and since our desk encounter, I opted to leave it on the stove top for him to find rather than call him down for it. Unlike him though, I didn't bother to leave a note to draw his attention. If he didn't see it, then tough luck.

Hearing his feet descending the steps at about half past seven, I quickly grabbed my portion and tiptoed my way through the lounge so that our paths wouldn't cross, and then, once he was safely in the kitchen and I could hear the sound of his knife and fork moving across a plate, I snuck up to my room to eat in peace.

As I got to my bedroom door I frowned and paused, seeing something hanging from the door handle. As I got closer I saw that it was a small travel hairdryer, and my eyebrows rose in surprise. Opening the door, I put my dinner down on the dresser and went back to retrieve the hairdryer, seeing a small note attached. "This is my sister's. It's too cold to wander around with wet hair." A faint smile curled my lips as I took the hairdryer inside and closed the door thoughtfully. So he might have acted detached earlier, but he *had* noticed my wet hair *and* clothes, and those observations had clearly troubled him enough to dig this out *and* order me to wear his clothes. Hmm. Perhaps there was a caring side hidden away underneath his cold front after all.

Chapter Seven
Allie

As ridiculous as it was, I continued with my avoidance tactics for the next two days, either holed up in my room or cooking dinners and being on guard the entire time, then sneaking through the lounge to avoid Sean when dinner time approached. Mind you, he made my job pretty easy for me by staying in his office practically all the time, anyway.

I had spotted him in the home gym yesterday when I'd been making my way downstairs. He'd been facing away from me and pounding out a run on the treadmill at a fearsome pace, a sight that had immediately caused my step to falter as I paused in the corridor and secretly observed him through the glass door. I was a bit of a health nut and usually dragged myself out for a run at least four times a week, so as I watched him on the treadmill I got a pang of envy, immediately missing my weekly tarmac time.

My craving was soon forgotten, however, as I refocused on the sights and sounds instead. Royal Blood's 'Out of the Black' blared from the speakers, and Sean was shirtless, sweaty, and just as gorgeous from the back as the front; muscular shoulders slimmed down to his narrow waist and then … wow. What an arse. The shorts he was wearing didn't disguise how firm and tight it was, and I watched in fascination as it bounced just a little with each frantic stride. Gosh, he was really going for it. I would class myself as a pretty good runner, but if I was on a treadmill going that pace I'd be flat on my face and flying off into the opposite wall before I'd even managed to take three steps.

Luckily, his focus was firmly on the BBC News on the television in front of him, so he didn't notice me watching him, mouth hanging open and eyes glued to his bottom. After indulging myself in a few more seconds of slack-jawed appreciation, I had hurried back to my room in a bit of a lusty daze.

So apart from that small glimpse of him, my evasive ways were working a treat and I hadn't had to speak to Sean once in nearly forty-eight hours. Admittedly, I was going a little stir crazy sat in my room alone, but thankfully I'd managed to get through to my mum earlier so I could properly let her know where I was. It had been so lovely to hear her voice that I'd nearly cried. She wasn't at all happy about the prospect of me missing Christmas dinner; it was a big family tradition in our house, but seeing as it was still snowing on and off and there was no sign of a thaw anytime soon, I just didn't see how I'd manage to escape. Christmas was just two days away, and as much as I disliked the idea, I was starting to miserably adjust to the fact that I would probably spend it here.

Taking some of my pent up energy out on cookery, I had managed to prepare meals on both nights so far without Sean disturbing me. Thank goodness he had a well-stocked freezer otherwise we'd both starve to death in the snowy wilderness. Unfortunately, as I was finishing off the final preparations for tonight's dinner I heard him coming downstairs earlier than usual, and in my desperate rush to avoid him I didn't have time to grab myself a portion as I had previously. Retreating from the kitchen, I dodged through the lounge empty-handed and sneaked upstairs, trying desperately to suppress my rumbling stomach. Damn it, I was really hungry, and unless I fancied facing up to Mr Moody, I wouldn't be able to eat until he had gone to bed.

The option of seeing Sean after his icy brush-off was too unpleasant to consider, so instead I wandered to my room feeling thoroughly miserable. I had my laptop with me, and would have loved to check my emails and Facebook, but I didn't know the password for Sean's WiFi access and there was no way I was going to ask him, so I killed more time reading.

Glancing at the clock, I saw it was nearly midnight, and as the house had been silent for some time now, I put my book down and slid from the bed before opening my door and creeping downstairs, praying that my empty stomach wouldn't growl too loudly and give me away. Clad only in my makeshift nightdress – one of Sean's huge T-shirts – the cool night air made my exposed skin pop with goose pimples, but I continued regardless, well and truly set on the task of easing my hunger.

I didn't want to risk disturbing Sean by turning on any lights so I felt my way along the unfamiliar walls, stubbing my toe more than once and cursing under my breath at this whole stupid situation. Finally, I found the corridor that led to the kitchen and held my hands out, expecting to feel the door at any moment. Instead, they settled on a solid slab of something firm and … warm.

Warm? Why was the door warm? The 'door' then moved swiftly, making me gasp loudly as in a split second strong arms had closed around my waist and pushed me against the cool of the tiled kitchen wall. Letting out a startled yelp of surprise, my confused, disorientated brain recognised Sean's smoky, spicy scent engulfing me just moments before the kitchen lights flickered on and I saw him looming over me and caging me in with his arms.

Blinking in the harsh brightness, I desperately tried to steady my erratic breathing, panting, before finally lifting my gaze to his face. His hair was tousled like he'd just woken up, but his narrowed eyes were alert and assessing me as he moved well within my personal space and gripped my waist, his shoulders hunched so he could maintain eye contact as he shifted his hips ever closer.

Close. He was very … close.

Swallowing loudly, I realised that if I just tipped my head forwards a tiny fraction I would be able to rub the tips of our noses together, but thankfully, sanity prevailed and instead I chose to gain a small amount of space by resting my head back on the wall behind me and simply watching him as our heated, quickened breaths mixed in the tiny distance between us.

Over the course of the two days of avoiding him I'd almost managed to kid myself that Sean wasn't as attractive as I'd first thought, but now it all came flooding back, especially seeing as the only thing he was wearing were those ridiculously sexy pyjama bottoms again. The heat coming from his exposed chest was incredible, seeming to reach me in waves and warm my previously chilled body within seconds.

This man really was something else: tall, toned, and handsome as sin, and once again my traitorous body reacted to his presence by heating with a furious blush as my anger with him seemed to simply melt away in his presence.

He leaned in close to my ear, and assuming he was going to kiss my neck I found myself wantonly angling it to give him better access. 'Why are you sneaking around my house at night, Allie?' he demanded, his velvety, quiet tone sending a shiver up my spine.

Surprised that he was speaking and not kissing me as I'd expected, I sputtered out an embarrassed breath at my stupid assumption. I had nearly capitulated to him instantaneously. I both hated and secretly loved how weak he made me feel. Blinking hard, I swallowed and licked my lips, refusing to show him how badly he affected me, even if I was positively thrumming inside from his close proximity. Lifting my chin defiantly I tensed my shoulders and narrowed my eyes.

'I was hungry,' I shot back obstinately, deliberately trying to ignore the way his thumbs were rubbing circles on my waist and making my legs go rubbery. Bloody man.

'You've been avoiding me,' he stated, and I lowered my head, feeling slightly guilty at my childish behaviour, before pulling myself up with a frown. I was *not* the one who should be feeling guilty. If he had any manners at all I wouldn't have felt the need to hide away from him. Besides, he hadn't exactly been sociably hanging around the house either, had he?

'I'm obviously an inconvenience to you so it seemed the easiest solution,' I muttered thickly, still averting my eyes and realising to my horror that my right hand had moved of its own accord and now rested on his lean hip. What the heck was I doing? Pulling my hand back sharply, I clenched my fists against the wall behind me and stared at his bare feet in annoyance.

I should leave. Scamper back to my room and hide again like the pathetic, hormonal wimp I was, but to do that I'd need to push past him, and given how strongly his presence affected me already, touching him certainly wasn't going to help matters.

'An inconvenience?' He made an almost amused grunting noise. 'That's not quite how I'd describe you ...' Sean murmured, but he left the rest of his cryptic sentence unfinished. The sexual tension between us was incredible, seeming to wash over me and causing my skin to ping like a constant series of red hot needles tickling me. Surely I couldn't be the only one feeling this chemistry?

Still avoiding his eyes, I stared down until the temptation to check out his pyjama bottoms became too much for me. They clung to the muscles in his thighs almost indecently, not to mention hugging the bulge that was beginning to form at his groin. *Oh God*. OK, so that clearly indicated that I *wasn't* the only one feeling this connection. Closing my eyes I tried to ignore his growing erection and stay calm, but for some inexplicable reason that ability seemed to completely escape me whenever Sean was around. Not that his arousal was helping me stay composed, because it was now starting to nudge hopefully against my belly.

I could barely focus as I stood frozen to the spot breathing shallowly and completely unsure as to what would happen. Or what I *wanted* to happen. After the cold way he had treated me after our last liaison I should be shoving him away, but as much as my brain yelled at me to do just that, my body was demanding I do the exact opposite and throw myself into his arms.

I did neither. Instead, I just stood there, well and truly under his spell. Sean didn't speak any more, but I watched in fascination as his right hand lifted and began to trail lazily across my T-shirt, circling over and around my body, never fully touching, just brushing over the cotton and teasing me nonetheless. It were as if he was exploring me and silently cataloguing everything he saw, and being well and truly in his thrall I simply stood there and let him.

Finally, his fingers traced the neck of my T-shirt, ran across my collarbone, and skated down the skin of my arm, briefly brushing the side of my breast as he went and causing me to bite back the moan of pleasure that threatened to escape my lips. Such minimal contact, but already I was so aroused and needy that I felt myself getting light-headed as his hand continued its tease and returned to my hip.

I was throbbing with need and so wet I had to clench my thighs together to try and find some relief. Rationally I knew I shouldn't be allowing him to touch me like this, not when he'd been so rude, but the attraction between us was just so incredible that I seemed to be helpless to resist him.

'Oh, Allie,' Sean groaned, as he lowered his head and nuzzled my neck, spreading a trail of kisses across my collarbone and behind the sensitive flesh of my ear. Now *this* is what I had expected him to do earlier.

If it was possible to die from massive over-arousal – which at this particular moment, it certainly felt like it was – then this man was going to be the death of me. I was all at sea; my head was telling me to push Sean away because he was clearly a jerk, but my body was speaking a whole different language – my flesh was tingling, my nipples had tightened, and there was an empty ache deep inside of me that was crying out to be fulfilled by him.

I was normally so sensible. Would it really matter if I gave in to my body just this once? After all, as soon as the snow cleared I'd be out of here and never have to see him again. Perhaps a little selfish pleasure wouldn't matter. And besides, after the telephone call had interrupted us the other day, we technically had some unfinished business to attend to …

Lust finally won out and I gave in to the desires welling within me, as with a moan I allowed my hands to unclench and slide around his bare chest to rub across his firm, warm back. Trailing up his heated skin I sunk my fingers into the hair at the nape of his neck, where I tugged urgently, encouraging him to raise his head for a kiss. Lifting up, our eyes met and I saw his characteristic frown was gone for once, instead replaced with unshielded desire, and I wondered if perhaps there was a reason he'd been previously guarded with me. But all thoughts were lost as his lips lowered to mine, his tongue lapping at my mouth, demanding entry, which of course I willingly gave with a lusty moan.

Stroking his tongue over mine, our heated breaths mingled. His naked desperately as his hands tugged me against him chest crashed into mine as his hands pulled me toward him so tightly that I almost struggled for breath. Considering the urgency of his actions, his mouth was the complete opposite, moving against mine so tenderly and carefully that I nearly sobbed out loud.

'You look really sexy wearing my T-shirt ...' he murmured, leaning back far enough to examine my attire. His right hand pulled up the hem of my temporary sleeping shirt, fingering it between forefinger and thumb with a thoughtful hum before gradually beginning to lift it up.

If I hadn't been almost frozen with anticipation, then I certainly would have giggled at his astonished expression a few seconds later when he discovered that I wasn't wearing any underwear. His eyes shot to mine, wide and desire-filled, before he growled his approval and bent to kiss me again, his mouth open and hungry as he slid a hand to my nape and held me in place while he explored my mouth with deep, lapping lashes of his skilful tongue. He didn't need to hold me in place; I wasn't going anywhere.

A long, garbled moan bubbled in my throat, escaping as a breathy whisper as he trailed a hand over my belly and down to tangle his fingers in the soft curls between my legs. A little sluttishly I found myself parting my legs to give him easier access, but honestly, I was so turned on that I was way beyond caring about how he might view my morals.

One of his fingers slid to my slit, and he began to rub at the warmth with a contented grumble, while his thumb pressed and circled my engorged clit. 'So wet ...' he muttered, seeming to love how affected by him I was. He might be a virtual stranger, but there really was no point trying to deny the reaction Sean sparked in me. I couldn't help but moan loudly as he slipped a finger insideme,, followed quickly by a second, before he began to rhythmically stroke my core.

Feeling braver – or perhaps he had just truly caused me to lose my mind – I reciprocated the gesture and pushed a hand over his firm stomach and inside the waistband of his pyjama bottoms, tentatively feeling and stroking at the red hot flesh I found there and causing him to thrust against me jerkily.

Groaning loudly, Sean paused for a second, his hand tightening in my hair, and eyes fluttering shut as he absorbed my movements and gently ground himself into my hand. Opening his eyes, I saw that his pupils were so dilated that his eyes looked almost completely black as he began to work a third finger inside me with a groan. This time I could really feel the stretch, but what an amazing sensation it was.

'See how your body accepts me? You are so fucking receptive,' he murmured as his fingers stretched me deliciously before he increased the pace of his movements as I writhed shamelessly against his hand.

I spoke before even realising it. 'Sean … please …' I whispered against his lips and as he raised his head I shivered at the intensity that glinted in his eyes.

'What do you want, Allie?' he asked gruffly against the skin of my neck, before lowering his head to greedily nibble and lick at the lobe of my ear again. God, I had never known that my ear was such an erogenous zone. His touch ignited my skin and caused me to shudder and tremble against him.

He was a whole different person now, caring and attentive, his characteristic frown and bad mood totally evaporated. Perhaps he had been annoyed that he hadn't got to finish things the other day, I wondered. Maybe that would explain his odd mood swings? I had certainly enjoyed the experience on his desk, but the interruption had meant he had gone unfinished. Pondering this, I wondered that maybe if I gave a little of myself to him he would start to open up to me.

'Take me. Please,' I gasped. 'However you want me.' He certainly seemed to like being in charge so I was hoping that handing over control might be the key to loosening him up.

At my words, Sean raised his face and moved his hand to grip my chin while staring at me intently. I could see anticipation glinting in the blue depths of his eyes, excitement causing his lips to twitch and cheeks to flush. God, what was I thinking? I'd just offered carte blanche on my body to a stranger. Jeez, he really *had* scrambled my brain. But before many more thoughts could flood my brain Sean stepped back and gripped the hem of my T-shirt suddenly, looking at me purposefully. Without another word, he peeled the material up over my head to reveal my trembling body, and after smiling darkly at my nudeness, he raised his hooded gaze to mine. 'So beautiful. And so many possibilities ...' he murmured, making my arousal and nerves climb even higher.

Without another word Sean placed his hands on my hips and spun me around, pulling me so I could feel his warmth pressed against my back. His head lowered, lips diving through my hair as I willingly tilted my head to give him better access to my neck. My hands felt useless, but I found myself gripping his fingers where they rested on my hips as he began to grind his erection into the small of my back. He was so hot and hard that I moaned out loud, now completely desperate to have him inside me. Sliding his fingers out from below mine he pushed gently on my shoulders so I bent forwards until I was leant over the marble kitchen top, the cold of the surface causing me to sigh as it clashed with my heated skin.

Pinning me down, he kept one hand pressed between my shoulder blades so my breasts swelled against the coolness beneath me, making my nipples harden further. Wriggling, I tried to find some relief from my burning arousal, but the almost painful friction of my nipples against the marble only seemed to cause my excitement to spiral higher.

Behind me, Sean spread my legs with a swift push of his foot on my ankle, so he had me splayed, pinned, and completely at his mercy. Logically, I probably shouldn't have liked this position quite as much as I did – I'd certainly never given over control to a man like this before, but he was so confident and capable that I had no issues doing so with Sean.

In fact, I loved it. Biting my lip, I stared out of the window beside me at the moonlit garden and falling snow, and as I felt his fingers exploring my opening I allowed myself a little smile. Perhaps it would be a merry Christmas after all.

All thoughts of Christmas were quickly forced aside as I felt the hard tip of his erection replace his fingers and push against me before I was suddenly filled in one long, deep thrust.

My eyes flew open at the delicious intrusion, but regardless of how turned on he had gotten me, I still found his width hard to accommodate, stretching almost to the point of discomfort. Almost, but not quite. I was definitely floating just on the pleasurable edge of the stretch. Someone let out a long groan of pleasure, but I was so hazy that I really didn't know if it was me or him, or perhaps both. All I knew was that I was stretched to capacity and loving it. Sean briefly sagged against my back, breathing heavily, apparently overcome with sensation, before keeping himself completely still inside me as he stood and took hold of my hips with gentle massaging fingers. 'OK, my gorgeous girl?'

There was that sweet endearment again, and although I'd never been one for pet names, I found that I really rather liked them when they came from Sean's lips. Pulling in a deep breath I released it slowly and felt my lower muscles relaxing and accommodating him more readily. 'You're really big,' I murmured hoarsely, immediately realising that that was probably the wrong thing to say to a guy like Sean – it would no doubt inflate his already large ego. 'But yes, I'm OK.'

After gently grinding himself inside me a few times to assist with stretching, he withdrew to the tip and began to thrust more purposefully. Thankfully, his movements weren't quite as ferocious as they had been in his office when he'd nearly split me in half, but they were certainly hard enough to have me seeing stars as his cock bucked against my g-spot on every thrust. His rhythm quickly became fast and relentless, dragging my body back and forth across the counter so my breasts were feeling well and truly teased by the unforgiving surface.

Keeping a firm hold of my hip with one hand, Sean used his free hand to gather both of my wrists and place them above my head. 'These stay here,' he informed me as he thrust into me again, causing me to groan at his easy dominance. Then, when he was happy that I was complying, I felt his hand tangle in the long waves of my hair, tugging gently as if he had wrapped it around his hand.

Looking at our reflection in the illuminated kitchen window I saw that that was exactly what he had done; a large chunk of my blonde hair was firmly wrapped around his wrist and gripped in his hand, stopping me from moving my head very far. To his credit, he wasn't pulling to the point of pain, merely seeming to enjoy the fact that he had me well and truly at his mercy. And boy, was that the truth. My brain struggled to understand how and why I had so willingly submitted to him, but I came up with no logical answer. Sean was the answer, him and the magnetic draw he had on me.

He was so commanding over the position that I felt myself slicken further, my body apparently loving the power he was demonstrating over me. 'Fuck, Allie ... so good,' he murmured as he pounded himself against me, now thrusting his hips with short, jerking thrusts.

I had offered him any position, but if I were truthful I felt a little disappointed; I was enjoying myself, yes, but I never climaxed when a man was behind me and after the amazing orgasm of the other day I had been hoping for another to remember him by. Just as this was flitting though my brain, Sean released my hair and seemed to raise his hand. I heard him lick his fingers before they wrapped around my belly and dipped lower to find my clit. He began rubbing small, hard circles with his fingers while keeping up the punishing rhythm with his hips, and I felt my stomach begin to clench with the promise of release. His fingers deftly tugged and circled my clitoris with firmer movements and an ever faster pace, until suddenly I was clutching the work surface and crying out as my body clenched around him in a series of spasms. My orgasm caused Sean's rhythm to falter, becoming less controlled and far more lurching, before he suddenly let out a roar and exploded inside me, his cock twitching like mad within my tightly clamped muscles.

I felt a shudder of pleasure rip though his entire body as Sean worked us down from our climax with several gentler thrusts, before he collapsed on my back, breathing hard and holding me tightly against him. One of his talented fingers continued to lazily circle my clitoris every now and then, causing me to jerk and twitch against his hand and tighten around his cock, a feeling he obviously enjoyed because he growled in appreciation and nipped gently at my shoulder with his teeth.

As I lay there breathing heavily and sprawled on the cool marble squashed below him, I became startlingly aware that this man seemed to have an ability to make me feel and do things that I had never experienced before. Firstly, I had never given over total control like that before, and secondly, no man had ever made me come when they were behind me, regardless of how much effort they put in. It was unnerving the way the Sean made me act with hardly any effort, but surprisingly not enough of a concern for me to dwell on at the moment.

Finally, Sean eased out of me, and just like last time I winced at the empty feeling it left behind. He had felt so good that I would have liked to keep him nestled inside of me all night. Turning my head, I saw him pulling off a condom and replacing his pyjama bottoms before he bent down and tossed me my nightshirt.

Where the heck had he got the condom from? Thank God he'd thought to use one, because I'd been so caught up in him that it hadn't even crossed my mind. Flushing at how easy I must have seemed to him, I dragged the T-shirt over my head, suddenly feeling tremendously self-conscious.

Crossing one arm over my breasts I hung the other around my stomach and onto my hip, standing with slightly hunched shoulders as I tried, and failed, to silently cope with my growing shame. Lifting my head, I watched curiously as I saw Sean go to speak several times, only to close his mouth on each occasion and then frown deeply as if something was suddenly bothering him. 'I'll let you get some food,' he said after an age, which made me close my eyes in disappointment and scrunch my shoulders even more. 'Use the house as you like, you don't need to hide away,' he added as he turned and left. I had assumed that now we had been intimate again he would let his guard down a little, but how naive that thought had been.

No, whatever it was that was keeping him closed off was still bothering him, and I had just allowed myself to be used. Again. Although technically I knew that wasn't true – I had been a willing partner. More than willing, and had no one to blame but myself. I knew what he was like and I had still allowed myself to go along with it, hadn't I?

One thing was for sure; I certainly wouldn't be making that mistake again.

Glancing down the corridor I watched his tense shoulders retreat away from me, his fists clenching and unclenching at his sides. He looked worked up about something, but seeing as he'd just had his way with me – rather vigorously, too – I couldn't imagine what he had to feel tense about. A warm feeling on my thigh made me glance away from him awkwardly and look down at my leg. Even with the condom I was still ridiculously wet down below, and I could see a shine of my spent arousal dampening my leg, a sensation that only added to my shame and feeling of overall embarrassment.

Breathing out a sigh that was almost a sob, I turned and gripped the counter until my knuckles went white from the pressure. Closing my eyes against the tears brewing I shook my head and quickly grabbed a handful of kitchen paper to roughly wipe myself clean. I was an idiot. Even with some exceptionally enjoyable kitchen sex, nothing had changed between Sean and I, except he seemed even more distant than before and I felt even more shamed about my behaviour around him.

Chapter Eight
Sean

It might have been the middle of the night, but as soon I left Allie in the kitchen, I found myself heading rapidly for my office, and not my bedroom as any normal person would have. Then again, if I were a normal, decent human being I wouldn't have fucked the life out of her and left her alone barely a minute later. But I had, my jumbled thoughts towards her causing me to turn and flee like a complete coward, and I now hated myself more than I ever thought possible.

Collapsing into my office chair, I logged onto my computer and sat back while it loaded. My eyes flickered shut as I tried to calm my heartbeat, but it was no good; I was still alert and aroused from our encounter, and probably would be for quite some time. Christ, that had been incredible. Admittedly, Allie had seemed a little shocked to see me at first, and perhaps a little defensive, but it had only taken a few minutes for her to melt against me as her exploring hands had encouraged me forward.

Remembering how wet she'd been, I groaned out loud. She was just as affected by me as I was by her. And responsive, too, so fucking responsive. Those little noises of pleasure she made had driven me wild.

The computer screen finally flickered to life and I wasted no time typing in the password to my security system so I could bring up the feed of the kitchen camera. I might have run away from her like a pathetic shit, but I still wanted to see if she was all right. I *needed* her to be all right.

As the camera feed filled my screen I saw with relief that she was still in the kitchen. Her back was to me, and she was hunched over the counter, completely motionless and still wearing nothing but that T-shirt of mine. God, she looked sexy, those long, long legs of her stretching bare to the floor, smooth and so tempting.

My eyes narrowed as I watched her pull off several sheets of kitchen paper almost viciously and bend forwards to wipe between her legs. Regret immediately simmered in my chest. I ran a hand over my face in exasperation about how much of a bastard I'd been. I'd fucked her, left her, and not even tended to her afterwards. She must fucking hate me. *I* pretty much hated me right now.

Desperate to see her face to try to judge her emotions I watched in rapt fascination as she tipped her head back to stare at the ceiling, then finally lowered her head and turned her body in the direction of the camera.

Despite our recent exertion she was pale as a ghost, lifting a hand to rub at her eyes with the back of her knuckles. I felt my stomach drop as I watched her. *Fuck.* She was crying. Or she had been; her cheeks seemed drier now, but she just looked miserable, self-conscious, and pissed off.

I scratched nervously at the back of my neck. What should I do? Go back down and apologise? But that would no doubt add to her embarrassment, and seeing as I had no idea what I'd even say to her, it would probably make me look like even more of a dickhead in the process.

After taking several deep breaths, Allie walked to the fridge and took out the bowl of leftover pasta from my meal earlier. OK, this was good, she was calming down enough to eat. I knew she must be hungry, because I'd deliberately gone down early to dinner hoping to see her. I'd seen on the security cameras from the previous two nights how she always scampered through the lounge to avoid me, and so tonight I'd tried to catch her out. Not that it had worked, of course; she'd simply gone without dinner. Yet another reason to feel guilty. Christ, this woman had me in complete tangles. On the one hand, I was desperate to keep her away because of my relationship issues, but then on the other hand I was practically yearning to be in her company. God, I was such a wreck.

Watching as she placed the bowl on the breakfast bar I noticed she didn't even bother to re-heat it, instead just slipped onto one of the stools before picking at the pasta shapes unenthusiastically. She must have eaten two tiny mouthfuls, maximum, before she pushed the bowl away miserably, chewed briefly on a fingernail, and stood up, tipping the contents of the bowl into the bin. Shortly afterwards, my screen went dark as she must have switched off the light and left the room, but stupidly I still found myself staring at the screen for a few more moments.

Throwing myself backwards in my chair, I let out a long, irritated grunt. So I'd fucked her, left her, upset her, *and* removed her appetite. I felt like the lowest, shittiest man alive. Which was probably because I *was* the lowest, shittiest man alive. This was not how you treated a woman, I knew that, and yet here I was, sitting away in my office while she wandered back to her bedroom alone and no doubt hating my guts. Fuck.

Curiosity had me rewinding the tape of our encounter. The first few minutes only showed half our bodies as we stood just inside the kitchen door and almost out of camera view, but still I watched, fascinated by the smooth skin of her arm that I could see and remembering the way her eyes had dilated and her cheeks flushed when she'd noticed my arousal.

She was so sweet, almost innocent in certain ways, but the sure, firm way she had cupped my erection and stroked me told me otherwise. My cock hardened now, as I watched where she had told me I could have her any way I wanted her. Fuck. That had almost done me in. I'd never had a woman demonstrate such trust in me, and it had felt incredible.

I wanted her in all ways, and deep down I was beginning to recognise a primal need in me that wanted her *always*. I'd never really met a woman that sparked my interest so deeply and affected me so dramatically, but she did. Allie. And now, after barely any conversation and just two brief sexual encounters, I was considering the possibility of a long-term future with her? It should sound crazy. But it didn't. It sounded amazing.

On the screen I now watched the moment where I had bent her over the counter and wrapped my hand in that long, tempting hair of hers. That moment had literally made my previous night's dreams a reality. I'd been worried that my tendency to dominate during sex might put her off, or scare her, but she had been just perfect, offering herself willingly, and eagerly meeting every one of my demanding thrusts with a push of her hips.

Closing my eyes, I sat silently for a second or two as my cock throbbed and jerked below the desk. I was so aroused that the temptation to jerk off was almost overwhelming, but I didn't. I couldn't. Instead, I let out a disgusted breath at my pitiful behaviour tonight and deleted the footage. After the way I had treated Allie, I didn't deserve a second of enjoyment, or even the pleasure of the memory of it.

Once the memory cards for the security cameras had been cleared, I shut the computer down and stood up to head to bed. Closing up my office for the night, I made my way downstairs to my bedroom, but paused as I passed Allie's door. I wanted to see her so badly that it was almost an obsession. Perhaps I needed to see her to persuade myself that she was fine, or perhaps it was just to slake the growing desire I had to be near her.

Standing there for several seconds, I finally gave in to the need to see her and pushed open the door a few inches. Holding my breath, I stuck my head in and saw that the lights were off, and that she was lying on her side facing me. I froze for a second, wondering if she were still awake, but from the deep breathing I could hear in the dim room, she was almost certainly asleep.

Cocking my head, I watched her in fascination, realising that this was taking my stalker-like tendencies to a whole new level, but really not caring. It was becoming clearer to me that the thing I *did* care about was lying in the bed a few feet away from me. I cared about her, and hated the fact that I'd treated her so badly. The more I allowed this to permeate my brain, the more I knew that I was going to have to do something about this whole situation. We might have only met a short time ago, but the connection between us was blindingly obvious, and I knew I needed to speak to her, perhaps explain why I had been so reluctant to let my guard down.

For now though, I would indulge myself. Approaching the bed, I crouched down so I was level with her face. Even in her sleep there was a frown creasing her brow, and I once again felt guilt begin to twist and burn in my stomach. 'I'm so sorry, my gorgeous girl. So sorry,' I murmured, knowing the words were useless when she was so deeply asleep, but feeling the overwhelming need to say them anyway.

Suddenly, looking at her just wasn't enough, and I found myself walking around the bed and crawling in behind her before I'd even realised that I'd done it. I moved as carefully as I could, hoping not to disturb her, and then gently folded myself around so my chest was pressed against her back and my head was lying near the nape of her neck, where I could breathe in her warmth and scent. Letting out a content sigh in her sleep, Allie wriggled herself backwards, deepening our embrace until we were well and truly spooning, and I couldn't help but grin. She was so warm, and she smelt amazing; all sweet and lush with just a hint of sweat and sex that remained from our frantic kitchen session.

Nuzzling my head into her hair, I breathed deeply, humming happily to myself. Regardless of my issues with relationships, I instinctively knew that this was where I was supposed to be. Here, with this woman in my arms. I didn't even care if she woke up. If she did, I'd just apologise and hope that she would let me hold her until she fell back to sleep. Then perhaps in the morning we could talk. If I could get my head screwed on straight.

Relaxing against her, I slid an arm around her waist and closed my eyes, loving the sensation of having Allie in my arms like this. It felt perfect. I wanted to keep and protect her. Although I was also bitterly aware that after the way I had treated her in the kitchen, the person Allie probably needed protecting from the most right now was me.

Chapter Nine
Allie

Christmas Eve morning was finally here, and I woke feeling moody, miserable, and overly warm. I was also tangled in the covers far more than usual, and so I flopped onto my back to try and ease the twists of material that trapped my legs. Letting out a huff, I finally untangled my limbs and looked at the bed in confusion. God, I had really thrashed around in here last night. Both sides of the covers were crumpled, and even both pillows looked used. How weird. Normally I fell asleep in one position and woke up pretty much in the same place the next morning. Although my subconscious had run rife last night, so I suppose that might explain it.

Grimacing as I recalled my dreams – or perhaps I should say nightmares – I wiped a hand over my face to clear the flopping hair from my eyes. As well as repeatedly dreaming about my steamy kitchen liaison with Sean, I had stupidly dreamt that he'd been with me in bed, cradling me against his body as he repeatedly apologised for his cold treatment. It had felt so real I'd almost been able to feel the weight of his arm around my waist and the heat of his breath on my neck.

How bloody stupid was I? Now, not only had I allowed myself to be used like his plaything – *twice* – I was dreaming up romantic endings to make myself feel better. Ugh. I was pathetic. Or at least I was when it came to him.

Letting out a disgusted grunt, I practically threw myself from the bed and trudged into the en-suite. As I flicked on the shower and waited for it to heat up I felt some remaining stickiness between my legs, which was yet another reminder of my sordid actions last night, and gave me further reason to scowl. I should have showered last night and washed away the memories of Sean from my body, but when I'd reached my room all I'd wanted to do was curl into a ball and cry, so that was exactly what I'd done. Now though, I seriously regretted last night's laziness because as I lifted my arms to remove my T-shirt I got a faint whiff of his smoky, woody scent lingering on my skin, and shivered from the deluge of memories it triggered.

After a long and rather painful shower – like last time, I took out my self-disgust on my skin by scrubbing it way too hard – I found that, thankfully, my washed clothes were now dry. Dressing in garments that actually fit me felt like a novelty after being swamped in Sean's massive things for so long, and I took a second to smooth my hands over my clothes – it was good to be able to feel my hips and boobs again.

Using the hairdryer that Sean had left for me, I dried my tresses, applied a tiny smidgen of makeup to improve my confidence, and looked in the mirror with a satisfied nod. At least I could look like myself today, even if my battered ego felt absolutely nothing like the calm, confident, headstrong woman I usually was.

It might be Christmas Eve, but as I opened my curtains I saw that there would be no Christmas miracle for me today, because there was more sodding snow falling outside. Seeing the thick, white flakes still dancing around, I cursed loudly before decisively deciding that I wouldn't hide in my room any longer. Sean was the one with the issues, not me, and if he wanted me out of his sight then he could be the one to flipping hide away. I was sick of these four walls, and I'd done nothing wrong ... except for get a little carried away in the heat of the moment last night.

Pushing my long hair back from my face, I huffed out a long breath. God, I couldn't wait to get the hell out of this place, away from Sean and back to my comfortable if somewhat boring life.

Making my way downstairs, I practically held my breath as I pushed the kitchen door open, but released a long, relieved sigh when I found it empty. Thank goodness for that. I was feeling way too snarky today to deal with Sean before I had any caffeine in me.

As I stepped into the large room my eyes were instinctively drawn to the granite worktop where we'd had sex last night. There was no evidence of our heated encounter, but I felt my nose crinkle as I imagined what hidden residues might be happily encrusting themselves to the surface at this very moment. Ugh. I probably should wipe the surface down. As my gaze lingered and my skin began to warm from the returning memories, I swallowed loudly before having to forcefully rip my gaze away, determined not to linger on thoughts of Sean and his superb sexing skills, or the way I constantly seemed to lose my wits when I was around him.

My stomach grumbled loudly, reminding me that I'd barely eaten last night, and so I immediately grabbed a banana to feed my poor empty tummy alongside some butter and jam from the fridge and two slices of bread from the freezer. Minutes later I had demolished the banana and was well through the process of brewing a pot of Sean's finest Columbian coffee as my bread defrosted on the counter – not the sex counter of course; I still hadn't gotten around to cleaning over *there* yet.

All in all, today was starting off better. The coffee was on, I was about to have a nice, peaceful breakfast, and best of all, I hadn't had any hormone-stirring, soul shaking encounters with a certain Mr Irresistible. Smiling as I inhaled the delicious smell now filling the room, I turned to pop my bread in the toaster, but was suddenly interrupted by the kitchen door slamming open as the man himself strode in from the hallway, casting a dark glance around and freezing when he saw me. My heart sunk – looks like I had jinxed my nice morning by entertaining brief thoughts of him. Damn.

We did that fleeting staring thing again, both of us frozen to the spot as our eyes locked and held, but I was first to break the electric link between us by blinking, and forced my head to turn back toward the toaster. I had no idea what the deal was with him always staring at me, but I wouldn't indulge him any longer. Even if a tiny deep down part of me did find the connection between us quite thrilling.

'G ... good morning,' I murmured almost automatically as a way to fill the awkward silence, but immediately chastised myself for interacting with him at all. And what the hell was I on about when I'd described the morning as "good"? It was snowing again, I was still trapped, and to top it all off I was a little sore between my legs from where I'd willingly allowed this miserable arsehole and his large appendage to shag me senseless. That made today about as far from a "good" morning as I could possibly imagine.

Sean merely continued to stare at me in reply, his shoulders tense below the material of the black, long sleeved T-shirt that he was wearing. Which, I noted despairingly, also happened to cling to his sodding muscles to near perfection. His jaw was tight as he blinked rapidly, but for a moment it looked like he was about to speak, before briefly dropping his head with a grunt and walking towards the fridge instead. Charming. This man's stunning lack of social skills knew no bounds.

'You're in a dazzling mood I see,' I muttered, more to myself than him, but in response I got a glare as he poured himself a giant glass of orange juice and took several long swigs. Stupidly, the movement of his throat as he swallowed drew my attention; that Adam's apple of his, so masculine and bobbing up and down as if tempting me to walk across and kiss it. Hmm ... I would start on his neck and work my way up his stubble covered jaw until I reached that sinful mouth of his ... *Fuck*! My bloody mind was going crazy again, and before I even knew it, *I* was the one staring, not him.

There was quite a high chance that I was probably drooling, too. Bugger. What was it about this guy that pulled me so strongly?

'I'm not really a morning person,' he mumbled moodily, depositing the carton back in the fridge, slamming the door, and ruining my throat appreciation session as he turned away from me so I was left staring at the ruffled hair on the back of his head.

'No kidding,' I replied tightly, turning to rescue my toast from becoming charcoal and buttering it furiously, only just managing to bite back the sarcastic comment that flew to mind. He obviously wasn't going to talk about what had happened last night, and there was no way in hell that I was going to be the one to bring it up.

'I couldn't sleep,' he suddenly admitted, his tone quieter and softer than before and making me abandon my buttering and look across in surprise to find him already watching me with a wary expression on his handsome face.

'How about you ... how are you?' he asked hesitantly. So *now* he was making small talk? My eyebrows flew up at his utter cheek. After shagging me not once, but twice, and effectively dismissing me after each bout, *now* he wanted to chat?

Glaring at him, I decided it was probably advisable to get away from Sean and his temperamental moods while I still had my sanity even vaguely intact, so I dropped the knife, leaving my toast uneaten. Funnily enough, with Sean in the room my appetite had disappeared now anyway.

'Oh, I'm just peachy,' I replied sarcastically, before picking up my coffee cup, shoving past him, and wandering into the lounge without another word.

Hearing the door click closed behind me, I sighed in relief and leant back on the wall to try and steady my breath. Even with my exhausting efforts at staying strong around him my body had reacted anyway by heating and going into overdrive, leaving me feeling a bit clammy and restless. This really was physical attraction at its most potent. And dangerous. Nodding my head, I scowled; I might not like to properly admit it, but there was no doubt that that man and his charms were a serious danger to the safety of my heart. Raising my free hand I rubbed at my chest in a useless attempt at soothing my hammering pulse rate, but managed nothing other than knocking my coffee cup and nearly spilling the contents.

As well as being a completely confusing, changeable, and miserable man, Sean clearly wasn't a Christmas person either, I thought sourly, looking around the undecorated room as I drew in long, slow breaths. There wasn't a single bauble or string of tinsel in sight. All in all, it was a truly depressing situation.

If I was where I should be today – enjoying the day at my mum's house – we'd all be gathered around the dining table with a Christmas tree twinkling beside us, carols on the radio, and our traditional Christmas Eve breakfast of baked ham and toast waiting for us. Thanks to Sean's interruption I didn't even have my toast to enjoy now. I felt so fragile this morning that the thought of my family was almost enough to make me burst into tears on the spot, but I'd cried plenty last night, so I instead gave myself a firm pep talk and let out a long, unhappy sigh.

Attempting to distract myself from this bout of melancholy, I placed my mug on a nearby coffee table and contented myself by looking through Sean's extensive DVD collection to find something to help my day pass. Seeing as it was Christmas Day tomorrow I wondered if I could get a little more into the spirt with a nice Christmas film – not that I expected him to own any.

From his domineering personality and outdoorsy vibe I had thought Sean would be an action movie fan, or perhaps into horrors, but as I looked across the titles I was actually quite impressed by the range of genres he owned; everything from off the wall art-house productions to black and white classics and modern day blockbusters. All alphabetically ordered too, Mr Control obviously liked his house as well ordered as his parking arrangements, I thought with a smirk.

Picking cases out at random to inspect the covers, I made sure to carefully insert them back in the exact same spots I'd found them – no point giving him something else to get moody about. One caught my eye and I re-examined the cover to see what had taken my interest. *Shooting Point*, a recent Hollywood blockbuster. Skimming the blurb on the back of the box I nodded my recognition – it was released last year, garnering fairly good reviews but I'd never got round to watching it. I quite liked a good action flick. Maybe I could watch this today. However, as I flipped the box over in my palm and gazed at the glossy cover again, my eyes narrowed, blinked, and widened as something suddenly dawned on me that had me slapping a hand over my mouth in shock.

Dropping the DVD as if it had burnt me, I stared at it in horror as I tried to take in what I'd just realised. *Oh my God, I was such a bloody idiot!*

'I wouldn't bother with that one, it's not one of my best,' drawled a voice from the back of the room, causing me to yelp and spin around to see Sean just inside the doorway. He was leaning on the wall with one hand tucked in the pocket of his grey jeans, the other holding a plate of toast slathered in jam – presumably my abandoned breakfast – and his feet crossed at the ankles. All in all he looked cool, calm, and sexy as hell as he watched me with vague amusement twinkling in his dark blue eyes.

Holding up the plate of toast, he raised his eyebrows and put it on the table next to my coffee. 'You skipped dinner last night, make sure you eat this.' I briefly wondered how he knew I hadn't eaten after our interlude in the kitchen, but my mind was still going loopy from the information I had learnt from the DVD residing on the floor by my feet. Glancing at the box again I felt a bit sick, and blew out a huge breath to try and clear my reeling mind.

I had *just* discovered this huge bombshell and he was calmly talking about food? Now? Seriously? Toast really was no longer my main concern, I was officially entering full meltdown mode. My cheeks were burning, my heart pounding under my skin, and my head felt woozy, which, all in all, was making my entire body decidedly unsteady.

'I ... I can't believe I didn't recognise you ...' My eyes flicked back to the DVD box again as I bent to retrieve it from the floor with a trembling hand. I cringed – it *really* was him. 'You're Sean Phillips ... as in *the* Sean Phillips,' I said, waving the DVD case that had his face plastered all over the cover.

I was literally in the presence of Hollywood royalty, and I could barely believe it. He was the real deal, a hugely successful actor, known around the world, and I was standing right here in front of him. He'd been nominated for Oscars, for God's sake – what had I ever been nominated for? Best playground games supervisor?

This was so surreal. My shock was muted slightly when the realisation that I had slept with him came back to me like a bucket of ice water had been thrown over me. Me and Sean Phillips, movie star and all round Hollywood heartthrob had fucked like bunnies on his sparkly kitchen counter. I was so in shock that I nearly laughed hysterically. More precisely, he'd held me down, eased my legs apart, and had his wicked way with me, but still, I had been an active, if somewhat restrained, participant.

Cait was going to go mental when I told her, and as I came to terms with the fact that this really *was* happening, that I really had slept with *the* Sean Phillips, I had to try my hardest not to grin. He was a modern pin-up; women everywhere wanted him, and I'd slept with him. *Twice.* If the unfinished business on his desk could be counted, which in my books it definitely did – well, there was penetration wasn't there? – Albeit brief, it definitely made it an official shag in my mind.

As my glee settled back to normal levels again, I risked a quick glance at him and suddenly felt like a complete idiot. How on earth had I not recognised him? I thought back to our first meeting and recalled that vague sense of recognition, but I suppose seeing him in his house, half-dressed, and out of context I just hadn't made the connection.

A small, amused grunt rose in my throat – who was I kidding? I'd been too busy ogling his fine chest to really give his face too much focus – *that* was why I hadn't recognised him. But as I gazed at his handsome face again now it was screamingly obvious who he was.

'It was actually quite refreshing that you didn't know me,' he said quietly, watching me carefully as I turned back to him fully. 'You weren't judgemental about me.'

A frown flickered on his brow as he continued to observe me, before a hint of a smile tweaked on his lips, causing my eyebrows to rise and pull my heartrate with them. I couldn't believe it – after days of constant scowling he had nearly smiled! But as I searched his face for that lovely expression again it was gone, almost too soon to even register, and I realised it was the happiest I'd seen him. He'd hardly even smiled when he'd been doing ridiculously naughty things to me, but I'd known he'd been happy then – or at least enjoying himself – from the appreciative noises and statements he'd made.

As we continued to stand there in silence staring at each other – again – I began to find this whole situation incredibly awkward. My face felt so flushed that I was surely glowing by now, and to top it off I had no clue what to say to him – not that I'd really known what to say to him before I'd found out who he was, but still. *Sean flipping Phillips*?

The knowledge of his identity was making my brain hurt as I tried to work out how to progress from this, but before I'd had a chance to come to any conclusions, I watched with rapt fascination as Sean pushed away from the wall and quickly closed the distance between us with large, leisurely steps of those long, long legs.

Swallowing loudly, I licked my lips nervously as I remained frozen to the spot and watching his advance, completely unable to do anything other than stare at him. Even the way he walked was sexy; that confident, cocksure stride making me want to tackle him onto the carpet and mount him there and then.

Tucking his hands in the pockets of his jeans, he then leant forwards, closing the gap between us further so his upper chest and head were just centimetres away. My nose was invaded with a full hit of his smoky spiciness as I breathed in, which combined with his closeness made a small gasp fly from my lips. I didn't know if it were one of shock or arousal, but to make sure I didn't do it again I held my breath, unsure what to expect from him and clutching the DVD to my chest as if my life depended on it.

He certainly seemed to have a thing about personal space – or more specifically, a distinct disregard for it – because Sean was now stood so close that I could clearly see every colour in his eyes; deep navy flecked with just a few traces of green and hazel that seemed to dance in the dark depths of his irises and edged with long, dark lashes that most women would be envious of. Perhaps it was his eyes that drew me to him so strongly, because they really were beautiful.

This close, I could also see some small creases on his forehead and between his eyebrows – frown lines no doubt, which given how much he scowled, really wasn't a surprise. Talk about hypnotic; he was so stunning that I just couldn't look away. In fact, I could quite happily stand there all day absorbing his appearance. It wouldn't even seem like a tiresome task if I were asked to count each individual bristle on his gorgeous stubbly chin.

'You used the hair dryer,' Sean commented quietly, breaking the silence as he lifted a hand and took a small section of hair between his finger and thumb before trailing it loosely through his fingers and nodding approvingly. I'd always loved the sensation of my hair being touched, and my eyes briefly fluttered shut as tingles scattered across my scalp. 'I'm glad. I don't want you catching a chill.'

How oddly observant of him, and quite a caring statement from someone who had, by now, shagged and deserted me twice. As we stood in our silent bubble, our eyes locked and breaths mingling, it felt exactly like his gaze was burning into me. Like he was able to see each and every thought in my mind, and absorb the feelings that he provoked in me. It was at once both incredibly thrilling and unnerving, but I just couldn't look away.

I wondered if his silence was almost his way of daring me to say something, but I couldn't speak. My throat was a useless bunch of clogged-up nervousness, and on top of that I was too busy trying not to tremble from the arousal flowing through my system and thumping between my legs.

Much like earlier, Sean parted his lips as if he were going to say something, before hesitating for a second, narrowing his eyes, and promptly snapping his mouth shut again. Closing his eyes for a second, he pursed his lips as if weighing something up in his head, before he rolled his neck with an audible click, released a long sigh, and reached around me, brushing against my shoulder and causing me to draw in a small rush of air.

'Try this one; it was bigger budget, more exciting,' Sean said blandly, holding out a DVD that he had just plucked from the shelf. Numbly, I took it from him, my brain beginning to shut down in disappointment. Every single fibre in my being told me that this man was trouble, dangerous not only to my body and its inability to refuse him, but to my heart as well. Yet, regardless of this belief, I had found myself hoping that he was going to touch me again, kiss me. But instead of being dragged into his arms and ravished to within an inch of my life, I had been handed a bloody DVD.

'Thanks,' I murmured huskily, but Sean had already turned and was leaving the room. His broad shoulders once again seemed to bristle with tension as he disappeared through the doorway and towards the hall. My lungs deflated in a rushed breath as I once again got some breathing room. Wow, he really was seriously uptight. Maybe I should recommend my yoga group to him, because he could certainly use some loosening up. Mind you, talk about loosening up – I should take a few moments to do that myself because after yet another encounter with Sean that positively seemed to tingle with sexual tension, I was feeling pretty wound up.

After recovering for a few seconds, I gave my body an all-over shake and turned towards the DVD player to load the disc. Watching Sean in a film probably wasn't going to help my lusty fangirl obsession with him one little bit, but seeing as he'd selected the movie, it would look rude if I didn't at least watch it. At least that's what I told myself, anyway.

Taking the remote control with me I settled back on the comfy sofa and looked at the plate of toast on the table as my stomach grumbled hungrily. I still couldn't quite believe that Sean had made me breakfast. Sean Phillips, movie star and all round famous person had made me toast. It was the most bizarre thought in the world. After giving a disbelieving shake of my head I obediently began to munch on a slice while I waited for the film to start. It had gone cold and crunchy by now, but the jam was excellent and I was so hungry that it didn't bother me in the slightest.

After just five minutes the toast had been demolished, and I was sat practically drooling over Sean in all his sexy, action-hero, widescreen glory. God, he was so attractive. I'd honestly never felt the pull of raw physical attraction before, but with Sean it was almost like he sparked some primal desire in me to give myself over to his will. That recognition partly annoyed my independent side, but also turned me on so much that I had to force images of him and his domineering ways from my head and cross my legs to ease the neediness there.

In an attempt to distract my mind from the glorious images on the TV screen – Sean toting a pair of hand guns while topless, tanned, and wearing only a rain-soaked pair of combat trousers that clung to his hips a little too well – I wandered across to the router and saw, to my delight, that the password was stuck to the side on a Post-it note.

Pausing the film, I dashed to my room to grab my laptop, jogged back downstairs, booted it up, and continued to watch while surfing the internet. After briefly checking my Facebook and replying to a couple of emails, my fingers sought out Google and before I knew it, I had typed in Sean's name. Rolling my eyes, I scrunched up my face in annoyance at my pathetic weakness where it came to him. So perhaps my laptop wouldn't be quite the distraction from Sean that I had first thought.

Sean was well-known enough that I already knew the basics about him from my occasional reading of celeb magazines over the years; he had become famous while still young, starting off in television commercials as a teenager, but had quickly been scouted and signed up to act in many films during his early twenties. Recently, he had made it big by playing the lead role in a series of big-budget action films, one of which I was currently watching.

But what I really wanted to know about was his personal life. Which I knew was stupid, and asking for trouble, but I couldn't help myself from wondering about the man behind the fame. I'd slept with the guy and was inexplicably drawn to him, so regardless of whether it was sensible to indulge my curiosity or not, the temptation to trawl the internet about him was just too great to ignore. Besides, I might learn something that would make the remainder of my stay here more tolerable. His temperament, for example. Was he a miserable sod all the time or just when I was around?

Unfortunately, the next hour didn't make comfortable reading. *At all.* It seemed from all I'd read that Sean had a reputation in Hollywood of being moody and unpredictable, with a fiery temper and tendency to lock himself away as a virtual recluse when not filming. Depressingly, it all seemed to ring true. Stupidly, I'd been hoping that underneath his prickly veneer there might be a light-hearted guy waiting to burst free, but it looked like I was going to be sorely disappointed.

As I read on, things only got worse. Most of the gossip pages I read painted images of him as a bad boy when on location, with rumours that he'd bedded many, if not all, of his leading ladies and left a trail of broken hearts behind him after using them and coldly casting them aside.

A lump the size of a tennis ball seemed to lodge itself in my throat as I grimaced and tried to absorb this thoroughly depressing news. Looking up to the television screen, I saw Sean's handsome face intently concentrating on defusing a bomb and realised with a pang of shame laced anger that I was no different to every other women in his life. He had used me for sex, and as soon as the snow was gone I too would be cast aside and forgotten. It was as plain, simple, and depressing as that.

Mind you, I could have said no during either of our encounters but I hadn't, so really, I was no better. I'd slept with him before I even knew his name, for goodness sake, it was hardly like I'd been expecting a long-term relationship to blossom from it. Just as well, because seeing who Sean was, that clearly would never have been an option. This thing between us, whatever it was, would be done and dusted in a few days. The confusing thing was the accompanying sadness I felt at this realisation – this should have been a short, snowbound fling. There was no way I should have allowed myself to get even marginally attached to him.

Sighing, I closed the celebrity gossip pages and went back to my initial search results, and a link that had caught my eye to a an article about Sean, written back in the days when he was lesser known and just breaking into his acting career. His girlfriend at the time had been an Elena Bortsova, a pretty Russian model, pictured with Sean. My lips curled fondly as I looked at the photo; he looked almost baby faced, his manly chin less defined and his forehead free of the scowl I was used to, because for a change he was actually smiling. My eyes left the picture of Sean and drifted to Elena. She was utterly stunning; long, black hair, perfect skin, and vivid green, almost cat-like eyes. It was easy to see how she had gotten her career.

Reading the article, I found myself leaning forward in interest as a frown creased my brow. Blimey, Sean's past was horrific– apparently Sean and Elena had been on holiday together in Greece when she'd been in a snorkelling accident and a boat's propeller had caught and killed her almost instantly. Blinking in shock, I sat for a second, staring again at the photograph of her. A beautiful girl dead before she'd even reached twenty.

Shaking my head sadly I finished reading the article, which said that Sean had never forgiven himself for not going on the snorkelling trip that day, and hasn't officially 'dated' anyone since.

Wow. Talk about an eye-opener. The date of the accident was given as nearly twenty years ago … had he really never dated anyone in all that time? Biting my lip, I sat back and frowned as my mind went into overdrive. If he had loved Elena and she had died so tragically and suddenly, I suppose it would certainly go a long way to explaining why he was always so miserable. Perhaps his reluctance to forgive himself also explained his casual attitude to the women he supposedly bedded too?

Running a hand through my hair I flipped the long tresses over my shoulder and pursed my lips. Who knew what went on inside that complicated mind of his? Certainly not me, that was for sure. He'd thrown me into a tailspin from the minute

I'd met him, and now, after spending several days cooped up together I still felt like I was plummeting to the ground at full speed whenever he was around.

Taking a break from my search, I placed the laptop on the coffee table and sat back to watch the end of the film. It was actually very good; action packed with a great storyline, but I found I just couldn't enjoy it, not when my mind was preoccupied with Sean and his dark moods. Although God knows why I bothered – he clearly wasn't interested in me for anything other than food and sex.

At the precise moment that the credits began to roll, I heard the door behind me squeak, and turned my head to see Sean entering the room. He glanced briefly in my direction, then lowered his head and moved to loiter by the large windows, his back still to me as he stood watching the snow fall with his hands rammed deep into his jean pockets.

My eyebrows rose in surprise at his near-perfect timing and I wondered if he had secretly been watching me and waiting for the film to finish. I quickly pushed such a stupid idea away with a dismissive grunt – this man was in no way organising his daily schedule around me, of that much I was almost certain.

I was getting quite familiar with the sensations that coursed through my body whenever Sean was near – the tingling hairs on my arms, thumping pulse, flushed skin, and rush of blood to my core as my arousal peaked – but familiarity didn't make it any easier to deal with. Especially when I had the view of his fine bum teasing me just a few feet away.

Standing up with a sigh, I decided to escape to the kitchen for a refill of coffee, but almost as soon as I moved, Sean turned and stared at me with those intense blue eyes of his, causing me to stumble to a standstill just a few steps in front of him. Swallowing loudly, I internally kicked myself for letting our eyes connect; that had been my mistake, because his gaze just seemed to somehow hold me captive.

He might be a movie star, and probably the most magnetically attractive person I had ever met, but after my depressing readings about his endless string of sexual conquests I decided that I needed to firmly keep my distance from now on. Having unplanned sex with him in the heat of the moment was one thing, but I was way too attracted to him to let it continue without putting my heart in serious danger.

Upping my resistance to the next level, I straightened my back and drew in a fortifying breath. It couldn't snow for much longer, so I'd just have to return to avoidance until I could escape. Not having to speak to him would help too, because that way I wouldn't have to hear his lovely raspy tones. Unless he started a conversation, of course, then I'd have to reply because I was a bit too polite to go for out-and-out ignoring.

With my plan set I ripped my gaze from his – an action that almost seemed to cause a physical pain in my chest – and turned towards the kitchen door. However, before I could take any further steps, Sean swiftly sidestepped so he was in front of me, blocking my path with his huge body and captured my shoulder with a surprisingly gentle grip. Instantly fire seemed to spread across my skin from his point of contact, weakening both my knees and my resolve to stay away from him, and I inwardly groaned as I desperately fought with my body's warring emotions.

'Did you enjoy the film?' he asked softly, tipping his chin towards the TV as his hand left my shoulder to reach up and stroke some stray hairs away from my face.

Shattered. That was the only word I could think of that adequately described what his touch did to my common sense. One brush of skin and I melted like some pathetic loser. As his fingertips touched my cheek again, I found my head marginally leaning in to his touch and only barely managed to hold back the groan of pleasure was rising in my throat. If only he was always as soft and caring as this. Although, ironically, I recognised that I would actually rather miss his domineering side if it disappeared altogether.

His almost sweet gesture simultaneously made me feel like yelling at him, throwing myself at him, and melting into a pool of hormones on the carpeted floor. Physical contact from this man was going to be the death of me, but I did my best to rein in my rampaging libido and try to look unaffected as I took a marginal step backwards but failed to dislodge his hand. He was so bloody confusing, and movie star or not, I'd quite frankly had enough of his cold shoulder and bizarre mood swings over the past few days, so I stiffened and forced my face to look neutral.

'The film was fine,' I said blandly, trying to ignore the way his fingers had lingered on my cheek and felt as if they were searing into my skin.

'Just fine? It got three Oscar nominations,' he joked lightly, and my eyes shot to his face at the sound of a small chuckle leaving his throat. A smile, oh my God, Sean was actually smiling. It was only a small one, but in the flesh it was so much better than it had been on the television screen and my heart leapt into gear. The expression warmed his entire face, and was almost charmingly boyish, causing a small dimple to appear in his cheek that I instantly wanted to caress.

As lovely as his smile was, it was all coming a bit late for me, and I just found this new side of him ramping up my annoyance as I shook my head while letting out a heavy sigh. 'I'm getting a headache trying to keep up with your mood swings, Sean. One minute you can't stand me, the next you're all over me. I feel like my head's going to explode.'

After a brief pause where he almost looked genuinely regretful, his new half-amused expression and dimple were back. I couldn't decide if I liked it or not. As appealing as he looked with the smile and little creases at the corners of his eyes, it seemed fake or forced. Staring at me intently, his lips twitched in amusement again.

'Am I keeping you on your toes?' he murmured. *Keeping me on my toes?* A bubble of annoyance expanded in my chest before swiftly exploding as his comment sunk in. The arrogant arse! How dare he play with my emotions like this, how bloody dare he? Finally getting up my resolve to break the physical link between us I shoved his hand away from my face, ignoring the sense of loss that hit me as our contact was severed.

'You're such an arsehole, Sean,' I whispered, shaking my head before stomping past him into the kitchen.

Making it to the safety of the empty room, I sagged against a counter, my trembling fingers clutching at the cool marble as my ears remained alert and on guard in case he followed me. After a minute had passed I decided that I was safe – for now – and tipped my head back from the stress of it all as my eyes fluttered shut. Holy shit. Talk about intense. My entire body was vibrating with a confusing mix of anger, lust, annoyance, and attraction.

I couldn't decide if this new, jokey, talking Sean was a better option than Mr Mean and Moody who never said a word to me and then randomly jumped my bones when he got the opportunity. God, what a mess.

Pulling in a long, wobbly breath I decided against more coffee and moved to the sink to get some water instead. Turning on the tap I tested the water temperature with my finger and while feeling distinctly numb, I filled a glass and took a few shaky sips until I felt more controlled. I could do this. I'd just managed to channel my inner confidence enough to knock his hand *and* walk away from him, so I could do it again. I nodded decisively, and decided to get my laptop and retreat to the safety of my room.

With one more sip of water, I placed the glass down, straightened my posture, and walked back into the lounge hoping I could grab my computer and get out quick. I might be channelling my inner beast, but hiding in my room was still an easier option than sharing the same breathing space as Sean, even if it was decidedly gutless.

My eyes immediately located Sean, who was now stood beside the sofa, still with his hands buried in his pockets but now with a slight slump to his usually proud shoulders. His eyes flashed to mine, looking a million miles away from the jokey man he was a few minutes ago, before turning away and seeming to focus on the coffee table again. Letting out the most almighty sigh, Sean's knees suddenly seemed to buckle as his six foot something frame sank down onto the soft leather sofa in a rushed heap. What on earth was wrong with him?

'You're right, I am an arsehole.' He dropped his head into his hands and rubbed his face. I was so shocked to see him crumple that I forgot all about my plan to escape back to my room. This wasn't how I'd expected things to go at all. Where was the cocksure, moody man I had gotten used to?

Unsure of how to respond, I stayed at a distance, running a hand nervously through my hair and moving to the bar area, where I rested myself on one of the tall stools and watched him carefully.

'You don't even know the half of it,' he said thickly, indicating to my laptop screen with a jerk of his chin. As my eyes followed his gesture I realised to my utter horror that my search about Sean's relationship with Elena was still on the screen.

Shit, shit, shit!

Cringing at being caught in my blatant snooping, I felt my cheeks begin to burn as I frantically tried, and failed, to think of a suitable excuse. Whichever way I thought about it, there was no excuse for that article about *him* to be on *my* laptop. Bugger.

'I … um … I didn't mean to pry …' Which was obviously a blatant lie, because if I hadn't wanted to pry, I wouldn't have been searching about him on the sodding internet. This was awkward. I couldn't believe I'd left my laptop lying around in his house like that – I was such an idiot sometimes. 'I was just curious about you … and that came up. I'm sorry.' I stumbled over my words, completely mortified to be caught looking into his private life like some stalker fangirl.

'Not as sorry as I am.' For a second, I thought he meant that he was angry at my snooping, but as he turned his head towards me I saw Sean's frown line was the deepest I'd ever seen it, making him look far older than his years as his face contorted with pain so palpable that I felt the urge to go and comfort him.

Holding my ground on the stool, our eyes met and held as Sean started yet another round of our mutual staring. This seemed to happen so frequently that it was almost becoming our 'thing'. A heavy, tense silence hung between us as his eyes burned into mine, before he finally shook his head and observed me thoughtfully.

'I don't know what it is about you, Allie, I barely know you … but you … you make me feel like I can open up. I'm starting to want things with you that I haven't allowed myself to want for a very long time.' Behind my ribs, a small explosion of happiness burst from my heart as it fluttered with hope, my chest expanding with the idea that perhaps Sean also felt this incredible connection between us. Could it really be possible?

Just before I did something stupid like throw myself into his arms, I thought it through again and brought myself harshly crashing back to earth. What the hell was I doing indulging my fantastical imagination where Sean Phillips was concerned? I'd literally just read about the string of women he had bedded and discarded – the very *long* string of women he had bedded and discarded. Was I completely stupid? This regretful, puppy-dog eyed, sympathy act was no doubt a strategy he had used on countless girls before.

'Oh, really?' I said, raising an eyebrow sarcastically and refusing to let myself fall for his smooth lines. He might be stunningly handsome and amazing at all things sexual – OK, *really* amazing – but I was savvier than that, and regardless of how much I was drawn to him, I would not allow myself to be added to his list of conquests. Well, not again, anyway.

Seeing my casual brush-off, Sean looked momentarily shocked, before frowning, standing, and turning his body in my direction. It looked like he was about to charge across the room and melt my defiance with some of his magical touch, but instead, both of his hands shot to his hair and ran through the dark locks until it was well and truly messed-up. Suddenly looking at me with oddly alert eyes, Sean rolled his neck and began to walk toward me, every one of his long, sure strides rising my defences until he was right before me and I was bristling with panicked awareness.

What was it with him and ignoring the usual etiquette of personal space? Could it be that he just couldn't help himself because he felt the odd magnetism between us too? Oh God, I'd never had so many conversations running through my brain at once – this man well and truly scrambled my usually logical thoughts. Once again his close presence set my body on fire and melted any vague resistance I might have to him. I drew in a shaky breath, desperately trying to cling to the last threads of my composure and not throw myself at him like I wanted to.

'I can see why you wouldn't believe me ...' Sighing as if he had the weight of the world on his shoulders, Sean shook his head as a torrent of emotions seemed to play across his troubled face. 'It's just difficult for me to explain.'

He stared at me for what seemed like an eternity, his eyes trying to convey some message to me that I was completely unable to decipher. As I sat there with my emotions on a full spin cycle, Sean must have opened and closed his mouth at least six times, on each occasion closing his eyes and clenching his teeth together as he went to speak, as if whatever it was he wanted to say was too painful or too difficult to vocalise.

To my complete shock, he gave up on speech and after blinking twice, simply leant in to softly place his lips on mine. His kiss was gentle, exploratory, and almost chaste, causing my heart to expand as warmth flooded my system from his tenderness. Moaning huskily, I parted my lips, beginning to give myself over to the slow seduction of this infinitively tempting man and his skilled kisses when my mind paused on that final though. Skilful kisses. Sean really was good at this, which presumably meant it was something that he had practiced quite a lot ... As I briefly dwelled on that, the rational part of my mind kicked in and reminded me about his string of ex-lovers and the broken hearts he had stomped on, causing me to pull back and sever the contact of our lips.

I might have allowed myself to sleep with him last night when I was clueless about his identity and lack of morals, but now I knew about his past I wouldn't be so careless again, and

I gave myself a mental slap around the face to collect some of the anger needed to repel him.

'Is this the only way you can communicate with people? Through a quick fuck?' I accused, straightening my back and desperately trying to ignore the way my lips were tingling from his kiss.

I watched as Sean's face fell in shock, but then almost immediately irritation seemed to bloom in his eyes. '*A quick fuck?*' he repeated slowly and clearly, causing both the 'k's at the ends of the words to click precisely from his tongue as he over enunciated them.

Swallowing loudly at how annoyed he looked, I felt my resolve beginning to crumble under his intense scrutiny. He hadn't blinked at all, not that I'd seen anyway, and as usual I found myself frozen and helplessly returning his gaze. God, this man could win a staring competition with a bloody statue.

I strongly suspected that I'd be helpless to resist his charms if Sean chose to kiss me again, so I hoped my bluntness might help protect my falling heart by deterring him. 'I read about you and your co-stars, Sean, and seeing as you disappeared straight after we'd done the deed last night it's fairly clear that's all I am to you too,' I said as brusquely as I could, but his intense look was making me start to falter in my words.

Widening his stance, he crossed his arms over his broad chest, and stared down at me, looking far more intimidating than I'd ever thought he could. But then his features briefly slackened and twisted, just as they had earlier when he'd been stood by the sofa. The speed at which he could change from cocky and domineering to withdrawn and remorseful was quite astonishing. 'You really believe that crap you read?' he asked quietly, jerking a thumb towards my abandoned laptop.

That was definitely a question he was expecting me to answer, but I didn't. I couldn't; my throat was thick from a mix of emotions, but on top of that, I was tired of all this strain, and as I watched his face I found I didn't even have the energy to muster up a head nod. This was exhausting.

My lack of reply didn't sit well with Sean, because after watching me for a second or two I saw the moment that his jaw tensed, eyes darkened, and his cheeks flushed. 'You barely know me, so don't you dare judge me,' he growled, his jaw working furiously as he gritted his teeth so hard that I actually winced. Jesus. For a second I thought it was anger flowing from him, but after watching his eyes flick nervously around the room I decided it actually appeared to be embarrassment. Perhaps even shame? Did he regret his casual treatment of the woman who had shared his bed? Was that why he looked like this?

Unfortunately, he was infuriatingly difficult to read, his tense body language and seemingly regretful expression not really aligning together. At a total loss for what to say, I simply remained silent, watching his apparent turmoil but not knowing what I could, or should, do to help him. 'You have no idea what you're talking about. There are things you don't understand ...' he muttered, but shaking his head forcefully Sean's eyes cleared marginally before he tipped his head to the side and gave me a thoughtful look.

He'd obviously decided we'd spoken enough on that topic because his troubled expression was suddenly replaced with a smirk and I was left in the odd position of wishing that his embarrassed self would come back – he might have been a little awkward and odd just now, but at least he'd seemed genuinely truthful. This smirky, arrogant façade appeared totally false, and if I wasn't mistaken, was just used to hide his deeper feelings. Whatever they were. God, this man was complicated.

'Besides, you enjoyed our "quick fuck" just as much as I did, Allie.' My mouth popped open to object, but I immediately found myself unable to lie out loud, because when all was said and done, I *had* enjoyed it. Every passionate, pleasurable, demanding minute of it. Instead of the denial I had planned, a short, huffed breath left my throat instead. I had more than enjoyed it – I'd loved it. I didn't admit this of course. No, I shook my head in rejection, knowing my weak denial wouldn't pass for one minute if he had any vague idea about reading body language, because clearly even now I was fully aroused and ready to go, and that was just from his mere presence in the room.

Watching my response carefully, Sean let out an indifferent grunting noise and reached up to tip my chin towards him. His contact and fragrance sent my body flying into alert, but even though I knew with every shred of common sense that I needed to move away from him, I just couldn't. It was like his hold over me turned my limbs to concrete and rendered them completely useless. Holding my chin firmly between his finger and thumb, Sean then lowered his parted lips toward mine, our eyes still locked as if he were asking for silent permission. He must have seen that I was torn but turned on and willing, because the next second he closed the final gap between us, his warm breath tickling me just moments before his soft skin pressed to mine.

As soon as our lips connected I felt the full, devastating force of his hungry, possessive desire. God, this man really was something else. His total confidence and ability to meld me to his ways sent a searing rush of heat straight between my legs and had me instantly craving more even as I tried to keep my mouth firmly shut against his advances.

His lips worked against mine for several seconds, lapping and nibbling as I clenched my jaw against my crumbling resolve. 'You don't want this?' he asked huskily, his heat rushing over my face as his lips hovered just above mine.

I knew Sean would stop if I asked him to, but I didn't ask, because truthfully, I didn't want him to. Ever. Drawing in several ragged breaths through my nose, I maintained my pretence for just a while longer by weakly shaking my head, but seeing as it was held within his grip I only really managed a pathetic wobbling. 'Oh no, I'm going to need to hear it verbally, Allie,' he demanded softly as I made a feeble attempt to move away from Sean and the magnetic pull he had on me.

As lame as my attempts were, I gave up almost immediately when I realised that the bar stool was blocking my backwards path and Sean's free hand was gripping my hip and holding me firmly in place. It would take significant force to get away, and I just wasn't strong enough, or intent enough to bother trying.

Instead I whimpered needily as he lowered his face so our noses were touching, and moved a hand to my breast and casually rubbed the pad of his thumb across the nipple. Oh God. One touch and I was a lost cause. Desire was zinging around my body, my nipple now hard and puckered and desperate for more as I squirmed pathetically, trying to look like I was resisting but really loving every second of it.

My aroused writhing caused him to stop immediately. 'You're not enjoying this?'

Yes! Yes! I'm loving it! I want it!, I wanted to cry, but I instead forced a stubborn shake of my head as a gasp of pleasure flew from my lips. I wanted it, Sean knew I wanted it, but this tease was ridiculously arousing and so I continued with my attempt at playing hard to get. Even as I was shaking my head, I could feel his thumb's presence near my nipple and I felt my body marginally arching towards him and completely giving my game away.

My eyes fluttered shut for the briefest of seconds before Sean gave my chin a gentle caress, his fingers trailing briefly along my jaw to my temple and back, a sign I took to mean that he wanted me to keep them open. Prying my heavy lids back up I found his blue pools still locked on mine.

'I'll stop if you want me to. Do you want me to stop, Allie?' he asked breathily, as his hand dropped between my legs and began to rub slowly against my knee and then higher. Just below the clothing my flesh was throbbing wildly. I knew I shouldn't respond to him, I knew there was a distinct chance that I was going to get devastatingly hurt in the long run if I chose this path of pleasure over sensibility, but I just couldn't help myself, not when it felt this good, and I finally gave in as my hands reached up to clutch at his shoulders. '*Oh God* ... no ... please don't stop, Sean.'

'You want me?' he asked, as he hunkered his shoulders down so we were at the same height and he was looking me directly in the eye. Too breathless for words, I nodded as Sean began to wedge his hips between my thighs, spreading them wider as his free hand splayed high up on my inner thigh both soothing and upping my arousal simultaneously. 'Verbally, Allie, let me hear it, my gorgeous girl.'

'Yes. I want you.' I didn't hesitate for a millisecond.

One second he was staring intently into my eyes, and then the next he was crashing his lips down onto mine and thrusting his tongue against my mouth with a low groan. Anxious to absorb as much of this man as I could in my time here, my lips opened to him immediately, allowing his tongue to lash against mine with almost desperate strokes as I returned his fervour with everything I had.

His free hand slid from my thigh to my bum, where he gripped tightly and tugged me forward so hard that there was not a scrap of space left between my groin and his thighs.

'See? That wasn't so hard to admit, was it?' Arrogant arse, but actually, he was dead wrong– admitting the way I felt about him *was* difficult, because if I fully accepted that I did have feelings for him, then I would be getting myself into all sorts of trouble when the time came to leave. I didn't say any of that. Instead I merely moaned against his lips and dug my fingernails deeper into his shoulders.

Running a wet swipe of his tongue along my jawline and up to my ear he nuzzled the sensitive flesh before whispering in my ear, 'And just so you know, the feeling is completely mutual. I want you, Allie, so much. I *need* you. Need to have you again.'

Vaguely, my brain latched onto his last words, and depressingly interpreted them as him merely wanting me for sex again, but even if that was all this turned out to be, I way beyond the point of stopping now. If this was just sex, then so be it. I'd never done anything as reckless as have casual sex with a virtual stranger before, so sod it. Maybe this was just my time to catch up on missed life experiences. 'Yes … take me again, Sean.'

Next to my ear, Sean let out a low, breathy chuckle that mixed with a grunt of approval. 'I don't usually make a habit of using dirty talk, but seeing as you started it, Allie, I'll have to … tell me you want me. How did you describe it? A quick fuck? Say you want it, Allie, *tell me.*' He was teasing me, using my own words against me, at the same time encouraging me by kissing behind my ear, making me shudder with pleasure and lean myself into his touch.

He was like water flowing over me; somehow his hands seemed to be everywhere at once. Between my legs, on my breasts, smoothing over my back, tangling in my hair, running down my arms. God, he just blanketed me. I struggled to gauge where he was touching me in each distinct moment, because he was just *everywhere*.

The room dissolved and life faded away as my entire focus tuned in towards Sean. 'I want you,' I whispered longingly, my hands now copying his and unashamedly roving over his hard body. I hadn't really had a chance last night, because I'd been pinned down at his mercy, but Sean certainly didn't seem to have issues with me touching him now, because groans of pleasure left his lips as my fingers explored and acquainted myself with the firm muscles of his chest and back.

'No. Say it, Allie. Like you did before. Say it.' I knew what he meant, but I was so unused to using swear words, let alone dirty talk during sex, that my face flushed from the very thought of it. God, I was regretting yelling the accusation at him earlier.

'Oh God, I want you to …' I tried again, but the words just wouldn't come out, it would sound so … sordid, so dirty. So good.

'Say it, Allie, come on.' His hips thrust against me and I groaned as I felt the hard warmth of his erection pressing against my abdomen through our clothing. I wanted this man so much it hurt.

Swallowing back my nerves, I buried my face in his neck to avoid his eyes and sucked in a lungful of his delicious smoky, spicy scent, finally feeling courageous enough to whisper the words he wanted to hear. 'I want you to f … fuck me.' In response, his hands gripped me tighter in keenness, making me feel even braver and pushing this to a whole new level by adding a further challenge. 'Fuck me better than any man ever has …' I added hoarsely on a moment of madness.

111

Sean let out a primitive growl at my dare as his lips claimed mine in a fiercely possessive kiss and he bucked his groin against me several times, our hip bones clashing almost painfully. His tongue delved into my mouth, well and truly dominating mine as his hands roamed around my clothing, skilfully loosening and removing as he went.

The undressing happened so quickly that I barely registered it, and then, before I knew it, I was naked and panting on the barstool with my leggings and knickers dangling from one foot and a very naked, *very* aroused Sean pressed between my spread thighs. He was clad in nothing but a condom, which he had hastily pulled from his pocket and donned a second ago before immediately continuing to kiss and caress my exposed flesh almost lovingly.

One of his hands danced across my skin, teasing my stomach, breasts, and ticklish ribs before dipping back between my legs and swirling around my clitoris with slick, swift circles. 'Christ, girl, you're so wet for me.'

My eyes rolled shut at his words as I smiled and simply gave myself over to the power he held over me. 'Conveniently, this bar stool also appears to be the perfect height,' he murmured against my lips as his hands settled on my bottom and began to massage the flesh, making my clit pulse needily.

I needn't have asked what the stool was the perfect height for, as Sean gripped my buttocks harder and pulled me forwards in one swift drag to impale me on his waiting cock. Bloody hell. Once again I found myself letting out a cry of surprise at his sudden delicious intrusion, but the sound mingled in my throat into one of lusty desire as Sean ground himself against the little bundle of nerves that had been so desperate for attention.

'OK, my gorgeous girl?' he asked urgently as he paused with his shaft buried fully inside me. The concern in his tone was incredibly touching, but surprisingly, I found that his size was less painful this time. Still stretching me, but just in a pleasurable way that allowed me to feel every inch and twitch of him inside me.

'I'm good.' Rolling my head back I let out a long, breathy moan. 'God, it's so good, Sean,' I panted, meaning every word. Perhaps I was just adjusting to him. That, and adjusting to the more regular usage, of course.

Withdrawing to the tip, I prepared for him to hammer home like he had the previous times, but instead, he reached up, cupped my jaw to bring my head up so our eyes met, and as he smoothed my sweat-dampened hair back from my face, he smoothly thrust his hips forwards to stroke his length back inside me almost lovingly.

This position was fantastic. *Fan-bloody-tastic*. Sean continued with his controlled movements and tapped my calf muscles to guide me to wrap my legs around him, which I did happily. Clenching my thighs around him only seemed to bring him even deeper within me. This position honestly felt like the most intimate we'd been yet. He seemed so deep inside me that he hit all the right spots with each gentle thrust, and my trembling g-spot was thanking the gods for the position Sean had chosen. As well as that, because we were facing each other I could look into his eyes as he claimed me, and see the mutual desire reflected right back in his blue depths.

This was some intense stuff. Surely this went beyond mere sex? Perhaps not for Sean, but I think it was fair to say that it certainly did for me. The intimacy of our liaison soon had me swelling towards a huge climax and as his movements became more furious and jerky, I came around him, crying out but managing to maintain our gaze as Sean continued to stare into my eyes and draw out my orgasm with his skilled movements.

In the past I'd often found that looking at my partner during sex was a bit embarrassing, and usually tried to avoid it at all costs, but Sean clearly had no such issues; he had barely broken eye contact once the entire time, and surprisingly, I'd loved the tenderness that it had created between us. In fact, I think the only time he closed his eyes was when he threw back his head to climax as he rammed himself inside me so forcefully that it sparked a second, smaller climax from me and had me whimpering and burying my face into his neck as my body quivered and the bar stool rocked from his fierce thrusts.

Unable to muster up the energy to move, I stayed where I was, clinging to him like a limpet, still on a high but starting to dread the inevitable moment where he would pull out and effectively dismiss me like he had the last times. Talk about a glutton for punishment. After his almost affectionate behaviour I had a sinking suspicion that cold behaviour from him now was going to hurt far more than it had before.

To my surprise, however, Sean nuzzled my neck and wrapped his arms around me humming contentedly below my ear. 'Hold on tight, gorgeous girl,' he murmured, causing me to frown in confusion, but comply immediately by wrapping my arms around his neck and clinging on. Then, with his impressively semi-hard erection still buried inside me, Sean gently lifted me from the stool, adjusted his grip so he was supporting my weight below my bum, and turned to carry me upstairs.

Every step he took with him buried inside of me caused my channel to pulse greedily around his thick cock, and by the time he had carried me to an unfamiliar bedroom – his, I assumed – he was groaning his approval into my hair and was rock hard again. With a low, amused-sounding curse he laid me down on the bed, gently pulled out of me with a slight wince, and set about pulling the soft covers up under my chin.

Flashing me a grin which looked far more genuine than the strange smirks I'd seen downstairs, he ruefully eyed his cock, which was now bobbing around hopefully, then disposed of the condom in a bin to his right with a low chuckle.

Dropping one hand onto the bed beside my head, he leaned over me and stared at me intently before grinning, dropping short, swift kiss onto the tip of my nose, winking, and disappearing into the en-suite, leaving me watching his retreating arse in all its tight, clenched glory.

A wink *and* a grin? I was a lucky girl. And after its second appearance, I could confirm that *that* smile was definitely one-hundred percent genuine. It had been just as spectacular as I had imagined, and far surpassed the fake, arrogant ones he had been throwing at me downstairs before our interlude on the bar stool.

He hadn't run away from me this time, which was both confusing and blooming brilliant – but what did it mean? After watching his retreat, I lay there for a few moments clutching the blankets beneath my chin and feeling completely confused by this turn of events, but also pleasantly surprised. Hearing running water I assumed he was cleaning himself up, and after a few seconds Sean reappeared with a washcloth in hand.

The washcloth was momentarily forgotten as I greedily soaked up the view of Sean striding back towards me stark naked and making no effort whatsoever to conceal his body or his impressively swinging manhood. My eyes were like pinballs, unashamedly roving across his beauty as I bit down on my lower lip to try and supress the swirling desire resurfacing within me. He was so close to perfection it was almost impossible for my brain to grasp, and clearly from his confident swagger and mild smirk, Sean was well aware of his flawlessness too.

Crawling into the bed beside me, Sean took a hold of the top of the duvet and began drag the covers away from my body, causing me to yelp, squirm, and try to cover myself again. All the while, Sean merely laughed at me, ripped them from my hands, and swiftly began trying to part my legs with his big palms. Gasping at this sudden – and completely unexpected – onslaught, I clenched my thighs together and scrabbled for the sheets again to try and regain my dignity. If I actually *had* any dignity left where this man was concerned.

'Stop squirming, woman,' Sean grumbled with a chuckle as he once again tried to part my legs with the washcloth clutched in one hand and dragging its warm dampness across my thigh.

What was he doing? It was all very well exposing myself to him in the heat of the moment, but now I was lying spread-eagled in broad daylight and it was embarrassing. Really bloody embarrassing. I barely knew him and he was trying to do what, exactly? Wash me? How weird was that? I was perfectly capable of doing it myself.

Pushing myself upright, I shook my head, sending my hair flying around me in a tangle of blonde strands as a blush reddened my cheeks until I felt them burning. 'I can do that,' I muttered, trying to take the cloth from him, but he pulled it back away from me with a deep frown and looking genuinely put out. Squinting at me in apparent displeasure, I saw none of his earlier light-heartedness. Sean's better mood apparently now a thing of the past.

'Obviously you can. But I want to do it.' Hmm. Did he think I was dirty or something? Perhaps he was worried that I might leak on his bed after our rampant bar stool liaison? Who knew? But it all seemed a bit strange to me. I'd certainly never had a partner try to clean me after sex before.

'Why?' I asked quietly, pulling the sheet under my chin as self-consciousness flooded my body and the flush from my cheeks spread down my neck.

Tilting his head, Sean observed me quietly for several seconds before leaning forward and placing an almost reverent kiss on my forehead. 'Because I want to take care of you,' he confessed in a barely audible whisper, before leaning back and looking at me nervously.

Oh. Well, I suppose that was certainly better than thinking I was dirty. Gosh. He wanted to take care of me? I wasn't entirely sure what to make of that, but inside my chest my heart certainly swelled a little.

Blinking several times, Sean finally let out a low sigh and dropped his head to his chest, his muscular shoulders slumping forwards for a few seconds, before he lifted his head and gazed at me with troubled eyes. 'The last times that we ...' he paused, wincing, apparently unsure how to continue, 'when I ... *fuck* ... I mean when we ...' His words trailed off as Sean sat back on his heels and ran a hand through his hair in apparent exasperation. 'When we had sex before, I ... I shouldn't have treated you the way I did by leaving you afterwards. I was a total shit to you, Allie, and I'm so sorry. I want to make up for it by looking after you.'

My eyebrows were almost in my hairline after that speech. Wow. At least he recognised that his behaviour had upset me and seemed willing to apologise, even if that apology was rather unorthodox and involved washing me. Seeing the hopeful look in his wary, blue eyes I briefly chewed on my lower lip before letting out a breath, releasing the sheet and laying back on the back bed in silent agreement. This was a little odd to me, so I was still tense at first, but when I heard his grumble of appreciation I relaxed as his warm palm gently encouraged me to open my legs for him. Throwing caution to the wind, I did, allowing them to splay open to Sean's prying eyes and gentle touch.

The small smile that played on his lips as he set about gently washing me was worth all of my previous embarrassment because his dimple was back, his face looking relaxed, happy, and utterly content.

This almost obsessively caring behaviour was a million miles away from the Sean who had fucked me over a kitchen counter and buggered off into the night. Not that I was complaining – this upgrade was far more preferable.

Watching the top of his dark head as it tilted with each careful swipe, I couldn't help but smile. This man was a complete mystery, but getting to know him was proving to be rather good fun.

As I waited for him to finish his silent task, my mind rewound his words again. As much as I knew I shouldn't, it was nearly impossible not to read too much into his apparently heartfelt declarations of regret. Saying he wanted to take care of me was probably no more than Sean's way of apologising for being a bit of a shit after our last two encounters – wasn't it?

Once the washcloth had been meticulously smoothed all around my sensitive flesh and upper thighs, Sean finished by sliding his forearm under my hips, lifting my back a few inches from the bed, and wiping the flannel right down the crack of my bum. Yelping in surprise, I squirmed in his arms, almost unable to believe what he had just done. Back there was somewhere that no man had ever been before, and his contact made me buck embarrassingly and clutch at his wrist as he tried to repeat the action.

'Like that, do you?' he murmured darkly, before smirking at me, winking wickedly at my astonished expression, and then thankfully tossing the cloth onto the floor before he could continue with a more detailed exploration of my nether regions. Blimey, that had been a bit unexpected. And as to whether I had liked it or not? Well, I wasn't really sure – it been a surprise, yes, but hadn't been unpleasant, so I wasn't really sure what to make of it.

Thankfully, Sean didn't actually wait for me to answer his embarrassing question and instead set about pulling the covers up around us. Tugging me into his arms, he gently arranged my body so that I was spooned against his big frame, with my back to his front and one of his arms wrapped around my waist, before he let out a contented sigh into the hair by my nape.

We snuggled for some time like this, and at first it was bliss. Against my will, I was developing some serious feelings for this man, and right now, this was exactly where I wanted to be. But the more time that passed, the more I began to worry about what would happen next. Sean was a serial seducer and had already proven that he could be perfectly heartless, distant, and cold when he wanted, so I needed to cut this short now and get away. It had been fun – more than fun – but I was well aware of the fact that I was starting to quite like my position in Sean's arms, which definitely was not a good thing for the long-term health of my falling heart.

Even though it was only early afternoon, I was starting to feel sleepy from our antics and felt a ball of nerves settle in my belly. Sean seemed happy– in fact, from the heavy breathing on my neck he might actually be asleep. But would he wake up soon, decide that his apology was done and kick me out?

Just the thought of his emotionless dismissals made me shudder and feel cold despite the heat of his arms. I couldn't, and wouldn't, let that happen again. Thinking that perhaps enough was enough, I made the decision to move back to my own room in the hopes that it would avoid any awkwardness later.

From his low, steady breaths it seemed like Sean definitely was asleep, so I carefully started to slide out from under his arm, hoping I could get away without disturbing him. But before I had even gotten a few inches away from his solid chest, his arm tightened around me and yanked me backwards so I was firmly encased within his warm embrace again.

'Where do you think you're going?' he growled, his voice sleepy, rough, and sexy as sin.

In a flash of moving sheets and hot, hard skin I suddenly found myself gently pinned below Sean, his thighs straddling mine, his arms effectively trapping me below him, and the weight of his semi-hard cock resting heavily on my belly.

As I looked up into two alert blue pools, I felt my cheeks flush guiltily. Oops. I had been caught in the act of fleeing, and Sean certainly didn't look as sleepy as he had sounded.

'Um … don't you want me to leave?' I asked curiously, trying to hide the excitement at the thought that he might want me to stay with him. It felt so good being held in his arms. Probably too good, but perhaps I could escape reality for just a while longer and stay with him for a short time more. It would sure beat going back to my freezing cold bed sheets for a post-sex snooze, that was for sure.

He stared at me intently for a few seconds, his face annoying unreadable, before his lips twitched into just a tiniest hint of a smile.

'No. Stay,' he murmured, looking down at me quizzically, as if he were also trying to work out what his answer meant. 'I … I like having you in my arms,' He said, simultaneously causing my heart to soar and my poor confused brain to become even more tangled as I tried to understand the inner workings of this man.

Hesitantly nodding my acceptance, I watched as Sean smiled happily, dropped a peck onto the tip of my nose, and once again settled the two of us in his bed, this time with him on his back and me laid across his chest.

'I need to catch up on the sleep I missed last night. No more trying to leave, OK?' he murmured, confusing me even more. Rather than start a Q&A session about what the heck he was thinking and feeling, I just gave in to another of his demands and nodded my head. 'You better be here when I wake up,' he muttered, shortly before his arm around me tightened and I heard a low snore escape his throat.

There was no way I could sleep now. This was all far too confusing to let me relax that much. Not to mention possessive – his words almost sounded like he was talking about long-term plans, but there was no way I could indulge my heart in fantastical wanderings like that. My poor brain could barely keep up with what was going on as it was, and I lay there for quite a while breaking down all possible reasons, options, and outcomes.

Depressingly, most of the scenarios I came up with ended with me experiencing some mind-blowing sex for a few days, falling head over heels for Sean, and then leaving here with a broken heart when the snow had cleared and he'd had his fill of me. Men could be shallow like that, sex really could be "just sex" for them, whereas women might claim that was the deal, but often viewed it from a far more emotional perspective.

At least, that was the case for me, anyway. It was one of the reasons I'd avoided one-night stands and 'fuck buddies' for most of my life. I'd learnt this lesson the hard way when at nineteen, I'd had a brief fling with an intense, charming, and slightly older man, swiftly falling head over heels and then discarded when he realised I wanted more than just sex. That had been an eye opener for me and left me an emotional wreck for months afterward.

Pursing my lips now, I scowled when I thought about it. It wasn't a million miles away from what was happening here; Sean was older, certainly intense and charming when he chose to be, and no doubt I would take months to recover from this encounter. Damn. After years of being sensible and selecting boyfriends with care, I had unconsciously allowed myself to slip right back onto the same path.

Despite my earlier belief that I wouldn't be able to sleep, gradually sleepiness softened my gloomy thoughts and eventually pulled me into a relaxing peace.

The two of us must have snoozed for quite some time, because when I woke up the room was darkening as afternoon turned to evening. I was still sprawled across Sean's chest; my head was over his heart, one hand was laying on the soft hair of his stomach, and my leg had somehow shifted in my sleep so it was now flung over his thigh.

As my mind became more alert my earlier panic returned, and I began to worry that our snooze had merely delayed the inevitable awkwardness that would fall between us, but before anxiety could fully settle in I re-evaluated my positioning and smiled. As well as being pretty forward with my feelings as I practically blanketed him with my body, he too was showing no signs of wanting me gone from his bed – one of his arms was cradling me against him, his hand gripping my hip just as tightly as before, as if he truly had meant his earlier statement about me not leaving him as he slept. As well as his firm hold on me, Sean's free hand was trailing gently through the long stands of my hair, following it from scalp to tip over and over again – and that wasn't something a lover would do if they wanted you out pronto, was it?

I hummed contentedly and snuggled closer. I loved having my hair touched, it always made me feel warm and sleepy and I couldn't help but angle my head closer to increase his contact. 'Your hair is incredible,' he murmured gruffly, his voice rough from sleep and sending a shiver of lust straight through me.

His hand finally released its tight hold of my hip, almost like he was now satisfied that I wasn't running away, and joined his other hand in smoothing over my hair from the scalp to the ends. 'Sleep well?' he enquired, and I was fairly sure from his tone that there was a smile on his lips.

Well, this was certainly a more pleasant wake-up call than I'd expected. I couldn't help but smile to myself as I shifted my body to look up at him. He was indeed smiling, and what a knockout it was; Sean's dimple was well and truly in place, his face looking relaxed and happy, and the floppy mess of his hair as it fell over his forehead was so endearing that I couldn't help my own smile widening into a broad grin.

I knew I shouldn't get carried away, but this cosy, affectionate wake-up was prompting me to develop a new sense of hope in this crazy situation. Perhaps he wasn't going to chuck me out after all.

'I did. You must have worn me out,' I joked quietly. Sean smiled along with me, lifting a hand and gently rubbing a thumb across my cheek before his eyes suddenly darkened and he began pursing his lips.

My whole body stiffened above him, I'd already worked out that this lip pursing gesture was some sort of sign that he was uptight or worried about something, but if that wasn't a clear enough indicator of his sudden mood change, then the tenseness of Sean's body accompanied by his flicking, agitated gaze was a dead giveaway.

Had I scared him off by being too affectionate? Perhaps I was giving away the fact that I was falling for him? Assuming that I was the cause of his sudden unease I tried to sit up, only to have Sean pull me closer to him, tucking my head into the nook of his neck and holding me so tightly it was like he was terrified that I was going to disappear.

OK, I was certainly confused now. He hadn't asked me to leave, though, and was clinging onto me for dear life, so I had very little choice but to relax against him.

As he felt my body go lax in his arms, Sean let out a sigh so long and deep that I couldn't decide if it was relieved or pained. 'I need to keep you close,' he muttered. A frown flitted to my brows. I didn't understanding what he meant, but now didn't seem an appropriate time to ask, so I stayed silent and went along with it. After all, being in his arms felt pretty fantastic, regardless of what random statements he might be making.

Snuggling into him, I gently rubbed at his chest with my fingertips, hoping to reassure him even though I didn't know the issue. 'Those articles you read earlier. I want to talk about them.'

Ah. So that was what was bothering him. Was this the moment he confessed that he only had sex with woman a few times and then left? Was I about to be turned out after all? My stomach did several somersaults, but I tried to remain calm and let him do the talking for now. Running away could come later if it needed to.

'The day that Elena went snorkelling and had her accident …' he began, his voice wobbling slightly. My eyebrows rose in surprise at the topic, because I'd assumed he wanted to talk about the string of broken hearts he had created, not the accident with his ex. From his tone and the slight trembling I could feel in his arms it was clear he was upset, and I frowned in concern, but chose to stay silent and let him continue.

'I … I told her I was tired and didn't want to go snorkelling because I had a hangover, but really, I was sleeping with another woman,' he confessed suddenly, his words coming out in a rush.

My eyes practically popped from my skull. OK, so we could officially add "cheater" to the ever growing list of "player" and "heartbreaker" for Sean's character description. My stomach dropped, and I suddenly felt quite sick. The accompanying pain in my heart at this news also told me that I was already in over my head with this man, but seeing as I was naked, in his bed, and in his arms while he went on some strange confessional, there really wasn't much I could do about it the at present moment. So he'd been with another woman when his girlfriend was killed – no wonder he still felt guilty.

'I feel awful, still to this day I blame myself for her death. If I'd been there I would never have let her go near the propeller, but instead I was balls deep and screwing some waitress.'

Gulping down my shock at his blunt honesty, I swallowed the huge lump that had formed in my throat and hesitated, completely unsure as to what to say or do. As irrational and insensitive as it was, I initially felt a pang of jealousy, but had to forcefully push that aside and consider how to respond. His

123

girlfriend had died, for goodness sake, I needed to get a grip on my emotions, not turn into some nutty green-eyed monster over some waitress.

It turned out I didn't have to say anything, because after drawing in a long breath, Sean continued, his voice low and rough. 'We were both so young. Elena and I had met on a film shoot and ended up fooling around a bit – we weren't ever officially dating, even though the press declared us as an item, but we were filming together for four months and hooked up every now and then. I suppose it was kind of a friends with benefits set up.'

Reaching up, he ran a hand through his hair in apparent agitation, scratching so hard at his scalp that I heard his nails dragging through the skin and winced before reaching over and taking his hand in mine, pulling it away from damaging himself further and interlocking our fingers. I don't know what prompted me to do it, but Sean paused, staring in apparent wonder at our joined hands for an age before licking his lips, looking briefly at me, and continuing.

'The day of the snorkelling trip, I'd been chatting to a pretty waitress at breakfast. She knew I was part of the acting team staying at the hotel and made it perfectly clear that I could have her if I wanted. I'll be honest, the prospect of a hot blonde in my bed beat a snorkelling trip hands down. That's why I wasn't there to help Elena. Perhaps it would still have happened, who knows, but I felt like utter shit. I've never dated properly since in case I fail like that again.'

Wow, so the speculation in that article I'd read really was true, Sean had never dated again since Elena. As traumatising as this conversation was, I couldn't help but wonder what Sean *had* done instead of dating, because he certainly wasn't lacking skills in the bedroom department. As much as I didn't want to think about it, that must be where the string of devastated women came into play – he didn't date, but he *did* fuck around. How depressing.

My gloomy thoughts made my body go limp in his arms, something Sean obviously picked up on, because he then rolled me backwards and manoeuvred himself so he was hovering over me, his blue eyes troubled but intense as they connected with mine.

'You need to understand that I was barely eighteen, sex was kinda new for me so I was taking advantage of the fact that I was getting plenty of offers. Elena and I both saw other people, it wasn't technically like I cheated on her because we weren't together. I swear I'm not like that now, Allie.' I hadn't meant to look sceptical, but I wasn't born yesterday; he was a Hollywood actor with looks to die for and a track record of being a heartbreaker, so his claims seemed fairly weak to me.

Blinking rapidly, he licked his lips and sighed. 'I'll be completely honest with you, after the accident I went off the rails for a few years, drinking heavily and sleeping around in the hopes that it might help to dull the guilt.'

Ugh. The thought of a young Sean on a reckless bender of women and booze was not a pleasant one, and I winced as various images of him developing his sexual skills with a flow of different women flooded my mind. I felt my earlier feelings of sickness returning with a vengeance and had to swallow hard to stop from gagging. 'What about now?' I asked softly, needing to know but dreading the answer.

He looked a little embarrassed by my question, his cheeks flushing as he pursed his lips again.

'I'm only human Allie, I have needs just like everyone else,' he whispered. 'As much as I might have avoided formal dating over the years I do occasionally indulge myself with a short fling here or there.' So I was a short fling? An indulgence? His words felt like they'd pierced me straight through the heart – it was what I'd expected, but not what I'd wanted to hear.

'As I said, I've been too scared to form emotional attachments in case I let someone down, but film sets are strange places; there are always crew members happy to have a no-strings attached one-night stand, so that's what I've done over the years. Always with women who wanted the same thing, only ever for one night with the same person, and never resulting in any broken hearts.'

Only ever for one night? He'd slept with me more than once ... did that mean something? Or was it more out of convenience because I was here and we were stuck together?

This was really unpleasant to listen to. I might be the one currently pressed up against his gloriously naked body, but it seemed that I was far from in the minority in that experience, and a small irritated huff of air left my lungs. 'I'm sorry, but I'm just being truthful with you, Allie. If it makes you feel any better, I hadn't slept with a woman in over a year before I met you.' Narrowing his eyes, he cocked his head as he thought and then shook his head, 'Actually, more like two years. I'm sure you're sceptical, but believe me, it's true.'

As incredible as it seemed, I did believe him. I had no reason not to, after all – he could have hidden his past from me, but he had openly admitted that he'd been a player when he was younger. Besides, he might be an actor, and a very good one at that, but I highly doubted he was faking; his eyes were glazed and sincere, and the look of utter desolation on his face when he'd been taking about Elena had been so real that my own eyes had begun to sting with unshed tears.

Nodding my head, I found myself biting the inside of my cheeks to try and stop myself getting too carried away and blurting out more than he would want to hear. 'I believe you,' I whispered simply, instinctively pushing myself up so I could place a quick peck on his lips. Raising one hand, I stroked his stubbly cheek and shook my head. 'The accident wasn't your fault, Sean, you need to forgive yourself. It was a horrible, horrible thing, but it could have happened regardless of whether you were there or not.'

I watched as he squeezed his eyes shut tight and felt a share of his pain settle in my own chest. 'Maybe.' His eyes opened, pupils dilating as he stared at me, his gaze softening along with the tenseness that he had been holding in his jaw. Stroking my cheek, a small smile curled his mouth that was so sweet it made my heart flutter wildly.

'I've avoided relationships, but I was attracted to you instantly. As crazy as this sounds, Allie, as soon as we met I felt a connection with you that I haven't ever felt before, and that terrified me.' Pausing, he pursed his lips and I couldn't help but follow his movements with my eyes. 'I hope this goes a little way to explaining why I was so brusque with you at first. I was doing the only thing I could think of to keep you at a distance. It was a shitty thing to do and I'm so, so sorry for the way I treated you. But my self-control failed miserably and attraction won out.' My self-control had been pretty pathetic too, I thought with a smile. 'I'm really glad that it did though,' he finished with a shy smile. I knew exactly what he meant, because I had done my own share of attempting to deny the connection between us only to fail miserably and melt into his hands.

'I felt it too, Sean. I mean, I still do, but on that first day it nearly knocked me down with the power of it. It's crazy.'

'It is, crazy and wonderful,' he admitted, smiling and looking incredibly pleased by my admission before he swallowed loudly and the smile fell from his face. 'I ... I don't want to let you down like that again, Allie. I couldn't bear that. I need to keep you safe.'

Wow. He looked completely serious and was almost talking as if this was a long term relationship and not just a few-day fling. No matter how much I wished that would be the case, I didn't let myself get too caught up in his words. He was full of emotion at the moment, his memories of Elena no doubt affecting his words, so I didn't pass comment, instead just nodding at him.

Letting out a long breath as if finally releasing some small fragment of his past, Sean lowered his forehead onto mine, closed his eyes, and simply seemed to breathe me in for a few minutes.

Finally blinking those gorgeous big blues of his, he rubbed our noses together and placed a soft kiss on my lips. 'Thank you for listening and not judging. It means more to me than you can imagine,' he murmured, before flopping onto his side and pulling me into his arms for a crushing hug. His cuddle this time had nothing at all to do with sex. It wasn't even a prelude to something naughty, but to me, the minutes spent in his arms were some of the best of my life so far. Perhaps this Christmas would be a good one after all.

Chapter Ten
Allie

Christmas Day morning literally couldn't have started off in a better way. First, I woke up snuggled against Sean's side with his arm wrapped around me as he possessively held on to me in his sleep again – how he managed to grip me so firmly and still sleep I had no idea – which made me grin as broadly as a Cheshire cat. Then, after drifting back to sleep for a while, I was woken by the confusing sensation of a delicious warmth travelling up my leg from my knee to my inner thigh.

As well as warm, my leg felt a bit wet, and I squirmed as I tried to work out what on earth was going on. Blinking several times, I began to properly wake up and glanced down to see a large lump in the duvet between my thighs, which appeared to be the cause of my warm, wet wake-up.

After wafting the duvet, I got a brief glimpse of Sean's dark hair by my stomach, before the covers were pulled down from my grip which left me lying there at his mercy as Sean continued his onslaught under the covers. I couldn't feel any other part of him touching me, so it was just Sean's warm, wet mouth that continued with the teasing as he gave me a morning welcome by exploring what seemed like every inch of my skin with his lips and tongue.

Giggling at the ticklish sensation as he nibbled by my knee, I tried to squirm away from his teasing exploration, only to hear a low warning growl before Sean pinned me to the bed more firmly with his hands. 'Stay still, my gorgeous girl, or I'll stop,' he mumbled from within his duvet cocoon, and even with the muffling effect of the quilt I could hear the edge of demand in his voice. What he was doing felt amazing and I didn't want him to stop – obviously – so I did as commanded and calmed my wriggling body, which caused him to let out a happy little sigh before continuing.

This happened several times, because no matter how much I knew he wanted me to stay still, there was only so much of his talented tongue I could take before I lost control and either gripped his head or flailed below him. Every single time he would stop, demand that I lie still, and only continue when I had obeyed him.

His self-control really was enviable, because mine was quickly fraying at the edges from his delicious torture as I climbed closer and closer toward the peak I so desperately craved, only for him to stop every single time I was about to come.

Eventually, after what seemed like hours of his incredible torment, Sean's hands and tongue left my skin and I watched as the duvet formed an even larger lump as he obviously sat up on his knees. Hearing the rip of a condom packet I experienced several seconds of almost unbearable anticipation before I felt his hot, hard frame crawling up my body.

His stunning face emerged from below the covers with flushed cheeks, ruffled hair, and a thoroughly wicked twinkle in his blue eyes which I couldn't help but grin at in delight. He looked the happiest I had ever seen him.

'Merry Christmas, Allie,' he murmured as he shifted to his elbows, aligned his shaft with my entrance, and pushed himself inside of me in one firm thrust.

He went so deep so quickly that my first Christmas greeting to him was a soft swear word at the suddenness of his intrusion, but then recovering myself with a gasp, I managed to shift slightly to accommodate his size and smile shyly up at him. 'Merry Christmas, Sean.'

Our rhythm was slow, relaxed, and exactly what I craved this morning. After a particularly barren spell in the sex department over the last few years I was surprised that all this sudden usage hadn't left me sorer, but surprisingly I was OK, and more than up for a Christmas round of naughtiness.

Pausing briefly as he hovered above me, Sean's eyes locked on mine, his depths glimmering as a slight sheen of sweat built on his forehead. 'You're the best Christmas present ever,' he murmured, before using his skilful hips to thrust smoothly in, rotate, and then pull out of me, making sure to hit all the right places, but at a tempo that while turning me on immensely, wasn't quite fast enough to take me over the edge. He was proving to be a master tease this morning, and if he didn't let me come soon I was fairly sure I would explode from delicious frustration.

But Sean didn't let me come soon, instead continuing his teasing until I was so frantic that I gripped his shoulders and begged him to take me harder, a comment that should have left me feeling mortified but didn't. That was the power he had – I had been reduced to desperate begging.

Seeming to enjoy my needy state, Sean grinned at first, looking mighty bloody smug, before his features softened and he nodded his compliance, hammering himself deeply inside me and causing us both to bark out noises of shock and pleasure. Taking me with more speed and force, he began to thrust deep and hard until our hips were banging together and our earlier gentle rhythm was well and truly forgotten.

Oh God. It was so good, so perfect. *He* was perfect. I would never get enough of him.

The sound of our pleasured moans and sweaty bodies moving against each other filled the still air around us, and after several more hard thrusts I came undone, screaming his name and gripping his back so hard that I no doubt left marks. With a throaty groan of approval, Sean bucked inside of me twice more before finding his own release and collapsing on top of me.

My arms dropped from his shoulders so they were flung above my head, Sean lay practically unconscious on my stomach and my body was still receiving lovely little aftershocks from my incredible orgasm. Wow. *Best sex never.*

Upon recovering, Sean propped himself up above me with a smile, looking well and truly dishevelled. 'Shower time,' he murmured, practically leaping to his feet, scooping me into his arms, and striding toward the bathroom before I had even realised that I had left the cosy confines of the bed.

Not complaining about my positioning in his arms I rested my cheek on his chest and hummed my contentment. This was obviously more of the 'caring' that Sean had talked about yesterday, and I was happy to allow him his way. It seemed that today, instead of just a quick wipe down with a washcloth I'd be getting the full works in the shower.

Popping me on my feet beside the bath, he ducked his head and ran a cheeky swipe of his tongue across one of my sensitive nipples, which made me yelp and clutch at his hair. I couldn't move back because I was trapped by the sink so I had little choice but to gasp and giggle as he repeated the same treatment to my other breast, his own laughter sending warm waves of breath across my tingling flesh before finally leaving me be.

Lifting his head, Sean wiggled his eyebrows playfully and turned to sort out the shower temperature, leaving me standing on wobbly legs and grinning like a giddy schoolgirl. Turning towards the mirror, my eyebrows jumped to my scalp as I took in my wayward appearance; my cheeks were red, eyes shining, and my long hair was an absolute mess of tangles. I looked a complete state. Or perhaps "thoroughly well fucked" would be a more appropriate description.

Satisfied with the water temperature, Sean ushered me under the soothing spray while he rooted around in the cupboard under the sink before producing two bottles and joining me.

Eyeing the white bottle in his hand I read the label and smiled – shampoo and conditioner. Perfect. And both of a brand that I recognised, unlike the masculine shampoo I'd found in the en-suite of my room. It was just what my poor bird's nest of hair had been crying out for since I got stuck here. Seeing my pleased expression Sean shrugged, suddenly looking a bit self-conscious. 'It's not mine, my sister left some things for when she visits,' he blurted. 'But this is good for long hair, right?'

Nodding, I suddenly felt a bit overcome with emotion at just how thoughtful Sean was being, and found myself hiding my glassy eyes by leaning forwards and placing a quick kiss in the centre of his lovely chest. 'It is. Exactly what I need to tame this wild mess,' I murmured, trying, and failing, to run a hand through my tangled hair.

'It's not wild. It's perfect,' Sean muttered, his voice so quiet that I wasn't entirely sure that I was supposed to hear his comment. But I had, and I absorbed it into my brain to treasure.

'Here, let me.' Moving behind me, Sean set about patiently untangling my hair, running his hands repeatedly through the strands and apologising softly every time he came across a particularly tough tangle and had to tug. This would have been much easier if I'd gone and got the brush from my handbag, but I rather liked being worshipped like this, and didn't want to break the spell by leaving the room, even if it was only for a second or two.

Once my hair was tangle free, I was treated to a full wash and rinse before Sean manoeuvred me slightly out of the water, applied the conditioner, and after consulting the bottle, told me firmly that I had to leave it on for three minutes. I then watched in greedy fascination as Sean began to soap himself down.

'Let me,' I offered, stepping forwards. I was immediately met with a frown.

'No, you need to leave your conditioner in and stay out from under the spray.' Pulling back the sponge, he continued to wash himself solo, leaving me pouting grumpily, but secretly supressing a smile at his bossy but caring demeanour.

I didn't complain about being a spectator because as much as I would have liked to have been involved in the washing process, Sean naked, bubbly, and slick was quite a sight to see and I couldn't tear my eyes away as his hands smoothed over his tight muscles. They were like saucers by the time he carefully began to soap his erect cock, and he flashed me a glance, smirking at my wanton look and continuing with a knowing smile flickering on his lips. God, he'd only just had me less than fifteen minutes ago, but I could totally go again, and clearly from the shaft he was cleaning, so could he.

Once he was washed, Sean squirted more shower gel on his sponge and stepped towards me, wrapping a warm, wet arm around my waist and beginning to soap my shoulders and arms. So he could wash me, but I couldn't wash him? Typical. Not that I was really complaining; this was bliss. He was incredibly thorough, not leaving an inch untouched, but when he rinsed the soap from the sponge and tried to move between my legs I tensed like last time with the flannel and tried to squeeze my legs together.

Glancing down at his stooped form, I saw the disapproving expression on his handsome face as he patiently waited for me to comply with his silent request. The disappointed look in his blue eyes told me that for whatever bizarre reason, he really wanted this, so I relented on a sigh, parted my legs, and let him do his thing, hearing a satisfied hum leave his lips as his hand dipped between my legs.

Chapter Eleven
Sean

Pulling a T-shirt over my head, I made a vague attempt at flattening my shower-dampened hair then turned away from the mirror to eye my bedroom with amusement. There was absolutely no mistaking what had taken place here; the rumpled sheets, carelessly discarded clothing, torn condom packets, and lingering scent of hot skin made it very clear that somebody had recently been indulging in a good time between the sheets. A very, *very* good time. And luckily, that someone had been me, I thought with a smug smirk as I bent to shake out the bedcovers.

After making the bed, binning the condom packets, and folding my clothing, I briefly sat on the side of the mattress and took a moment to think back over all that had occurred between Allie and I. One thing was for sure, that last conversation had certainly all gone a lot better that I had ever hoped, or expected. In fact, I could barely believe how amazing the last ten hours had been. Blowing out a long, thankful breath I thought of Allie and how amazing she had felt in my arms and in my bed. Right on cue, I felt my cock give a twitch and looked down with a rueful smile. The bloody thing just wouldn't calm down at the moment, seeming to be either half-mast or fully hard ever since Allie had arrived. It was a wonder I wasn't dizzy from lack of blood to the brain. But with our relationship seemingly moving in the right direction, I suspected my lower anatomy wouldn't be getting any respite just yet. Not that I was complaining in the slightest; I'd learn to cope with being lightheaded if I meant having Allie around.

I'd been so nervous yesterday when I'd initiated the conversation with Allie that I'd resorted to acting like a complete dick, making stupid, teasing comments in an effort to hide my anxiety. Wincing, I recalled my flippant remark of "Am I keeping you on your toes?" and shook my head as I remembered the appalled expression on her pretty face. Where the hell that had come from I have no idea, but I was still surprised that Allie hadn't slapped me for it. I certainly deserved a good clip round the ear after the inexcusably casual way I'd treated her.

Christ, when I'd seen that article about Elena on Allie's laptop I'd thought I was going to vomit. All the feelings and guilt that I'd tried to bury over the years had come crashing back on top of me so suddenly that I was still amazed that I *hadn't* thrown up. I'd never confessed my past to a woman before. A few close friends knew the full sordid details, and my family had a fairly good idea of what had gone on with Elena that day, but I'd never told them about the waitress. But I'd never told a woman.

Amazingly, Allie had taken it all in her stride. OK, so she'd looked a little troubled when I'd told her about my wild years, but after that she had just been so supportive, and thankfully, had seemingly forgiven me for my callous treatment over the last few days. Just the simple act of sharing my burden with her seemed to have made my guilt feel lighter already. It was incredible. Rolling my neck to check for the usual tension I held there I smiled – it felt looser than I could ever recall.

I had no idea what I'd done to deserve her, but I was so bloody grateful that Allie had turned up to cover that shift.

Leaning down, I picked up the damp flannel that I had used on her last night and grinned. My gorgeous girl had looked so hesitant when I'd said I wanted to care for her, but her eventual trust in me had been incredibly endearing, and prompted me to feel like the king of the world for a few minutes while I tended to her. Her embarrassment about letting me wipe between her legs had made me smile, because clearly she'd had no issues with me being between her legs while we were having sex. Maybe I'd freaked her out a bit with the washing thing. Chewing on my lower lip I nodded my head. Yeah, that was probably it. It was, after all, not something I'd ever done with a partner before, but looking after Allie, taking care of her, and tending to her just seemed to be a natural instinct. Luckily for me, she had agreed in the end, because I had a feeling that those would be difficult urges for me to suppress.

The memory of being between her legs predictably solidified my cock again, and it was now tenting out the front of my tracksuit bottoms like a bloody homing missile. But God, Allie was just perfect. A groan left my throat as I closed my eyes, replaying every image I had of her stored in my mind. Soft skin and always so wet and ready for me. Not forgetting her breasts. Christ, they were perfection; pert, responsive handfuls that tasted so good I would happily feast on them every night for the rest of my life. There wasn't an inch of her I didn't adore. Even her long hair turned me on. Grinning at just how horny I was, I shook my head with a smile and adjusted my trousers to ease some of the tension. It wasn't a particularly successful tactic, but it would have to do for now. Besides, there was no way I was having a wank when I had Allie and her receptive little body waiting for me downstairs.

Standing up, I gave my crotch a brief rub to try and calm my throbbing hard-on and then wandered into the en-suite to chuck the washcloth into the sink before turning back and surveying my room again. It looked better now, neater and less like the seedy sex den it had resembled earlier. As I gazed around, it occurred to me that Allie was the only woman ever to step foot in this room. I'd never brought a woman up here. Thinking about it, I'd never entertained a woman at this house, either. All of my less salubrious encounters with the opposite sex had occurred in either a hotel or while on set somewhere around the world. This house in England was my retreat from the world. No-one came here except for my closest family and friends, and as such the only females to visit thus far were my mother and sister.

My pondering was ceased when I suddenly heard a peculiar noise seeping up from somewhere downstairs. Intrigued, I walked to the bedroom door and stuck my head out, tilting my head and straining my ears to listen. It was faint, but I could definitely hear Allie singing Christmas songs, and I grinned. Bing Crosby was flowing from her tongue. Or perhaps I should say "crucifying", because from the tuneless yodelling I could hear, Allie was butchering poor Bing's famous tune.

Grinning in amusement, I left my previous thoughts about my history in the bedroom and headed off to find the cause of my present happiness.

Chapter Twelve
Allie

Now showered, dressed, and every single nook and cranny of my body spotless – and I really do mean *every* nook – I was in the kitchen about to try and work out what I could cook for Christmas dinner. After all the sex Sean had showered upon me, we both needed something fairly substantial to replace the burnt calories, so I was hoping to find a joint of meat in the freezer.

Deciding to continue this morning's festive spirit, I turned on the radio in the kitchen and retuned it until I heard the familiar crooning tones of Bing Crosby singing 'White Christmas' on Radio One. Glancing towards the snow covered garden, I smiled contentedly. It was one of my favourite Christmas tracks, but this year it was also very appropriate.

Humming along with Bing, I set about scouring the fridge, freezer, and cupboards for possible menu options. There was no turkey, because apparently Sean hated it, and we were fast running out of fresh ingredients. I hated using frozen food. I rarely ever did at home, but here, after days of being snowed in, there was little choice. Digging in the huge chest freezer in the garage I had found a bag of roast potatoes and a beef joint, which I now had out and defrosting, some slightly bendy carrots in the fridge, a can of peas, and all the ingredients needed for Yorkshire puddings – so a roast beef dinner it would be. It wouldn't be the most fantastic Christmas dinner ever, but at least it would be slightly special, and given the circumstances, it was the best I could do.

Christmas sex with an incredible man, shower time adoration, and now cheesy Christmas songs on the radio. I sighed happily – this day couldn't get any better. As much as I had longed days ago for a family Christmas, now that things

139

had developed with Sean I was more than content to be spending the day with him. Besides, I could see my family next week when I got out of here.

I was midway through belting out my best accompaniment to Mariah Carey's 'All I Want For Christmas Is You', when I became aware of Sean entering the kitchen and grinning. Glancing across at his glorious beaming face, I felt myself flush bright red – he was no doubt laughing at my tuneless wailing – so I quickly snapped my mouth shut and gave him a rueful look in return.

Squirming with embarrassment under his intent gaze, I tried to supress my smile by pursing my lips just as he always did, but then brought myself up short. Gosh, had I picked that trait up from him? I certainly don't think it was something I'd ever really done before … Hmm. I needed to be careful – if I was copying his mannerisms already then I was definitely getting myself way in over my head.

'All you want for Christmas is me, eh?' he asked, strolling towards me with that cocksure stride and a twinkle in his eye. Yes, it was, but luckily I'd already had him, I thought with a smile, recalling my lovely Christmas wake up. Sean's cheeky tone and wink made it obvious that he was thinking the same thing and my smile broadened. I then felt an unwelcome twinge of sadness settle in my chest as I registered that I wouldn't have him for long. This thing between us was no doubt going to end when the snow melted, but I really shouldn't allow myself to dwell on that. This was my chance to be reckless for a change. I needed to grab it with both hands and push my gloominess aside.

Unaware of my sudden melancholy, Sean rested his hands on my hips and dipped down to place a quick kiss on my nose. 'Well, your wish is my command. I'm all yours, my gorgeous girl,' he murmured, before moving his lips to my mouth and taking his time to softly reacquaint me with his talented tongue.

He was mine. For today at least, I thought with a sad smile against his mouth.

Once I had shelved my gloomy thoughts, our Christmas Day proceeded fantastically; there might not have been any Christmas decorations or presents – although sex with Sean was practically a gift in itself – but we spent the morning listening to Christmas songs on the radio while snuggling up together in front of a roaring log fire which Sean had built, and lit. Perhaps that was where his mildly smoky, spicy scent came from. Whatever its source, I loved it.

At lunch time we ate the beef roast, and it was delicious if I do say so myself. Actually, considering my limited ingredients, it had turned out far better than expected; the meat was succulent and tender, the potatoes crispy and moreish, and after devouring four of my Yorkshire puddings Sean had pronounced them to be the best he'd ever eaten, which had pleased me no end.

Our afternoon then slipped into one of pure indulgence as we snuggled together on Sean's huge sofa for a post dinner snooze before we began to watch the *Die Hard* – selected because we'd missed all the good films on television, and it was the closest thing Sean had to a Christmas movie. Besides, once I'd mentioned in passing that I'd never seen that particular Bruce Willis film, he had stared at me in shock and then insisted we watch it so he could "educate me on Christmas classics". The cheeky bastard.

The television was on, the room was cosy from the fire, and we were relaxing together, which was ideal for a lazy day like this. Given how new this intimacy between us was, I felt surprisingly comfortable with him, and found myself able to push away my worries about what the future might hold for us and just absorb the current bliss.

Lifting his arm, Sean patted around on the sofa until he located the TV remote, then pressed pause, and placed a kiss on my temple. 'Let's talk,' he suggested.

Nodding my agreement, I snuggled closer to his chest and waited for him to start the conversation, only to find him lying below me quietly. That was fine by me; there was plenty I wanted to talk about.

'So what's your next film project?'

Below me, I felt Sean's chest rise and fall sharply as he let out a sigh, almost as if he was disappointed that I was choosing to talk about work. After a short pause he shifted me slightly in his arms and replied, 'I was supposed to be flying out to Canada tomorrow night for a week's film shoot. It's an advert for a series I filmed last year, but judging by this weather, I won't be going anywhere.' The idea that he had to leave tomorrow struck me in the chest way harder than it should have done, and I instantly felt myself tense in his arms. It was nearly over. My scintillating snow-bound fling with Sean would be coming to an end incredibly soon.

'Then after that I have a few weeks' break before I'm heading to LA to shoot the next season of *LA Blue*. They've just extended our contracts for at least another two seasons, so I'll be back and forth quite a bit.' Pushing aside the sudden sadness that had settled on my mind, I nodded. Ah, yes, *LA Blue*. I'd read an article about it just last month when I was in the hairdresser's – it was a police drama that was hitting the big time. Critics were describing it as "one of the best dramas to ever grace the small screen", but I hadn't yet gotten around to watching it, and now after this fling with Sean, I might try and avoid it.

In fact, once I'd gone back to my real life I think I'd be trying to avoid *anything* that might remind me of him and make me realise what I'd had so briefly as mine. Roast beef dinners would definitely be off the menu for a while, as would *Die Hard* films, sponges in the shower … ugh, the list just went on and on.

It was stupid, really, because we'd met less than a week ago, but the feelings Sean had stirred within me were so potent that I already knew I was going to miss him terribly.

'So, enough about me. I want to know more about you,' he said, breaking the silence as he rolled me further onto his chest so that he could access my long waves of hair. Adjusting my loose ponytail onto my spine he slipped the hair tie off and began to rhythmically smooth his hands down the strands.

The repetitive sliding motion was almost lulling me off to sleep, and I had to force my brain to engage and remember his question. 'Oh, OK. There's not much to tell. I'm quite boring, but fire away. What do you want to know?' I asked, causing Sean to snort out a laugh at my comment.

'You are far from boring, Allie,' he corrected me, his strict tone making me laugh. I *was* boring when compared to him though – he was flying off to LA to shoot a TV series, and what would I be doing? Oh yes, going back to school to teach another term with my year threes. Hardly comparable lifestyles – although I didn't bother to say it out loud again.

'Start with your name. Is it short for something?' His hand was still stroking down the length of my hair, something he really seemed quite fascinated with, so with a contented sigh I let my eyes flicker shut as I relaxed against him, completely at ease. My nose wrinkled as I considered his question.

'Yeah, my name is Alexis, but I hate it, so I've always shorted it to Allie.'

'Alexis? That's quite a unique name, but I don't see why you hate it; it's pretty,' he mumbled against my temple, but I huffed, remembering how all the kids at school had called me "posh" for years, and then of course there were the boys, who upon discovering that Alexis could also be a male name had spent endless hours taking the piss out of me.

'It is, but I prefer Allie. My dad is a bit of a history buff, I'm named after some Greek poet.'

'It's more exciting that my name. I can't even shorten it,' he murmured before falling quiet again.

We had laid in companionable silence for the last few hours as we'd snoozed and watched the television, but below me, I suddenly felt a change. Sean became noticeably tenser, and I could feel his jaw working against the top of my head as if he was chewing nervously on his lip. Pushing myself upright I looked at him and found him doing exactly that – his lip was being chewed frantically between his teeth as his concerned, frowning face looked up at me warily.

At the sight of his unease, I felt my own eyebrows pull together nervously. 'What's up?'

His blue eyes narrowed for a second before Sean guided me into a sitting position and pulled himself up to join me, his shoulders still bunched and his jaw continuing to work endless. 'How old are you?'

Oh, was that it? I'd been expecting some horrible statement or strange confession or another heart wrenching tale perhaps, but all he wanted was my age. 'Twenty-six. Twenty-seven in July.'

Nodding his head, I saw him briefly flinch and draw in a long breath. 'I'd guessed as much, but I was secretly hoping you might be a bit older.' My eyebrows went from furrowed to rising significantly. Was I too young for him to have a casual fling with? Or did he just prefer his women more mature?

'Well, I'm sorry to disappoint you,' I muttered petulantly, folding my arms and well aware that I sounded just as immature as he had made me feel.

Running a hand though his hair, Sean shook his head. 'I didn't mean it like that, Allie. Christ, what man wouldn't want you? You're a beautiful, intelligent, funny, twenty-six year old. And gorgeous to boot. I just meant that I'd hoped you might be slightly closer to my age so you weren't concerned by the age gap.'

Oh. Age gap? I knew he was older than me, I suspected late thirties, but it didn't bother me in the slightest – I'd always had a thing for older men. There was just something about their calm maturity and experience which I found a huge turn on. And physically speaking, Sean was in better shape than any man I'd ever dated, and probably would ever date, so I didn't understand why he was worried. Especially seeing as this thing between us didn't ever really stand a chance of progressing beyond his house. As soon as the snow had melted I'd be going back to school and he would be going back to his star-studded life of glamour and movies. I couldn't see why he was getting so worked up about it.

'It doesn't bother me,' I said simply, telling the compete truth, but he looked decidedly sceptical.

'I am significantly older than you, Allie. It matters,' he whispered, leaning in to trace his thumb down my jawline. The intensity of our connection once again had me breathless, and as I tried to draw in some air I found myself desperately wishing that he really did want something more long-term between us.

'Not to me, it doesn't.'

Sighing heavily, he smiled at me thinly while shaking his head. 'You are so fucking sweet.' Another sigh had his shoulders rising and falling harshly before he pinned me with an intense gaze. 'How old do you think I am?'

Ah, he was deflecting it, was he? I was fairly sure thirty-eight was the correct answer, but not definite in that knowledge. I hadn't specifically Googled his age in my searches because it really hadn't bothered me enough to do so, but he'd said he was eighteen at the time of Elena's death, and I think the article on the accident had been dated from 1994, which would make him thirty-eight if my maths was correct. Which it frequently wasn't. Or was the article dated 1998? Shit. I couldn't remember. Bugger. I didn't want to make a faux pas and increase his paranoia if I said he was older than he was, so I erred on the side of caution. 'Thirty-four?' I guessed.

Watching his reaction carefully, I saw immediately that underestimation was the wrong thing to do, because his face now looked even more stressed as he winced and shifted himself across the sofa away from me and crossed his arms. 'Thirty-eight?' I asked, hoping for the life of me that I wasn't wrong again.

Flashing me a wary glance Sean nodded slowly, scrutinising my reaction the entire time. A twelve year gap. It was hardly the end of the world. This reaction in him was all very bizarre, and my mind kept returning to the faint possibility that might want more from me than just a casual fling. Could it be possible? It would certainly explain his behaviour, but it just seemed so unlikely that I pushed it away before my fantastical imagination could go into overdrive. Again.

Rolling my eyes at not only my stupid thoughts but his defensive posture and withdrawn expression, I decided to try and lighten the mood. This thing between us might only last until the thaw, but we may as well enjoy it while we could.

Crawling across the gap he had created between us, I straddled him, bringing my hands up to rest on his shoulders so we were eye to eye. 'Sean, I. Don't. Care.' I emphasised each word slowly and clearly. I wanted to say that we were perfect for each other, and that his age didn't matter because the way he made me feel was so incredible. But I didn't. It was way too soon to be throwing those types of thoughts on the table.

'Christmas is my favourite time of the year and you're starting to spoil it with your tantrum. Can we go back to our film and snuggle like we were before?' Blinking at me several times, Sean cocked his head and examined me quizzically, before finally seeming to believe me as he smiled tentatively, his posture relaxing and eyes beginning to twinkle again. Phew. Disaster averted.

'Your wish is my command, gorgeous girl.' Then, wrapping his arms around my waist he manoeuvred us so we were laid out full length on the sofa and pressed play on the remote again so that Bruce Willis could get back into action saving Christmas Day.

The film had ended a while ago, the credits long since finished, leaving the TV screen blank and the room quiet. Below me, Sean snored softly, so I decided to leave him to catch up on his sleep and go to burn off my Christmas dinner.

Now that I no longer had to hide away in his house I was quite looking forward to using the home gym, and jogged up to my room energetically to see if I had any suitable clothing for a work out. Narrowing my eyes, I looked at my pitifully pathetic options – I had trainers at least, because I'd been wearing them the day I arrived, but as far as suitable gym wear went, that was about it.

Dressing in the only outfit really available to me, I stood and appraised myself in the long mirror in my bedroom. The sight had me doubling over in near hysterical laughter until I was wiping away tears with the back of my hand – I was wearing trainers and socks, nothing on my legs, and one of Sean's gigantic T-shirts; that was all.

In short, I looked ridiculous.

In addition to the gargantuan T-shirt, I was also wearing my normal bra, which wasn't ideal but was relatively supportive and so would have to do. As long as I avoided anything overly bouncy like star jumps, I'd be fine. I could always wash it afterwards and dry it off on the radiator. Besides, I was sure my new, happy Sean wouldn't be complaining if I went braless for a few hours, I thought with a smirk.

Fingering the gigantic T-shirt I realised it was probably quite dangerous to attempt a run in a garment that was so oversized, so I pulled the belt from my jeans and tied it around the middle before pursing my lips and glancing in the mirror again. OK, so now I looked even stupider, but at least I wouldn't catch my arms and end up falling over.

Pushing aside my concerns about my appearance I made my way to the gym. Looking around properly for the first time I saw it was small, but perfectly formed, containing just a treadmill, rowing machine, weights bench, stack of towels, and an iPod dock, complete with metallic blue iPod. Picking it up I scrolled through Sean's music as I stretched for a few minutes to warm up, and found it positively stuffed with choice – he had everything from classical to rock, pop, and right through to some seriously heavy metal on here.

Opting for something I often ran to at home I selected one of my current favourites from Imagine Dragons, set it playing, and stepped onto the treadmill.

Considering I'd had several days off my usually strict regime, I was pleasantly surprised by how well I was managing. The display on my treadmill now read thirty-two minutes, and although I was sweating, I was running pretty fast and still relatively in control of my breathing, so all in all, this wasn't a bad effort at all. Mind you, with all of the super sexing Sean had been throwing my way in the last few days, he'd probably been a major contributor to helping maintain my fitness levels.

This thought had me grinning broadly as I ran, but the next second the door to the gym surged open so suddenly that it bounced off the wall with a thunderous crash, causing me to yelp in shock and stumble. Bloody hell! I'd nearly fallen off the sodding treadmill. Stabilising my wobbly legs I managed to continue my run, but watched in the mirror and saw Sean burst in, his eyes frantically flickering all over the place before they settled on me and softened in apparent relief.

'There you are,' he exhaled, long and low, and bent forwards onto his knees briefly as if recovering from some horrific shock. But to be honest, *I* was the one recovering from a horrific shock – the banging of the door had nearly made me pee myself in terror, and I was completely amazed that I was still managing to run. What the heck was wrong with him?

Standing up again, he appeared to make a visible effort to regain control of himself, as he loosened off his shoulders with a roll and came to the side of my treadmill where I could look at the beauty of the real Sean, and not the reflection in the mirror. Staring at me for a few seconds he blinked, and then sighed. 'I woke up and you were gone.'

Right. OK. That was pretty weird. Seeing as we were still snowed in I couldn't see exactly what he was panicked about, but clearly from the strained expression on his face he was, so I tried to think of a suitable reply.

'Usually on Christmas Day we go for a long walk in the afternoon,' I began, slipping my words in between my quickened breathing. 'But seeing how thick the snow was, I thought I'd go for a run. You were sleeping, so I didn't want to disturb you.'

Nodding slowly, Sean digested my words, then glanced at the read-out on my machine and startled me by reaching over and pressing the red stop button. Before the roller had even come to a standstill he was scooping my shrieking body up into his arms so my legs were wrapped around his waist with his hands under my bum to support my weight. 'Run's over. I need to be inside you.'

What? He sounded almost agitated, but the passion with which he seemed to crave me had me instantly melting into his arms and looping my hands behind his neck. Stuff the treadmill, sex with Sean would be much more fun.

Striding from the room he began to trot up the few stairs towards the bedrooms, all the while supporting my body as if I weighed nothing. 'I can walk, you know,' I informed him on a quiet giggle, relaxing my head onto his shoulder and giving in to his caveman demonstration.

'I know you can. But I want to do it,' he replied, using the same phrase as he had when I'd told him I was perfectly capable of washing my privates after sex. So this carrying must be another of his ways to take care of me then, and a further example of his regret for treating me so badly.

I was actually becoming rather fond of Sean's slightly controlling, caring ways. It was definitely something I was going to miss terribly when all of this came to an end.

My wayward, sad thoughts were stopped when Sean made it to his bedroom and approached the bed, making me tense and squeak in his arms. 'At least let me grab a quick shower first,' I yelped, mortified that he would be peeling off my clothes any minute now and discover the sweat-laden body beneath. I'd run for over half an hour – there was definite rinsing required.

'Fussy woman,' Sean tutted irritably, but did eventually divert his path by taking us into the en-suite and, to my surprise, walked us both straight into the shower area before finally placing me down on my own two feet.

'Is this the newest statement in running gear?' he asked in amusement as he stepped back and checked out my outfit. Giggling, I looked down at myself and burst out into a full belly laugh. 'No, but it was the best I could do under the circumstances.'

'You should approach Nike, I'm sure they'd like this design,' he added on a smirk, before nodding and beginning to undo my belt, humming to himself as he did so, apparently simply happy to have me here. 'Once again, may I say just how fucking sexy you look in my shirt,' he murmured as he tossed my belt aside and dropped to his knees to remove my knickers, trainers, and socks. Clearly I wasn't going to be allowed to shower on my own then. But that was fine; as long as I could rinse away the sweat before he started anything naughty, I'd feel fine about it all.

'Arms up, gorgeous girl,' he whispered, dropping a hot, open mouthed kiss on my temple. Obeying him immediately, I raised my arms as he peeled the T-shirt up my body until my head popped free, but instead of removing it fully from my arms, he chuckled a low, dark laugh and reached up to loop the head hole over the protruding shower head.

What the hell? I was now stood damp with sweat, dressed in only my bra, with my arms tangled in the T-shirt and stretched above my head. Tugging them, I found I was well and truly trapped, an outcome that had Sean standing back and looking mighty pleased with himself.

'Be still, my gorgeous girl, or I'll make you explain the broken shower to my plumber if you pull it from the wall,' he whispered. To my surprise, he looked and sounded completely serious, so his threat stopped me instantly, and I stilled and looked at his mischievous face. I couldn't believe him. Well, I sort of could. I mean, it was Sean, and he'd proven himself to be a bit kinky already, but still, tying me to the shower?

Collecting all of my clothes, Sean stepped out of the large shower cubicle, placed them on a chair, and swiftly undressed himself. As he pulled off his jeans I saw he was predictably hard, the image of me trussed up in his shower apparently rather a turn on.

'I've changed my mind about being inside of you. I think I want a taste of your body instead ...' he murmured as he stepped back towards me and flicked a glance down towards my groin.

Oh God. He couldn't seriously want to go down there after I'd run for thirty minutes and not showered! We barely knew each other! I really wasn't at that level of intimacy yet. I wasn't sure I would ever be at *that* level of intimacy. 'But I'm all sweaty! I need to wash!' I whined desperately, pinning my legs together as firmly as I could.

Sliding a hand though my hair, Sean gripped softly and slammed his lips down onto mine in a brutal kiss, his tongue instantly sending me to orbit with its skilled twists and turns as his other hand lowered to my bra. He didn't even bother to undo it, just yanked both cups down until my breasts popped free, my nipples already hard and seeking his touch.

God, his wild behaviour was such a turn on that I could feel my core start to convulse. 'I'm aware of that, and, quite frankly ...' he whispered against my lips, before leaning down and licking one sweaty nipple with a full, flat tongued swipe, '... I don't give a fuck.' Shifting to my other breast he repeated the same move, before groaning in pleasure and running a swipe up the valley at the centre of my breasts. 'You taste fucking fantastic.'

Well, when he put it like that, who needs a shower? The way he spoke and practically worshipped me with his hands and mouth, allowed my self-consciousness to fully slip away and be replaced by an almost frantic coiling at my core, my channel clenching and desperate to be filled.

I didn't care about the sweat anymore. What sweat? All I wanted was him, desperately.

Dropping to his knees, Sean gripped my thighs and spread them so wide that I nearly lost my footing on the slippery tiles. Then he bent my left leg and looped it over his shoulder before lunging forwards and immediately pulling my clit into his mouth. A distorted cry left my lips and I jerked so hard from the surprise that my back hit the shower control behind me and caused the jets to spring to life above us. Yelping in shock at the cool water pouring over me, I quickly calmed again as Sean glanced up and grinned, his hair now plastered to his face from the spray and his eyes twinkling happily.

'I'm that good, huh?' he asked in amusement, before getting back to his task and exploring me with his tongue. Arrogant bugger. But I couldn't really say anything, because he really *was* that good.

The water began to warm up and my head rolled back under the spray as his mouth continued to lick, suck, and nibble on my quivering flesh, his tongue disappearing inside me on several occasions and making me jerk in surprise every time. 'Are you sore from all our activities?' he asked softly, his tongue still lashing at my clitoris while two of his fingers began to gently explore.

'A little,' I admitted, but not sore enough that I couldn't go again.

'We'll just stick to two or three fingers then,' he conceded, pressing one long digit right up inside me as he spoke, curling it so it immediately zeroed in on my g-spot. It was heavenly and my eyes fluttered shut only to snap open again as my mind went back to his words … *we'll just stick to two or three fingers* … how many would he have used if I'd said I wasn't sore? Four? His entire hand? There was no way I would fit that in, his hands were like spades. Thank goodness I'd told the truth.

I felt his second finger enter me and he began circling the two digits in a delicious rhythm that he accompanied with licks and flicks of his tongue. Soon I was levering myself on my one standing leg so I could increase the speed and pressure of his thrusts against me. I was close. *Really* close. It wouldn't take too much more to send me over the edge.

'Can you take another?' he asked gruffly from between my legs. He wanted to put another finger in. He'd managed three once before, but it had been a bit of a tight squeeze.

I swallowed hard. To be honest, I had no idea if I could take another. I was hugely turned on, and the two thick fingers already inside me were certainly moving with enough ease. 'Um, I have no idea,' I replied honestly. 'You can try if you'd like.'

'Oh, I would very much like to,' he muttered thickly before beginning to press with a third finger. It took him a bit of manoeuvring and pushing, but then I heard Sean give a hiss of appreciation and I suddenly felt my body give as his fingers slid inside. My eyes rolled shut at the sensation of fullness and I let out a low, lusty moan. I was full, but not sore, so that was just fine by me.

'Christ, Allie, you look amazing like this. God, you're close too, I can feel every spasm of your muscles.' His voice was the grittiest I'd ever heard it, but he was right, I was close. I was so turned on I was ready to light up like a Christmas tree. All I needed was just a touch on my clitoris and I'd be a goner. As if reading my mind, Sean's mouth lowered towards me again, and as his three fingers continued their smooth, knowing thrusts in and out of my body, his tongue laved across my clit in a stoke so firm and perfect that I exploded instantly, my body jerking wildly and clenching at the intruding fingers as if trying to suck them into me forever. My orgasm seemed to go on and on, as Sean sucked on my swollen clit and worked me down in ever slower strokes until I was sagging forwards and desperate for support.

Holy shit. Talk about intense.

Ever so slowly, he pulled his fingers from within me, my body immediately feeling the loss of him as he lifted his hand to his mouth and made a show of licking them clean, digit by digit, his eyes never leaving mine. I watched in fascination, but nearly laughed at his unnecessary actions; we were in a shower after all – he could easily have rinsed them off under the water.

'Mmm. Tasty.' He pushed himself to stand with a wicked glint in his eye and finally set about removing my hands from above my head. The T-shirt fell to the shower floor with a wet splat and then as my arms dropped, Sean began rubbing some life back into them.

Wedging himself forwards, he pressed me against the wall again, his hips and erection pressing into my belly to support my weight as he continued to stroke my arms. 'Don't ever be embarrassed in front of me again. You hear me? I like you however you come; sweaty, dirty, or freshly showered, I don't care. You need to understand that.'

Oh. OK. I swallowed as if I had just been chastised by a teacher, and obediently nodded my head.

'Can you stand on your own now?' he asked, which sounded like a stupid question, but was actually incredibly valid because just seconds ago I had been in a near state of post-orgasmic collapse.

'I can,' I confirmed with a small, shy smile, which he returned before reaching for a bottle of shower gel.

'Let's get you cleaned up,' he murmured, before he began humming happily to himself as he dispensed some gel into his hand and began gently soaping me up. I had been about to inform him, yet again, that I was more than capable of looking after myself, but upon seeing the completely relaxed, happy, and content smile on Sean's face, I didn't. If taking care of me made him look that peaceful, then who was I to intervene?

As well as washing my body, I was once again treated to a full shampoo and rinse, the conditioner once again coming into play as my hair rejoiced in just how well it was being treated today. I really felt well and truly worshipped.

Coming to stand before me again, Sean smiled down me. 'All done.' He placed a soft kiss on my forehead as I tried to get hold of the shower gel to return the favour, but a thought occurred to me.

'Why didn't you take me?' I asked curiously. In the gym he'd said he needed to be inside me, which I'd assumed meant his cock. The monster hard-on he'd had throughout our shower was still squashed up between us now, so clearly he was keen.

'I was going to, but I was worried you'd be sore, and I know that I can get a little carried away so I thought it safest to stick to my mouth and hands. Besides, I love exploring you. I can't get enough of you, Allie.' There he went again, saying things that made my heart soar but my brain worried. I needed to be very, *very* sensible where it came to Sean, and not allow myself to get too carried away with the things he said. He was a passionate man, and clearly had no issues expressing himself where it came to sex, but that was a long way from wanting to commit to me outside of the bedroom, and I'd do well to remember that.

Distracting myself from dwelling on the negatives, I instead reached down between us and slid my hand around his throbbing erection, eliciting a hiss of pleasure from Sean as his eyes instantly dilated with desire. My quest for the shower gel was now forgotten as I set my mind on an altogether different task. Closing my fingers a little tighter, I felt his cock jerk in my palm as Sean let out a groan and flopped his head onto my shoulder.

'Easy girl, I'm really close. Making you come has got me incredibly turned on.' Yes, I could feel that. He was hard as steel in my hands, and twitching and jerking so frantically it was almost jumping in time to the pounding heartbeat I could feel in his chest.

Applying just the slightest pressure on his shoulder with my free hand, I managed to create enough space between our bodies to allow me to slither down the wall until I was crouched at his feet.

Looking up, I saw Sean eyeing me, his wet hair falling over his brow as his interest quickly turned to a look of lusty desire, leaving his lips parted in anticipation. Palming his cock in a better grip I saw a drip of excitement already on the tip and immediately leant forward to lick it away, cupping his sack with my other hand. He let out an almost pained growl and sank one hand into my hair, gripping at the soaking strands in desperation. He hadn't been kidding when he'd said he was close; his balls were already drawn up tight to his body and I could feel the tension buzzing in the muscles of his thighs and stomach.

Gazing up at him, I licked my lips provocatively. 'Don't pull out, not until you're completely finished. Understand?' Whoa! Where did that come from? I was usually so tame. But as crazy as it was, I wanted to taste him, just as he had tasted me. Trying to back up my challenge with a cool, calm look I met Sean's gaze and saw his eyes nearly bulging from his head in shock.

'Christ, you're going to make me come just by talking if you keep saying things like that,' he gurgled, his voice thick and strained. Smiling shyly, I felt satisfaction bloom within me. Sean was usually the one to shock me with his sexual prowess, so it was nice for me to be the one in charge for a change. Maybe I was discovering a new side to myself. Allie Shaw: sex goddess.

Gripping the base of him, I opened my mouth wide and immediately took as much of his length as I could, sliding him

155

across my tongue until he hit the back of my throat. Well, he was super aroused, so there was no point going for a long build-up – he was way beyond that.

'Holy fuck!' he barked, his free hand slamming onto the bathroom wall as he leant over me and began helping me with my rhythm by thrusting into my mouth. The fingers in my hair began to grip tighter, and I knew from his frantic movements that he really was about to go, so I sucked as hard as I could, gripping him tightly with my fist, and put in a final effort to send him over the edge.

With another curse, Sean suddenly pushed my head forwards at the same time as thrusting so I ended up taking him even deeper than before, and just as I thought I might gag on his size, I felt him jerk against my tongue as he began to come in hot, thick bursts into my throat, with a roar loud enough to shake the bathroom mirror leaving his chest.

After several gentler, jerky thrusts he then leant back far enough to slip his length from my mouth and immediately bent to scoop me from the shower floor.

'Fucking, fuck, Allie, Jesus,' he breathed hotly into the hair by my ear. 'I'm sorry, I got carried away. Did I go too deep?'

'Shaking my head, I smiled reassuringly and licked my lips. 'No. And just for the record, you taste delicious as well,' I added cheekily.

Sean's eyes widened before he shook his head in apparent wonder. 'You are incredible, woman.' Carrying me from the bathroom he laid me on the bed and leant to kiss me gently on the mouth before nuzzling his face into my hair. He was murmuring under his breath, words mostly incomprehensible but occasionally sounding like 'I'm never letting you go.' Then suddenly he was gone, heading back to the bathroom, before returning with two large towels.

Had he really said that? If he had, then I'm not sure I was supposed to hear it. And surely he couldn't have mean it, anyway? Laying there while he dried me off, I obediently allowed him his way, even parting my legs when he tapped on my inner thighs to prompt me to splay them for him. My complicity earned me a huge grin, and I noticed that as a reward he was extra gentle as he padded away the moisture from the over-sensitised flesh.

Once again, he insisted on drying my bum for me, even adding a weird little tickle, which made me yelp and slap at his hand and instantly caused him to smirk. Dirty bugger. I still found the whole washing and drying thing a bit weird, but when it made him this happy it seemed easier to just give in and let him have his way. Besides, underneath all of my independent thoughts, I actually rather liked it when he cared for me like this. I probably liked it all a bit too much really, but I'd deal with the aftermath of my feelings later.

Chapter Thirteen
Allie

Boxing Day morning came and I woke up in Sean's bed. Letting out a huge yawn, I stretched, immediately realising that my ability to move my limbs meant I wasn't welded against his body like usual. Rolling over I saw the bed was, in fact, empty, as was the room itself, leaving me alone. Sean had been so insistent that I always be there when he woke up that I'd assumed the deal went both ways, but apparently not. His sudden absence left me feeling a little vulnerable as my overactive mind went into overdrive – was he simply in the gym for his morning run, or had he had his fill of me and decided that it was time to make a break between us?

Chewing on my lower lip, I felt his side of the mattress and found the sheets completely cold, which further fuelled my nerves. Pushing myself upright I decided to check the time, because I knew he always did a run around ten, which could explain his absence. There was no clock that I could see, so I flopped over onto my stomach and reached for my mobile which was on the bedside table.

Ten thirty? God, I never slept in that late. I suppose the almost non-stop sex with Sean must have worn me out more than I first thought. At least the late hour explained his absence from the bed – he'd no doubt got up after becoming bored of waiting for my lazy arse to wake up.

Sliding from the sheets, I pulled back the curtain to bring some light into the room and saw that the morning had broken bright and clear. The sky was blue and I smiled at the beautiful day, before realising that as well as the covering of white that I had become used to, I could once again see the cherry red of my car's roof, patches of brown gravel, and the vivid green of a holly bush beside the driveway.

Blinking several times as I surveyed the front garden, I noticed that rivulets and drops of water were running off trees and bushes. As obvious as it was, it took me a second to comprehend the sight, but once I did, it settled in my stomach like a lead balloon – the snow was melting.

I was free to go home.

So that was it. Last night had been the last I would spend in bed with Sean. Leaning forwards, I gripped the edge of the dresser to support my weakening legs and drew in several long deep breaths in an attempt to calm myself. No more Sean. The thought almost made me frantic with panic, but what else could I do? Now the weather was clearing he would no doubt be leaving for his film shoot today as originally planned, and I would have to drive away and start the process of mending my breaking heart.

Looking again at the clearing driveway I shook my head. There was no longer any cause or reason for me to stay here, not any realistic reason anyway – a bout of lust for the sexy as sin house owner and some far-fetched dreams of a fairy tale outcome didn't count.

When I'd initially gotten trapped here all I'd thought about night and day for those first forty-eight hours had been leaving, but the relief I'd have felt then at being free didn't emerge at all now. In fact, if anything, I felt quite sick at the thought of leaving Sean.

Sighing heavily, I unclenched my fingers from the edge of the dresser, took three steps backwards, and sank onto the side of the bed. Closing my eyes, I tried my best to be realistic about this – all in all, it had been a pretty incredible few days with Sean. I'd got to spend time with a real life film star, had one of my best ever Christmases, and to top it all off I'd had some amazing, out-of-this-world sex. I needed to roll all of that up into my memory and appreciate what we'd had for what it was; a quick, enjoyable fling.

Blushing, I licked my lips and grinned. If I was being truthful I needed to rephrase that last thought; we'd had a quick, amazing, mind-blowing, best-orgasms-ever fling. My giggles faded with a small sigh. Unfortunately, it didn't help much that Sean was obviously one of those people who got carried away in the moment and professed all sorts of things he didn't really mean, which had been nice to hear at the time, but made leaving now even more of a bitter pill to swallow.

Regardless of all the seemingly possessive statements he'd made to me over the last few days, there was no way in the world that someone like Sean – a Hollywood heartthrob – would be interested in more than a quick fling with someone like me, a normal, everyday school teacher. He'd even said as much himself when he'd described how he indulged in short flings every now and then whenever he felt horny.

Rubbing my hands over my face I contemplated what I should do next. My wistful imagination reminded me that I didn't have to be in school until next week, so technically I could stay with him for a few more days if he wanted me to … but then I shook my head. He would be leaving for work today, even if I didn't have to. Now the snow was clearing, his flight would no doubt be back on track. I could stay for today, but would I end up being in the way? Surely he'd have packing to do, and various other things to sort out. Chewing on a fingernail I glumly decided that I should leave this morning.

Right now.

The more I thought about it, the more the idea of leaving Sean made me want to curl up in a ball, pull the duvet over my head, and cry. Despite my attempts not to, I'd gone against all my brain's sensible advice and fallen for him hook, line, and sinker. What an idiot. The searing pain in my chest told me that the feelings I had developed went way beyond lust, but at the moment, when I had to get away with my composure still intact, I couldn't even begin to process what exactly it was I felt for him. I had a fairly good idea, but the 'L' word wasn't one I could even dare to think about. Besides, was it possible to feel *that* emotion after just a week with someone?

Wincing, I realised that this could all be about to get *really* awkward, *really* quickly. Continuing the assault on my fingernail I immediately rolled my eyes and dropped my hand back to my lap – that was Cait's nervous habit and I always used to moan at her for it. Satisfying myself with a long, deep breath, I tried to predict what would happen if I told Sean I was leaving – he would no doubt be all kind and nice about my departure, telling me he'd had a great time, and maybe even trying to console me by swapping phone numbers or suggesting we stay friends.

I, on the other hand, would probably fall to pieces.

Groaning, I leant forward on my knees, trying to calm the sickly feeling swirling in my stomach. I decided that it was cowardly, but the easiest option would be to pack up and sneak out. Could I get away with it? I suppose it would depend where Sean was, but he seemed to start most days with a two-hour training session in the gym, so if I was lucky I could get away before he was finished.

Packing up the minimal amount of possessions I had, I then folded the clothes that Sean had loaned me and after debating it for at least ten minutes, caved and wrote him a quick note thanking him for his hospitality and the amazing time we had spent together. I resisted the temptation to leave any contact details – it would be easier if we made a clean break. And besides, if I left my phone number I'd spend the next few months on tenterhooks waiting for a call that would likely never come.

As quietly as I could, I made my way through the house and was amazed when I actually made it to the front door unnoticed. Propping the note on the counter beside the door I placed my hand on the lock to open it and eased it back surprisingly quietly. Unfortunately, my hopes of escaping an awkward goodbye (where I would no doubt get far more emotional than Sean) went up in flames when I heard a sudden loud crash and rushing footsteps.

'Allie? Wait! You're leaving?' Sean called urgently, as he burst from the kitchen doorway and jogged across the large expanse of lounge towards me. I was instantly hit with a bucket load of guilt as I saw the disturbed look on his beautiful face, as he pursed his lips in that quirky habit I'd quickly gotten used to.

Clearly my stealth skills weren't as good as I'd hoped. Or perhaps I'd secretly been hoping he'd catch me. Who knew? I was in such a state that I was barely maintaining my breathing, let alone deciphering the mass of confusion in my brain.

Shuffling awkwardly on my feet I smiled weakly at him, feeling my chest tighten in a way that told me that I'd definitely fallen harder for this guy than I should have allowed. 'Yeah … I … uh, well you'll be flying off to your film shoot tonight and I need to get back …' Bugger, my voice sounded as lame as my excuse.

Stepping closer to me, well within my personal space as he always did, Sean looked down at me with an unreadable expression on his face, his blue eyes clouding over as he frowned. 'I can't believe you were going to leave without telling me,' he murmured, my stomach dropping as I realised that the expression on his face was a mixture of hurt, confusion, and disappointment.

His reaction confused me; I'd genuinely believed he'd want to get back to his normal life now our snow-enforced tryst had come to an end, but his upset made me feel so ridiculously guilty that I only just held myself back from throwing my limp body into his arms in apology.

Stifling a groan, I thought about just how good having his arms around me would feel. Too good, I thought miserably, and that wouldn't help either of us in the long run.

'I didn't want to … I just thought … it might make things easier if I slipped out.' I hated my own words, but it was the only way. If I allowed myself to hope that more could come of this I knew I'd only get hurt in the long run. Better to try and stay strong now. But now that he was here, smelling all smoky and spicy and delicious, it was so much more difficult than I thought it would be.

Inclining his head to one side, Sean still looked a little put out and now I felt really awful – not to mention awkward. He was staring at me as if trying to see through my skull and read my mind, and the intensity made me cringe. This was the very reason I'd wanted to sneak away, to avoid a scene like this.

'Plus, a plough went up the road about half an hour ago and your lovely neighbour seems to be clearing your driveway for you,' I said weakly, with an attempt at an amused expression, trying to lighten the mood as I indicated with my thumb to the guy outside shovelling snow like his life depended on it.

Momentarily distracted from my departure, Sean's eyebrows popped up. 'Really?' His tone lifted as he leaned around the curtains to watch as the heavy-coated man continued shovelling fiercely at the layers of snow in front of the garage. Finally a small smile curved his lips,

'Ahh, that's Sam. He's my gardener in the summer but I pay him all year round so he randomly turns up and does jobs for me throughout the year.'

Turning back to me Sean sobered his face and began to fidget on the spot. 'Look … before you go, I need to get your number.'

I sighed heavily and allowed a sad smile to slip to my lips. Just as I had predicted. Sean was doing the honourable thing and trying to make me feel better about leaving. *This* had been my main reason for wanting to leave undetected.

'Sean, we've had fun, especially since you stopped acting like a bear with a sore head, but you don't have to try and make me feel good by pretending it was more than that.' I was a realist, and as much as I'd like it to be the case, I knew that a film star dating a schoolteacher wasn't ever a likely combination.

Instead of replying, Sean stared at me in surprise, his eyes widening and then narrowing as he practically scowled at me. 'Fun?' he asked in a low, choked growl.

What did he want me to say? That he was the best I'd ever had? That I was going to miss him so much that I felt like I was dying inside? That I might very well have fallen in love with him? Or was he just looking for an ego boost? Was "fun" not a good enough adjective for him? He was acting so strangely that I had no idea. Then again, I barely knew him, so how could I ever properly judge what he was thinking?

'A lot of fun …' I added weakly.

His scowl deepened, as did the intensity of his eyes, and after briefly rolling his head forward for a few seconds, he raised it to reveal a clearer expression.

'Stay for the day with me?' he asked hopefully, but I immediately found myself shaking my head. 'I can't Sean ...' This was already the hardest thing I'd ever had to do, staying for another hour or so – and no doubt experiencing another display of his fantastic sexual skills – would only make it more difficult.

There was a long pause where he simply stared at me thoughtfully, blinking rapidly as he chewed his lips between his teeth so hard that they turned white. 'Fine. You're right, you should leave,' he finally conceded with a shrug.

I felt my stomach drop at his confirmation as Sean tilted his head, cleared all traces of his scowl, and shoved his hands into his pockets. Talk about awkward. It was definitely time to leave. As I turned away, he suddenly caught my elbow in a firm grip and suddenly spun me around to pin me against the wall, his body caging me on all sides.

Whoa. He'd flipped me so fast I'd barely registered it, but now I was suspended between his hot, hard body and the wall with my arms pinned firmly by my sides and his breath fanning across my lips. He smelt like mint, and I suspected he'd recently brushed his teeth. 'I'm still going to need that number,' he murmured, before his lips smashed down onto mine so fiercely that I let out a small sigh of shock.

His tongue used my sigh as an opportunity to dive into my mouth, tangling with mine in a kiss so frantic that I was quickly writhing below his touch as I did my best to keep up with him. This had to be his idea of a goodbye kiss, because he was injecting so much passion into it that I could barely function after just a few moments of his attention.

Pulling back, he smirked at my no doubt dazed expression and then curved his mouth into a small, sweet smile that made my heart squeeze ridiculously in my chest. God, I was going to miss him so much. Stepping further away he kept me half pinned with his left hand while his right moved to a small cabinet next to us and began to rummage around in the top drawer. The way he kept a grip on me almost made me think he was scared I would run away if he let go of me. Pulling out a pad and a pen, he handed them to me and finally gave me a bit more space.

Glancing at the notepad I sighed, and gave in with a weak smile. 'Fine.' I shook my head, positive that Sean was just trying to make my exit less uncomfortable by requesting my number, but scribbled it down nonetheless. 'I won't hold my breath,' I teased lightly with a limp smile, secretly dying inside. What I wouldn't give to live in a world where we had similar lives and a relationship between us was a possibility.

'I wouldn't if I were you, providing the weather holds so that I can fly out. I'll be filming up in the hills in America so I probably won't have reception, but ...' He paused, reaching out for the phone number, but instead grabbing my wrist and tugging me against him again. 'I will call. Make sure you stay safe until I get back.' A flicker of concern crossed his eyebrows, then he lowered his lips to mine and I found myself helpless to protest as he gave me such a tender goodbye kiss that I'd never, ever forget it.

Chapter Fourteen
Sean

Fuck, fuck, fuck. I flung both of my hands into my hair and dragged them through until I felt several strands ripping out between my fingers. I couldn't believe I'd just let Allie walk away. Scrap that, I couldn't believe she'd *wanted* to walk away. Did she really view the last week as no more than a fling? A fling that had been just *fun*? Had I totally misinterpreted the connection? Or was Allie just hiding her feelings to try and avoid getting hurt? It was this latter that I was clinging to as I watched her give me a fragile smile and wave as she climbed into her car, started it, and pulled off down the driveway.

Pulling out my mobile I hurriedly added her number before I could lose it, only just resisting the temptation to call her immediately. My eyes fell on the now-empty driveway and the ragged holes that Allie's wheels had dug in my immaculate gravel on the day she had arrived. She had obviously spun her tyres so furiously that she'd managed to rip right through the gravel, sand, *and* underlay, so I'd forever have weeds growing through in those areas now. I thought I'd be irritated about the ruined patches – I *should* have been irritated – but for some reason, even they didn't spark a strong enough reaction to pull my thoughts away from Allie's departure.

Breathing in deeply, I stepped back inside, shut the door, and leant back on it before allowing my legs to buckle as I slid down to sit on the floor. Christ, I felt sick. Resting my elbows on my knees I dropped my head forward as I thought back over the last week and the chaos that Allie had unintentionally brought into my life.

As soon as I'd laid eyes on her I had instantly felt an unknown connection, and then when I'd let my guard down

167

and allowed myself to experience her, *really* experience her, it had been totally incredible.

She was exactly what I had been waiting for my entire life, but at the same time the very thing I'd always dreaded. I cared for her, and that frightened me. The experience with Elena had left me terrified of properly falling for someone and letting them down the way I had her, and now here was Allie. She was quite possibly my "someone". She was my perfect woman in every sense of the word; kind, funny, sexy, clever, and seemingly just as affected by me as I was by her, but that just meant that my worst nightmares were all coming true because she'd only just left and already I was panicking about where and how she was.

Jesus, I was a complete mess.

It was then that I noticed a folded piece of paper on the sideboard next to the front door. Frowning, I picked it up, seeing my name on it in unfamiliar, curly lettering. It must be from Allie. Christ, she really had been planning on leaving without saying goodbye. My chest hurt with that thought, and I found myself rubbing it before opening up the paper.

Dear Sean,

You certainly made this a Christmas that I won't easily forget, so thank you. I've left like this, without telling you, because it seemed the easiest option for both of us. We had fun, didn't we? But I didn't want to make it awkward by pretending it was ever going to be more than that.

Thank you for your (eventual) kind hospitality during my stay.

Allie x

Standing up numbly I shook out my arms in an attempt to stop the trembling in my limbs and tried to breathe slowly and calmly to help my rising panic subside.

We had fun, didn't we?

Didn't want to pretend it was ever going to be more than that.

Snorting with disbelief I ran my eyes over her words again. *Thank you for the hospitality*? The fucking hospitality? *That* was what she thanked me for? What about the intense connection between us, the hours spent talking, and confessing my inner fears and deepest secrets? Had that meant nothing to her? It certainly had to me.

I was buzzing with anxious tingles, my whole body vibrating with the need to go after her, grab her, and show her exactly how hospitable I could be. Fuck. Working off my nervous energy I began to prowl around the living room. As I passed the fire I screwed up the note and scrap of paper with her phone number on it and mindlessly tossed them into the flickering flames as I continued to weigh up what the hell I was going to do.

Was I letting lust blind my judgement? Had our week really been just that? A desire fuelled frenzy brought about by the circumstances of our snow-enforced closeness?

The more I thought about her sad, but resolute face just now, the more I began to doubt myself. Perhaps she *was* being the more realistic one – after all, my schedule for the next year was going to be crazy busy, and based mostly in America, which was hardly ideal grounding for a new relationship with a woman based in the Peak District.

Plus there was the differences in our lives; I was always moving around with my career so a relationship would never have been the easiest of rides for her. On top of all that, there was the age gap. I was knocking on forty and she was still young, free, and single. If she got involved with me she'd likely miss out on a calm, stable relationship, kids, and everything else she deserved.

Fuck. This was torturous.

My need to hear her voice was spurring me to call her, so opening my phone I brought up her contact details, but hesitated as my thumb hovered over the call button. After another second of hesitation, I scowled, then pressed my thumb down on the delete button instead, removing Allie's number, and her presence, from my life. It might feel like the worst decision ever, but it was no doubt the best for both of us in the long run.

Chapter Fifteen
Allie

Several weeks had now passed since I'd left Sean's house … two weeks, five days, and twelve hours, to be precise, and I was seriously pissed at myself for pining over him like a schoolgirl with a crush.

Pouring out a bowl of cereal, I slopped some milk on top, managing to get half the carton over my hand in the process as I let out a long, heavy sigh. Rinsing the milk from my hand, I turned off the tap and stared into the garden in a trance. All this moping around was making me sloppy and lethargic. I seriously needed to dig out my spunk, get running again, and re-ignite my usual confidence.

As I expected, Sean hadn't called. Of course he hadn't. He was Sean Phillips' movie star, heartthrob, and all-round sex god – why would he bother to call little ol' me? Despite what he'd said about not being a player anymore, I now firmly believed that I'd been well and truly fooled. No doubt taking a different woman to his bed was such a regular occurrence for him that the lies had slipped easily past his lovely lips. He'd probably forgotten all about me by now. If only the same could be true for me.

Making a dismissive noise with my lips, I rolled my eyes as I corrected my last thought – he'd probably forgotten about me the second he had closed the door and returned to his star-studded life.

After making such a fuss about getting my phone number and then laying me with that stunning, final, melt-worthy kiss, I'd stupidly allowed myself to believe for a while that he actually might call, and as a result had answered my phone with pathetic enthusiasm for at least nine days. But now a cold reality had set in – there was not going to be a call, and now I was simply in the process of trying to get him out of my mind and move on.

Unfortunately, after the few days I'd spent with him, that was quite a lot harder than I had hoped it would be. In fact, he may well have ruined me for other men for quite some time. After all, when you've been with a man as confident, handsome, and intensely passionate as Sean, I suspected that dating a regular guy might turn out to be a bit of a fall down the expectation ladder.

Bloody men. Or more specifically, bloody man. Singular.

Flopping down on the sofa, I began to attack my bowl of cereal as I switched on the television to distract myself, but was instead immediately met with Sean on the screen. Really? So now as well as spending half my time recapping our week together and generally moping over him, I was starting to hallucinate about him too?

Blinking hard to clear my mind, I opened my eyes and looked at the television again, realising that Sean really was there, sat on the *Good Morning Hollywood* couch and talking to the stunning host, Jessica Leighton.

Talking of stunning, he didn't look so bad himself, his arm casually draped along the back of the couch, one long leg bent at the knee and resting on the other, and wearing a navy three-piece suit and white shirt. My stomach clenched at just how gorgeous he was as my eyes greedily ate up his appearance. Unlike the unruly locks I had been used to seeing, his hair had been persuaded into some sort of deliberately ruffled style – no doubt by dozens of delighted, flirtatious make-up girls backstage. His brow was slightly dipped into that serious, intent expression I recognised well, and his chin looked to have at least a day's worth of stubble on it. In short, he looked utterly edible.

Scrabbling to grab the remote and turn the sound up, I heard Sean's low, raspy voice for the first time in weeks and it sent a delicious tingle running down my spine which simultaneously made me want to slap myself around the face for being so pathetic. As much as I wanted to turn the television off, I found myself completely unable to, as I continued to watch enraptured, cradling my forgotten bowl of cereal as it turned to a soggy mush.

Such was my desperation to soak in his image, I realised that I was sat like a goldfish, barely even blinking. It was like I was addicted to him. Sean was my drug, and was proving to be a bloody hard habit to kick. From what Jessica was saying, it seemed Sean was doing some sort of promotional interview for his latest series, but as he finished discussing the plot Jessica leaned in, pouting her cherry red lips and narrowing her perfectly mascaraed eyes seductively.

'So, Sean, any leading lady in your life at the moment?' I knew that as well as fishing for gossip, Jessica was dropping a really unsubtle hint about all the rumours that Sean had a habit of sleeping with his leading ladies. I grimaced as unwelcome images of him in bed with other women flashed in my mind. Would he care for them like he had me? Ensuring they got pleasure as well as him? Washing their hair and drying them off too? Probably. It was no doubt just his usual repertoire. My face crumpled at the thought. I once again remembered his adamant statement to me that he didn't sleep around anymore ... but he was way too good in bed to not be practicing his skills on a *very* regular basis. Bloody liar. Snorting out a dismissive grunt, I scrunched up my face in annoyance at how easily I'd given in to him.

Obviously reading straight through Jessica's line of questioning, Sean gave a rare public smile, but it was the fake almost smirky one he'd first given me, and not the real, dimpled show-stopper that I'd discovered was the true Sean smile. Even though it shouldn't have done, the thought that he wasn't giving Jessica his real smile pleased me immensely.

'Well that would be telling, wouldn't it?' he said with a soft hum, apparently happy to tease.

Jessica looked a little stunned for a second, then disappointed at the immediate lack of gossip. 'That *is* a mysterious answer, Sean, I'm sure there are plenty willing to take the part though.'

Ugh. She was blatantly flirting with him, and I absolutely hated her for it. Leaning forwards, her perfectly manicured fingers touched his knee as she giggled with a flutter of her eyelashes that practically made me gag. God, did she have no shame? Her bright red nails briefly rubbed higher over his trouser-clad thigh, making me glance down at my own hands in distraction. Unlike Jessica's perfect hands I had short, closely-trimmed nails, and the remains of some marker pen on my palms from an art lesson I had taught yesterday. How glamourous. Not. Once again I was reminded of the cavernous gap between famous people like Jessica and Sean and regular folk like me.

Now utterly depressed, I clenched my stupid non-perfect hands into fists and turned my attention back to the screen just in time to see Sean's response to her groping. He had tolerated Jessica's touch for no more than a second or two, before giving a thin, fake smile and discreetly shifting his leg away, which delighted me.

Apparently sensing she should change tack, Jessica sat herself up again and persevered with her questioning. 'When you're not filming, you seem to practically hide yourself away in your big house in the English hills. What's the reason behind that?'

On screen, Sean uncrossed his long legs and shrugged, looking thoroughly bored with the interview and keen for it to finish. 'Movie sets are chaotic places, so when I'm not on one I like peace and quiet.'

Nodding thoughtfully, Jessica leant forwards again, no doubt trying to tempt him into looking at her abundant cleavage which was practically spilling from her low-cut top. To my glee, Sean didn't bite at all, his eyes resolutely set on her face. 'So you haven't got a fair lady hidden away up there who keeps you occupied?' she joked lightly, still doggedly persevering with her trawl for gossip.

Sean seemed to visibly tense, his face looking impassively blank for a few seconds before the fake smile was back on his mouth. 'Afraid not, Jessica.' He paused again, and I watched in fascination as he tilted his head and briefly pursed his lips. 'I did have one recently, but unfortunately, she escaped.'

Jessica paused, looking momentarily stunned, before throwing her head back and laughing. 'Sean, you are so funny!' giggled Jessica, obviously assuming that he was joking, but my breath had caught in my throat at his words. Oh my God. Had that been a comment about me?

At that very moment Sean turned his eyes away from Jessica and looked into the camera. For a second it felt like he was looking directly through the lens and into my eyes, leaving my head reeling and my chest impossibly tight as I struggled to draw in a breath, managing only a pathetic wheeze. He had made no attempt to contact me in the two and a half weeks, so surely that comment had just been an off the cuff remark?

After sitting in confused silence for a moment or two, I let out a frustrated scream, switched the television off, and threw the remote control at the wall, sending a cascade of batteries and shards of plastic flying everywhere and leaving an impressive crack in the plaster.

Bloody bastard. Even when he was thousands of miles away he still managed to haunt me.

In the time I had spent moping last week I'd tried to consider it all logically, and had realised that I barely knew Sean at all, so had come to the conclusion that it must just be the attention and sex I was missing, not the man himself. I mean, realistically, I didn't know anything about Sean at all. Not real, proper, personal stuff; I didn't know his favourite food, colour, or music. I didn't know his idea of a perfect day, or his favourite travel destinations. All I really knew was that he was amazing in bed, could be temperamental, domineering, and sometimes heart meltingly sweet.

Hoping to rectify my brooding singleness, I had arranged a night out with Sarah to try and get back on the horse. Excitingly, even Cait was going to be joining us because her belated Christmas trip to the UK had come about after all. Really, she was travelling from the Far East over to Los Angeles and wanted to break up the flight with a week's touchdown here, but I wasn't going to complain. It had been over a year since the three of us had been out together and I was so excited.

As well as a girly catch up, tonight was my first night out since leaving Sean's house. I obviously wasn't planning on sleeping with anyone – I wasn't usually reckless enough to jump into bed with strangers, that was just the effect Sean had had on me – but I did intend to do some drinking, dancing, and even a little flirting to try and boost my flagging self-confidence.

Determined to put him out of my mind once and for all, I dumped my cereal bowl on the coffee table and stalked upstairs to plan what I would wear for my night out.

After selecting an outfit – my favourite little black dress – I then donned my trainers and decided to burn a few miles by going for a mind cleansing run.

So here I was, sat atop a brown, studded leather bar stool in Monk Cocktail Bar. Earlier, I'd run around the woods until my legs were sore, buried myself in a few hours of school work, and then spent an hour getting myself ready while listening to music loud enough to block out any thoughts of Sean. Sean? Sean who?

Looking around, I smiled. This place was as close to a trendy London bar as you could get around here, and considering I essentially lived in the middle of nowhere, it was an absolute lifesaver and all round awesome find. The bar was one of several properties set within a beautiful old terrace and had exposed brick interiors, quirky furniture, brilliant music, fabulous cocktails, and best of all, a late licence until midnight.

Neither Sarah nor Cait were here yet, running traditionally late as always. Sarah lived close to Cait's parents, so they were coming together, meaning that if Sarah was late – as she was every single time we went out – then Cait would be too. About five minutes ago I'd had a text telling me that Sarah's babysitter – her mum – had just arrived so they were on their way. She'd also asked me to order some drinks for us all before happy hour ended at eight, so after perusing the menu, I absently signalled a barman over.

As he wandered across I gave him a closer look and felt myself flush when he gave me a most stupendous grin and a cheeky wink. Hmm, perhaps I should add "handsome servers" to the list of this place's qualities, because this guy was a real cutie. Sparkling green eyes, dimples in his cheeks, and a contagious grin. Nowhere near as handsome as Sean, but at least there were no scowls or irritated lip pursing in sight.

Blinking away the infiltrating memories of Sean, I forced a smile onto my face and continued my appraisal. His hair was blond, with that deliberately messy look that indicated he probably took hours to perfect it with wax in front of his mirror before leaving the house, and he was wearing jeans, a white shirt open at the neck, and a black waistcoat. All in all, rather nice. And he was young too, probably my age, or perhaps even a year or two younger, which after my recent experience with over-confident, unreliable older men, was just fine by me.

'What can I get you this fine evening?' he asked with a soft, Northern accent and another smile, and for a crazy second I vaguely contemplated replying with 'you', but decided that that was *way* too over the top for me, even if I was supposedly on a drinking, flirting, forgetting-about-Sean mission.

'Three Thyme Sides, please,' I said instead, naming our usual – gin cut with lemon, infused with thyme and some orangey taste that finished it all off perfectly. Let's face it, who cares what's in it if it taste great?

'Three?' he enquired with a tiny narrow of his eyes that told me the he was either interested in me and disappointed that people were joining me, or merely trying to work out if I was attempting to get around the happy hour rule of one drink order per person. 'Are you thirsty or is someone meeting you?'

It was the latter then. Silly me. Clearly my fling with Sean had scrambled my brain so I now imagined that all men who smiled at me were actually interested in me. 'My friends are on their way, they'll only be two minutes.' Nodding, he flashed me a wink, and went about making our drinks as I watched his bottle twirling in admiration.

There was an excited shuffling of high heels to my right and hands landed on both of my shoulders as Sarah greeted me with her usual flamboyant style, and Cait simply rolled her eyes in the background. 'Girls' night out!' Sarah whooped gleefully, and I couldn't help but grin as I slid from my stool and embraced her, then flung my arms around Cait.

'Oh my God, it's so good to see you both. Cait, it feels like it's been ages,' I murmured, feeling tears prick at the back of my eyes as I hugged my friend fiercely. Gosh, I had missed these two so much. With Cait away travelling and Sarah having a business to run and her son to look after, we hardly ever all got together anymore.

'It *has* been ages,' Cait confirmed lightly. 'But you still look gorgeous as ever,' she said with a smile, stepping back and hanging her coat over a bar stool.

Glancing at my friends, I saw Sarah dressed up in a lovely red, sleeveless dress that was tight around her body but flicked out to float just above knee level, a similar length to my own black dress, while Cait was the most formally dressed of the three of us in a pair of black trousers and a pale pink blouse. She looked beautiful, but basically all of her skin was covered – as it always was. An observer might think this was as a result of the cold January weather, but I knew better. Cait never exposed great quantities of skin in public, not ever, because of a particularly traumatic experience with her ex-boyfriend that left her extremely fragile around men.

This careful dressing was one of many protective measures Cait had implemented since Greg the twat, and was one of her ways to try and limit unwanted attention from men. It never worked though, because no matter how many layers of clothes she wore, Cait's beauty always shone through.

'Where do we start? We have so much to catch up on!' Sarah giggled happily as she haphazardly attempted to drag a stool in her huge high heels. She was the most brilliant mum, but bless her, when Sarah got a chance at a night out she was in her absolute element and went full out with outfits, effort, drink consumption, you name it.

'Drinks, and then gossip!' I declared, seeing the barman putting the finishing touches to our drinks. Not that I was planning on sharing *my* gossip ... that was still a bit too fresh and painful, but hearing my friends chat would be great distraction.

'Sounds like a plan,' Cait agreed, picking up the drink being slid toward her by my cute barman, who I noticed she completed blanked by staring at the drink instead. I don't know how she did it. I understood why Cait didn't date, but she never even allowed herself to so much as check out a guy.

Maybe if I had her discipline I wouldn't be in this mess, I thought with a sardonic twist of my lips.

Luckily, Cait distracted me from allowing my thoughts to sink further when she raised her glass and chinked it against mine. 'Well, I don't have any man gossip, obviously,' she said with a subtle roll of her eyes, acknowledging her rigidly single status, 'but I headed across to Laos for Christmas, which was quite an experience. They don't really celebrate Christmas, but it was really hot so we spent a great day going out on a boat with a local fisherman. We swam, helped him pull in his nets, and barbequed the catch on the beach with his family later that day.'

As Christmas experiences go, that must have surely been unforgettable. A niggling feeling settled in my stomach and I had to struggle to keep the smile on my face – spending Christmas Day in bed with a Hollywood star had been pretty unforgettable too.

'Wow. We had a quiet one, just Mum, Dad, gran and gramps, and me and Scott,' Sarah said. 'I was still ill with flu, and by that point poor Scott had caught it too, so it was probably miserable for the rest of family! God, it really hung around, I was ill for a full fortnight.'

'So glad you're well enough to come out tonight,' Cait said, giving Sarah's arm a squeeze as I agreed with a nod.

'What about you, Allie? How was Christmas with Master of the Mansion?' At Cait's words, I practically sprayed out the mouthful of cocktail I'd just sipped, and had to blink wildly to try and clear the bubbles from my nose.

Master of the Mansion? Sean?

Actually, given his large house and preference for intensity and control, it was quite an appropriate description. But, why, oh why, had Cait brought that up? I'd been praying that she had forgotten our phone call, but I suppose being snowed in with a stranger *was* pretty big news. Seeing as I'd spoken to Cait before I knew who Sean was, not to mention before anything had happened physically between us, it was actually quite a lot bigger news than she would be expecting.

Looking at Sarah, I tried to give a nonchalant shrug, but I clearly failed because it turned out all jerky and accompanied by my cheeks rapidly flushing – she didn't know anything about my time with Sean because she'd been too sick to speak to me. We hadn't seen each other since I'd returned home, and seeing as I was trying to forget about Sean, I hadn't bothered to call her and ask for details about him either.

'Master of the Mansion?' Sarah asked in confusion. 'Have you been seeing someone, Allie?'

'Umm ... no. Not really,' I muttered, knowing that my cheeks were the colour of ripe tomatoes as my friends stared at me curiously.

So much for my plan not to talk about Sean. Judging from their expectant faces, there really wasn't going to be any getting away from it. Where to start?

Swallowing hard, I tried to decide what to tell them, but Cait jumped in and started it for me by turning to Sarah and filling her in. 'When I spoke to Allie a few days before Christmas, she was at the big house in the country where you'd asked her to cover that cleaning shift for you.' Biting on my lower lip, I watched as Sarah nodded. 'Well, it had snowed so hard that she'd got stuck there. Just Allie and the owner. Allie described him as 'stunning'. Would that be about right?' Cait asked Sarah, but all I could focus on was the stunned expression on her face.

'You got stuck there? *With Sean*?' she asked in a hushed whisper, to which I nodded a bit shakily. 'How long for?'

'Until Boxing Day,' I whispered, causing her eyes to gape so wide that her expression now screamed "oh my god", even though she appeared stunned into silence.

'Sean? So you found his name out?' Cait asked, sipping her drink with an appreciative hum.

'Yeah ...' I replied, suddenly remembering my irritation with Sarah for not warning me who the owner was. 'That reminds me, missy,' I said, pointing an accusing finger at Sarah's chest. 'You could have bloody well told me who he was! I mean, he's famous for God's sake, a little forewarning would have been nice!'

Sarah blushed, but was still grinning broadly, clearly in her element and loving every minute of my discomfort. *Cow.*

'Famous?' Cait chipped in, looking more and more curious by the second. 'Who is he?' Before I could respond to Cait, Sarah gave a shrug.

'Technically, I wasn't allowed to tell you who he was.' Seeing my continued stare she held her hands up in surrender with a chuckle. 'Calm down, Allie, you're going to blow a gasket! When I got the job I had to sign a confidentiality agreement at the agency to say I wouldn't blab about his address or sell any photographs of his house. But seeing as you met him I guess it doesn't matter if I talk to you about him.'

A confidentiality agreement? Given who he was I suppose it made sense. He hadn't made me sign one when I'd left, though, and he'd not sworn me to secrecy either. Did that mean he trusted me? Or that he'd just forgotten?

'You two are driving me nuts!' Cait suddenly yelped. 'I'm here too, you know! Now will one of you please tell me who the heck this *Sean* guy is?'

'Umm ...' I began vaguely, but paused as I saw Sarah scrabbling in her bag and pulling out her phone. Knowing how much Sarah loved her Google searches, I had a pretty good idea what she was about to do. And then, as expected I watched as she pressed a few buttons and thrust the phone in Cait's face, presumably showing Cait images of my Master of the Mansion. I giggled briefly again, biting on my lower lip.

181

'Not just any old Sean, *this* Sean.' As Sarah squawked at a stunned looking Cait, I closed my eyes and hung my head a little. Just thinking about him had completely squelched any desire I might have had to flirt with anyone else tonight. He was it for me. At least, at the moment he was, although I seriously needed to put some effort on getting him out of my brain because it was pathetic how much of my time was spent thinking about him.

I watched as Cait's face blanched of colour at her recognition of him. 'But that's ... I mean, he's ... famous ... Sean, as in Sean frigging Phillips?' Cait spluttered, sounding and looking about as shell-shocked as I must have done the day I discovered his identity. I could understand her shock. It was rather a lot to take in. I'd still barely absorbed it, and I was the one who had met him and bedded him. I shivered as I remembered just how thorough he had been with me during our last time together, and then sighed heavily.

Oh, God. I had been right earlier – I was ruined for anyone else.

'Yes. I hadn't realised it was him when I spoke to you,' I limply explained to Cait.

'I can't believe you didn't know him straight away! He's famous, Allie!' Cait replied, looking more animated than I'd seen her in a long time.

Nodding in agreement, I sipped my drink. I still couldn't believe I hadn't recognised him quicker. 'I know. I think it was seeing him out of context that threw me. I mean, you never expect to find yourself in the house a famous person, do you?'

'*I* can't believe you didn't tell me!' Sarah shrieked, butting in and waggling an accusing finger at me, the sudden onslaught of attention making me feel defensive and edgy. Not to mention emotional.

'I tried to call you,' I responded snappily. 'But you didn't answer your phone.' I gave a guilty shrug, 'We've not spoken about it since because you were ill, and I've been trying to forget about him.'

'Wow. You got to spend Christmas with Sean Phillips. I think that trumps my fishing trip and beach barbeque,' Cait mused as I desperately tried to think of a way of changing the subject.

'Wait a minute … back up …' Sarah said slowly, her eyes narrowing as she held out a hand to stop Cait from saying anything more, and then turned her beady eyes onto me. 'You said you've been trying to forget him. Why would you need to forget him if you just spent a few days together?' Her eyes were intent now as she watched me carefully, and I tried not to outwardly flinch at her scrutiny. 'Oh my God … something happened between you two, didn't it?' she demanded, making my stomach plunge and taking my shoulders along with it as I dropped my chin onto my chest in defeat.

It just wasn't in my capabilities for me to deny it any longer. I'd hidden the secret for over two weeks now and it was eating me up inside. Sighing heavily, I lifted my head to the curious gazes of my friends and then slowly nodded. 'Yes,' I whispered, my one word answer immediately causing Sarah's eyes to flash with triumph, and Cait's to widen like saucers.

'This calls for more bloody drinks, and then you, young lady …' Sarah said, pointing a finger in my direction, '… are going to fill us in on every single detail.'

'Ugh. I'm not sure I want *every* detail.' Cait said, creasing her face up in mock disgust as Sarah batted her arm and signalled to a barman. 'Shut up, Caitlin. *I* want every detail, even if you don't,' Sarah warned, her use of Cait's full name indicating just how determined she was. Marvellous, I thought dryly. 'Now, you two go and grab that booth over there. Come on, look lively …' She wafted at us with her hands in an impatient "hurry up" gesture, and I rolled my eyes in response. I hadn't seen her this motivated for ages. 'Bums on seats, I'll get the drinks in.'

Obediently following her demands, Cait and I trailed towards the empty booth and slid in, exchanging an amused glance once we were settled. 'You don't look massively happy, so I assume things didn't work out like you wanted?'

Cait asked gently, causing me to cringe and shake my head sadly as she reached out and gave my hand a squeeze. She was always the more tactful of my best friends, bless her. 'You don't have to talk about it if you don't want to, I'm sure we can deflect Sarah,' Cait added with a kind smile.

On one hand, it was probably going to be horrendous talking about my time with Sean, and would no doubt undo all the effort I had been putting into forgetting him, but then on the other side of things, I had been clamming it all up inside me for weeks now and it might be quite cleansing to get it out. Maybe it would help properly kick start my healing process.

In the end, I opted for spewing my entire story in all its ugly glory – right from Sean's initially grouchy ways to our magnetic bond, his incredible lovemaking, and the soft words he'd uttered to me when I'd left and he'd promised to call. I'd finished my story with a screwed up face as I miserably explained how I'd pined for him even though he had never bothered to call.

Throughout my tale my two friends looked on in curious fascination with the occasional sympathetic wince, swear word, or gasp thrown in for good measure. It took exactly twenty-three minutes to dish all the details about my tryst with Sean – and in the end, Sarah really *had* wanted every detail possible, with her even asking me to describe the dimensions of his family jewels. I had declined, of course, merely giving a smug smirk, and saying 'plenty big enough.'

Finishing the dregs of my third drink, I shrugged at them, trying to look nonchalant but probably failing miserably. 'So that's it, really.'

After a second or two of staring at me Sarah gave me sympathetic look. 'You fell for him, didn't you?' she asked softly, causing me to sigh, almost sob, and nod my head once.

'Only a bit,' I lied, meaning *a lot*. 'But I'm a tough cookie, I'll get over it. And hey, at least I can tick "saucy fling with a film star" off my bucket list,' I added, trying to lighten the mood.

'That you can. Wow,' said Sarah, still looking shell shocked. 'I wish I could meet him. I've spoken to him once on the phone and that man has a seriously sexy voice, but every time I've actually been at his place he's been away.'

Typical. Lucky me, being there the one time Sean was home early, I thought bitterly. I honestly wish I'd never met him. As much as I had enjoyed myself with Sean at the time – and I had *really* enjoyed myself – I was now so hurt about it all that I think I would rather have skipped the entire week with him completely.

Seeing my expression, Sarah reached out to squeeze my thigh understandingly. 'Sorry. I didn't mean that. Of course I don't want to meet him after what he's done to you. He sounds like a total shit bag.' That was about as supportive as Sarah could get, so I gave in and smiled at her with an eye roll.

'Whatever, don't worry about it. It's over now. Shall we dance?' I suggested, suddenly feeling the need to expel some nervous energy and get us firmly off the topic of bloody Sean Phillips.

'Yes, yes, yes,' Cait replied enthusiastically, practically dragging me up, which made me laugh, because she never actively chose to dance – or do anything that attracted attention to herself – so this was obviously her way of trying to help put an end to the stressful conversation.

No sooner had we all stood up that Sarah's phone began ringing with her unmistakable siren ringtone. It was a fast, repetitive honking that was so irritating you just had to answer or smash it to pieces. I *hated* it. 'You still have that annoying tone?' I asked with a wince, only just avoiding the temptation to put my fingers in my ears.

'It's the only one I can hear when I'm at work and hovering,' she replied defensively as she dug in her bag looking for it. The tone was loud enough, it couldn't be that hard to find the bloody thing. 'You go and dance. Let me just check this isn't Mum calling about Scott and I'll join you.'

Cait and I nodded and made our way to the small dance floor as Sarah rushed to the exit, still digging in her bag. "Counting Stars" by OneRepublic had just come on the speakers and I grinned and spun towards Cait. 'I love this song!' We began to dance as Cait listened and then shook her head, a blank expression on her face. 'I like it, but I've not heard it before.' Seeing my surprised look she grinned. 'I've been living in a rainforest in Vietnam, Allie, there's not that much chart music to be had over there.'

'Ah. Of course. Well, I have this album, you'll have to have a listen; it's excellent.'

Sarah arrived back a few seconds later, grinning from ear to ear. 'Everything all right with Scott?' I asked.

'Yep, it wasn't my mum,' she said mysteriously, just as the song's chorus came on and she started to jump up and down, grabbing our hands and forcing us to stop talking and join in with her overly exuberant moves. It was all a bit over-the-top for a small bar in Buxton, but I was letting my hair down, so what the hell.

After ten minutes of grooving away to some tunes I was starting to flag. 'I need a drink,' I panted as we practically staggered off the dance floor. Glancing back at the bar, I saw the blond waiter looking in my direction and flushed, finally acknowledging the fact that he'd been watching me dance. If I really wanted to get Sean out of my system, maybe he was the way to do it.

'I think I'll chat with that blond barman, I think he might have been flirting with me earlier,' I murmured, looking away from him with nervously. My mouth might be saying the appropriate things to help me get over Sean, but my stomach was on a completely different wavelength, rebelliously churning at the idea of even talking to another man.

Sarah's brow puckered slightly as she gave me a warning look. 'I don't think that's a good idea Allie. Rushing into something will only make you regret it later, babe, especially if you're still hurting from Sean.'

I was quite tipsy now, and feeling particularly reckless, so I raised my eyes in a dismissive "whatever" gesture. As far as I was concerned, Sean Phillips and his godliness could go to hell. 'Yeah well it's not like I'm ever going to see him again, is it?' I replied huffily, spinning away and making my way to the bar, trying to ignore the fact that she was probably right.

After five minutes talking to the handsome cocktail server, James, I had discovered two things: one, he *was* indeed interested in me, his looks and flirting left me in no doubt of that, and two, Sarah *had* been right. As ridiculous as it was, even talking to James was making my chest tight with guilt, and the thought of actually doing more than that almost made me feel like I was being unfaithful to Sean, which made me stutter like an idiot.

This was beyond stupid. I'm sure Sean was having no such difficulties with the opposite sex since our snowy week together. He'd no doubt warmed his bed with a different girl each night, and yet here I was practically paralysed just talking to another man. Ugh. This train of thought was making me feel distinctly sick what it prompted in my head, so I hastily excused myself from a confused-looking James and went back to the girls.

Returning to our table I flopped down next to Sarah, feeling tired, drunk, and defeated. 'I was right, wasn't I? You're still thinking of Sean?' she asked softly. Puffing out a breath that inflated my cheeks, I nodded glumly.

Despite my obvious distress, Sarah seemed just as jovial as she had after her phone call earlier, which actually irritated me a bit, but led me to assume that it had probably been a man calling her. Sarah was never, ever, short of a date.

I'd been dwelling on Sean for far too long tonight, and I was now starting to feel well and truly miserable, although I suppose that could be down to the copious amounts of gin I'd consumed, and selfishly found that Sarah's giddy state was only making me grumpier. Some friend I was. Mind you, it was getting late now, nearly eleven thirty, so perhaps it was just tiredness setting in.

'One more drink?' I offered, in a gallant attempt at remaining sociable, but in response I saw Sarah check her watch, narrow her eyes, and flash us a glance.

'Actually, it's late, we should probably get off.' Sarah never, *ever*, finished a night before closing time, but I wasn't going to argue, and felt stupidly relieved that I could finally go and sulk in private. After donning our coats, we said a fond goodbye, exchanging tight hugs as we made our way to the pavement outside and the small line of available taxis.

'Allie, I'll see you in Los Angeles!' Cait called, doing a little jig on the pavement with a happy giggle as they jumped into their cab and I got into mine alone. Los Angeles, the city of dreams. I couldn't wait. Maybe I could find a new dream to fill my head while I was over there too, and get rid of the constant images of Sean that filled my mind during the long, dark nights.

Ten minutes after the cab had dropped me home I was showered, changed into my pyjamas, and cradling a mug of decaf tea in my hands as I gazed around my lounge. Stupidly, now I was home I wasn't tired anymore. Just miserable. The excitement of seeing my friends had been dimmed by the quiet emptiness of my house, and as I sat on the sofa with my ears ringing from the silence, I seriously regretted smashing my television remote. My set was old and could only be operated directly from the remote, so as well as being down in the dumps I couldn't even watch television to provide some background noise.

I glanced at my laptop and considered attempting to download something, but it was already late and my connection was dreadfully slow so it would be too late to watch by the time it downloaded. Instead, I popped my tea on the coffee table and wandered over to my bookcase in the hallway, dragging my feet.

If I could read for ten minutes I might just manage to fall asleep on the sofa. It usually did the trick when I was feeling a bit restless. Crouching down on my haunches I began perusing the well-worn spines to see if anything took my fancy. I'd read most of these books at least three times, but perhaps there was something I'd missed. Just as I was about to pull one out, my doorbell rang, making me jump so much that I tumbled sideways and landed in a gasping heap on the floor.

Pulling myself upright I hastily shoved my hair back from my face and frowned at the closed door, suddenly jumpy and nervous. Who on earth could it be at this time of night? Edging myself toward the door as if it were made of some radioactive material, I cautiously leant to peer through the peep hole and then sucked in a fast, shocked breath as I saw the very last person I expected to see.

Sean.

Holey moley and slap me silly … Sean was on my flipping doorstep. All six foot something of him, wearing the same navy suit I'd seen him in this morning on the television, and leaning on the wall beside my door with a broody, weary expression as he stared fixedly at the door.

Stupidly, instinct made me duck away from the peep hole – not that he would have been able to see me through it. My mind went into complete overdrive. Why was he here? Surely that could only be a good thing? Couldn't it? More to the point, *how* was he here, when I'd never given him my address?

Clutching at my chest I squeezed my eyes shut and tried to take an even breath, but failed and ended up almost panting instead. My heart was hammering at my ribs so hard that it actually hurt. Was it possible to have a heart attack from longing? It certainly felt like it.

Gripping the wood of the door, I tried to calm myself before I looked like a completely neurotic mess in front of him. Who was I kidding? I *was* a completely neurotic mess, there would be no hiding it.

After a few more seconds of wheezing and chewing on my lip I gave a short huff and ran my hands over my face. It was no good, I simply couldn't calm myself, but if I crouched here for much longer he'd think I wasn't in and go away.

What if he was already turning to leave?

Panic spurred me into action, and so rising from my ducked position I used a shaky hand to practically rip the chain back and yank the door open as I tried to stomp down the hope that was spiralling in my chest like an out of control Catherine wheel.

The door flew open and bounced against my hallway wall, probably denting the plaster in the process, but I ignored it, my desperate eyes focused straight ahead at the man now stood before me. The frown was back between his dark brows, but it didn't matter–he could be gurning for all I cared; he was here, and that was all my brain and body could focus on.

I didn't care how, or why, he was here, because he was, and it was the most amazing sight I'd ever seen. After standing there staring at each other for several seconds – him, calm and cool, and me less composed as I gaped in open-mouthed shock – I suddenly lost all thoughts of my earlier anger toward him as rational behaviour flew out the door and causing me to fling myself up at him.

Staggering slightly at my sudden attack, a small grunt of surprise left Sean's chest as I wrapped myself around him like an octopus, but he soon recovered his balance, supporting my weight and pressing his face into my hair before taking a long inhale.

My legs twined around his waist, arms wrapped tightly around his shoulders, and I buried my face in his neck, searching for his reassuring scent. Breathing in I got a nose full of smoke and spice, and a hint of clean sweat mixed in, but it was just as good as I remembered. Oh, God. This was amazing. I suddenly felt like I'd come home, which was ironic seeing as we were stood in my own doorway.

Neither of us spoke for several minutes as we both silently seemed to agree that this quiet, entwined moment was completely necessary. Words could come later, all that mattered for me right now was that he was here in my arms and seemed to be embracing me back equally as hard.

I loved him so much.

Blinking over his shoulder at this sudden stark thought I stared into the dark, cold night and bit down hard on my lower lip. God, I did … I actually loved him. Real bone deep, stomach leaping, heart-thumping, all-consuming love. My accelerated breathing started to puff in the air and I wriggled slightly in his arms as the cold, and the shock of my realisation suddenly made me pop with goose pimples all over my body.

Tangling one hand in the long strands of my hair, Sean smoothed it down my back as he continued to breathe close to my ear. I could have sworn he whispered something which sounded distinctly like his old nickname for me – 'My gorgeous girl,' – before he leant back slightly and smiled down at me hopefully, his eyes twinkling and creasing at the corners in that way that I so adored. 'Can I come in? Or have I lost visiting rights by not calling?'

I was so shocked by his presence that I only managed a tiny, spasmodic nod, my tongue simply not responding to my brain at the moment as I struggled to comprehend his appearance.

'You're shivering, so I'm going to take that jerky thing as a nod of agreement and get you inside and out of the cold,' he told me with a minute smile, and I sighed happily as I relaxed against him and let him do his caring thing and carry me across the threshold before toeing the door shut behind us. 'Not that I would have taken no for an answer anyway,' he added jokingly as he shifted me slightly in his arms. An amused snort left my throat at his words. The arrogant bugger. But God, I had missed his handsome face and cock-sure ways.

Once we were inside, Sean slowly lowered me down his body until my feet were on the floor, and began rubbing his palms up and down my arms to warm me. My eyes rolled shut from the pleasure of the contact, my body seeming to come alive again under his touch as our intense connection kicked itself back in gear and had all my senses coming alight.

After a few seconds he stopped rubbing and used a hand to tilt my chin up so our gazes collided and his intense blues sliced through me. My breath left my lungs instantly. The fact that one glance from him could render me so immobile just illustrated how incredibly strong our connection still was.

The power this man had over me really was phenomenal.

Gradually, reality began to seep back into my brain and I suddenly realised that we were still both crammed into my small hallway, so I stood away by the bookcase and flapped an arm in the direction of the lounge. 'Come in properly!' I squeaked. Squeaking? Oh dear, I was definitely flustered. I tried again to breathe in and out a few times and calm myself.

I also seriously needed to try to stop my brain jumping to every conclusion about why Sean might be here, most of which were far-fetched ideas of him being here to sweep me off my feet and beg me to take him back. Mind you, I'd just been hoisted up in his arms, so he'd already done the sweeping me off my feet bit, hadn't he? Although technically *I* threw myself at *him*, so he probably hadn't had too much choice in the matter. Bugger, my brain felt like mush with all these thoughts speeding around it.

'Would you like a drink? Tea? Coffee? Or I've got some wine if you'd like a glass? I don't really drink beer, so I don't think I've got any in …' Now as well as arm-flapping I was babbling like a crazy woman. Crikey, I was so nervous it was a miracle that I was still stood upright.

'Allie.' Sean said my name in a voice so low and firm that I instantly stilled and turned my wide eyes up to him nervously. 'Calm down. We can have a drink later, if you want, but first we need to talk. OK?'

Swallowing loudly, I nodded and turned to lead the way into the lounge. It normally wasn't good news when someone said the dreaded "we need to talk", was it? Oh God, was that why he was here? To dump me officially and make sure I didn't go running to the press with juicy stories of our fling?

Using firm hands on my shoulders, Sean guided my useless body towards the sofa, swivelled me around, and ushered me into a sitting position, before joining me and taking one of my hands. I stared down at our joined fingers, my skin buzzing from the dry warmth of his palm. He was holding my hand. That had to be a good sign, didn't it? Or perhaps it was just to stop me thrashing out and slapping him when he broke bad news to me.

Ugh. Instead of trying to predict the outcome, I tried to clear my mind and just let it play out. Our thighs were touching. My sofa too small to really accommodate both of us, meaning that the heat from his close proximity was now seeping into my skin and reminding me of just how explosively good we had been together.

Unsure of what to do, I clung onto him, my fingers twining with his as I desperately hoped that this wasn't going to be the last time that I saw him.

Sean stared at me for several moments, his eyes sweeping over my face, before he sighed and his shoulders slumped slightly, taking my stomach with them as it plummeted to my boots at his deflated look. 'I am so sorry about these last two weeks,' he murmured grittily, his eyes still lowered to our joined hands. 'I wanted to call you, Allie. Every single day I wanted to. But I was an idiot.' He had wanted to call me? Hope surged inside me, and now, instead of sinking to my boots, my heart was soaring so fast and so high that I felt quite dizzy.

Shaking his head, I watched his lips thin as he chewed them frantically between his teeth. 'When you left my house, you seemed so ... so adamant that what we'd had was just a fling ...' Pausing, he drew in a another ragged breath, his eyes troubled and dark and making me desperate to correct him, to tell him that I'd assumed *he'd* wanted a short fling, which was why I'd left like I did, but my throat was constricted with growing tears and I couldn't speak.

'And then I saw your note, and it was so ... *dismissive.*' Guilt swept over me as his eyes flashed to mine, a glint of annoyance tinting the blue before clouding over again. 'I threw your number in the fire and deleted it from my phone in a fit of anger,' he admitted, looking incredibly sheepish. Wow. I had no idea that my leaving like that would have caused such a reaction in him, but as selfish as it sounded, I was so glad it had, because surely that proved that he also cared for me too?

'I missed you so much,' he suddenly admitted, pinning me with his laser-like eyes. 'After panicking that I had lost all ways to contact you it suddenly occurred to me that you knew Sarah, and I tried to call her, but there was no fucking phone reception on set.' Dragging a hand through his dark hair, Sean dropped his fingers back to encase mine once again, leaving his hair a spiky mess on his head. The urge to arrange it more neatly for him crossed my mind, but there was no way I was going to willingly break the contact of our joined hands – they were like my lifeline, his vitality gradually bringing me back to life. Through our connected skin I could feel the tension brimming inside him, his wrists giving the occasional flick and spasm as him muscles clenched and unclenched.

'I've never been so frustrated in my life, and then filming ran over to nearly two and a half weeks.' Closing his eyes, his grip on my hand tightened until it was almost painful and I winced. 'Not knowing if you were safe was driving me insane,' he muttered under his breath, almost sounding as if he were talking to himself, before opening his eyes and continuing. 'I had an early interview this morning and then I jumped straight on a plane to Manchester. I called Sarah as soon as I landed an hour ago, got your address, and I've literally come straight here from the airport.'

Wow. That was some determination. Not to mention long-haul travel time. All for me.

Suddenly, this made sense of Sarah's earlier phone call and subsequent excitement in the bar. It was Sean who had called her, which was why she'd been so giddy, and also explained why she had insisted we leave when we did, because she knew he was on his way over. She could have warned me! I was wearing penguin pyjamas, for goodness sakes. Penguin. It was hardly the sexiest of looks. If I'd been prepared for his arrival I would have worn something decidedly more revealing and sexy than these old things. I was going to have some serious words with my friend when I next spoke to her.

'All I kept thinking was how I'd said I'd call in a week and then couldn't. I could see in your face when you left that you were sceptical that I'd phone you, so when I wanted to but couldn't, I felt like utter shit. I felt so awful leaving you hanging, Allie, please believe me.' Sean pulled his standard move of shuffling across the sofa so he was right inside my personal space, his body turned sideways so we were as close as our seated position allowed before he used a thumb to gently caress my jaw and lower lip until my eyes fluttered shut and an embarrassingly needy whimper slipped from my mouth.

Our faces were so close we were almost touching, and his warm, minty breath fanned across my skin and making me sigh with pleasure. 'Open your eyes, my gorgeous girl,' he ordered softly, and like the slave to him that I was, I complied immediately. He was really here. I couldn't believe it.

'I haven't been able to stop thinking about you, and I don't just mean the sex ... although that *was* incredible,' he added with one of his characteristically roguish grins which nearly made me swoon on the spot, but then his expression sobered and shook his head. 'But it's you, Allie, just everything about *you* ...'

Everything about me? Blimey. This was a lot to take in. My face must have been a picture by this point as I struggled to comprehend his words. It truly seemed that Sean felt the same way about me as I did about him, which was totally amazing and at the same time as seemingly unbelievable.

I was no doubt gawking at him very unattractively, so I mustered up the energy to close my mouth as I gazed up, not even knowing what to say. These last ten minutes had been completely, astonishingly miraculous, and so many things were swimming around my head that I was struggling to decide what to say first. To be honest, I couldn't quite believe that it was really happening, the only thing stopping me from losing it and completely falling apart into a blubbering wreck was Sean's intense gaze which was locked with mine and keeping me sane.

Clearing his throat, Sean closed his eyes and appeared to wamt to say more, causing me to hold my breath in anticipation. Leaning forwards, he rubbed his nose around mine, a gesture so sweet that I smiled and closed my eyes again. 'I know you were doubtful about us working because of my job, but we *can* work, Allie. I'll make us work, I promise. Can I have a second chance?' A hiccupy, wet sob broke from my throat as I nodded frantically and clasped at his hands desperately.

'I've missed you so much, Sean.' I sniffled back my tears of happiness, hating the way that I always seemed to cry when I was happy. It was so inconvenient, and rather got in the way of deep and meaningful conversations. 'Yes, of course you can have a second chance. Not that you need one, if anything, it's me who should be apologising.' I watched as he frowned, his forehead puckering in the middle and drawing his eyebrows together. Lifting my hand, I smoothed the creases of skin with my thumb, his eyes closing and head pressing into my contact with a small hum of pleasure that made me grin so broadly my cheeks hurt.

'When we were together and things got ...' I blushed, remembering back to our first encounter on his desk, '... more intimate ... I knew I felt something for you,' I whispered, my words causing his eyes to open in surprise as he blinked slowly several times, his penetrating gaze drawing me in. 'The thing was, I kept telling myself that you wouldn't want more, that I would just be an unwanted complication in your busy life.' Sean's mouth opened, presumably to protest, but I laid my finger over his parted lips. 'You're famous, Sean, and our lives are worlds apart, it just didn't seem feasible ...'

Frowning he shook his head. 'But, Allie ...' he began, and I instantly silenced him with a firmer pressure of my finger. He relented and silenced, but the frown that I was so familiar with remained firmly embedded on his handsome face and telling me he wasn't happy with my enforced silence.

'*But ...*' I said, emphasising the word and raising my eyebrows, 'the time we've been apart has been hell. I started to think I'd never get over you, and now like magic you're here telling me you want to be together.' Blowing out a long breath, I smiled at him and pressed my lips to his in a long, chaste kiss. 'It might be tricky with your work, I know that, but I'm willing to try if you are. In fact, I can't think of anything that would make me happier.'

'Thank God,' Sean murmured on a rushed whisper, as his hands slid up to tangle in the hair by my nape. 'We *will* make it work. Fuck the rest of the world. I have to have you. You're mine now,' he growled, causing my chest to squeeze with joy. Clutching at my head, he pulled me forwards to smash his lips down onto mine in a gesture so possessive that I immediately melted into his embrace. I had missed him and his over the top gestures so bloody much.

Leaning back a fraction, Sean ran his fingers through my hair, carefully pulling a section of strands out to the side and examining them with a frown. 'You've cut your hair,' he grumbled irritably, 'I liked it long,' which caused me to laugh loudly, because while I had indeed had it cut last week, I'd only had the split ends off – two inches maximum – and so it was still hanging way down my back and far, far away from being short.

Looking back to my amused expression, Sean ran his gaze across my face and with a soft smile of his own, leant in and gently licked his tongue over my lower lip, which was no doubt swollen from the passion of his previous onslaught. 'I ... I've never said this before, Allie, because I've never felt it, but our time apart made it very clear to me that ...' He swallowed, his thumb moving from my hair to cup my face in his warm palm before he closed his eyes. '... that I've fallen in love with you.'

OK, retract my last statement, because hearing *those* words had made me even happier than I had been.

Sean, however, was unaware of my glee and sighed, still with his eyes squeezed shut and so totally unaware of the goofy grin spreading on my face. He loved me? I felt like jumping up and down and whooping my joy from the rooftop, but he continued before I could even move a single muscle.

'You deserve better than me, but I promise I won't let you down, Allie, I'll keep you safe ...' On his final words his voice cracked, and it made me realise how big a deal this was for him – he'd never dated since the accident with Elena, and now here he was professing his love for me and promising to keep me safe. Holy shit. This was some seriously deep stuff.

We'd only met three weeks ago, was I ready for this? Love and words of forever? It was pretty full on, but when I looked at Sean something just clicked into place. I'd never met anyone like him – with all his eccentric, caring, dominant traits that I adored, and that was before I even considered the explosiveness of our physical connection, which bypassed anything I'd ever experienced or dreamed of having. I loved him too, so much, so there really was no question of whether I would give this a chance or not.

Now that mini panic attack had passed, I slid my hands around his neck and yanked his head down for a desperate kiss.

'I love you too,' I whispered in between kisses, 'I love you, love you, love you.' Each repetition of my words made me grin wider and wider against his mouth until I was almost unable to continue kissing him. Almost, but it would take something pretty monumental to make me stop kissing this incredible man altogether.

Sean let out a groan, which I assumed was from happiness and then, with my lips still practically melded to his I tried to ease his concerns. 'You don't need to be a better person, Sean, just be yourself, that's all I want. Now stop speaking, and show me how much you love me.'

With a growl of approval, Sean stood upright and scooped me into his arms before I'd even realised that I was moving. 'Oh, I can certainly do that,' he murmured in a dark, deliciously promising tone.

'I was going to give you a tour,' I murmured, secretly hoping that he would turn down the tour and just get on with ravishing me.

'A tour can wait. Just tell me where your bedroom is,' he muttered, sounding decidedly impatient and making my pulse leap with desire.

'Up the stairs and at the end of the corridor,' I replied breathily, clutching my hands behind his neck. 'I can walk, you know,' I added with a small smile, remembering back to the last time he had insisted on carrying me.

'I know, but I want to do it,' he replied quietly, using the exact phrase he had used last time. Glancing up at him I found him looking at me with a tiny flicker twitching at the corners of his mouth as though he were remembering the same moment, and I couldn't help but crane my neck up to peck him on the lips.

'What was that for?'

'Just for being you,' I murmured. 'I'm so glad you're here.' My voice cracked as I felt my throat begin to tighten with further tears and gave up speaking in favour of resting my head on his shoulder as he carried me up the stairs and into my bedroom.

Laying me carefully on the bed Sean stood back and began to shrug out of his suit jacket, which even after a full day's travelling was barely creased. 'My flight today was twelve hours, so I need a shower before we reacquaint ourselves properly,' he informed me on a smirk.

I nearly laughed out loud at my hypocrite of a man, because I distinctly remember when he'd abducted me halfway through my gym session on Christmas Day and not allowed me to shower properly before he'd commenced licking me all over – even though I'd practically begged him for a quick rinse. It seemed to be one rule for him and another for me. But I had to say, where Sean was concerned, I didn't care, as I was promptly distracted by the image of him peeling off his white shirt, giving me a first glimpse at his gorgeous chest. And besides, a freshly showered and wet Sean Phillips was one of my favourite sights, so I wouldn't complain at all.

Once he had dispensed with his trousers and boxers – making himself well at home by dumping them in my laundry basket – he turned to me and revealed his beautiful body and impressively erect cock. Gosh, he was *very* pleased to see me, wasn't he? Coming to stand by the side of the bed, Sean held out a hand to me as his eyes glittered. 'Join me.' It was a command that I happily obeyed as I practically jumped from the bed and whipped off my pyjamas in a millisecond. I certainly wouldn't be putting those ratty things back on after my shower, that was for sure. Of all days to pick the penguin pyjamas, I had picked today – talk about embarrassing.

Dragging me back onto the landing, Sean quickly located the bathroom, started the water, and checked the temperature. Stepping into the shower, he pulled me with him, the space suddenly seeming rather small with us both squashed in. Not that either of us seemed to mind; after weeks apart extreme closeness was good. My little walk-in cubicle certainly didn't compare to Sean's gigantic wet room, that was for sure, but at least it was big enough for us both. Just.

Grabbing my shower gel Sean grinned down at me. 'Now, my gorgeous girl, it might be late, but prepare for a sleepless night because you are about to be well and truly worshipped.' My eyebrows shot up as I grinned up at him. Oh goody, a Sean style worshipping session – my favourite.

First an amazing Christmas, and now the start to my New Year was looking pretty good too, and all because I'd covered that cleaning shift for Sarah. Boy, did I owe her big time for getting ill that day!

Chapter Sixteen
Allie

'Rise and shine, baby.'

I was warm, cosy, deliciously sleepy, and wrapped up in a fluffy duvet. Mornings didn't get better than this. If I rolled over, I was pretty sure I could fall back asleep within a minute, which seeing as it was Sunday, seemed a perfect idea. But as I tried to shift my hips I came up against a heavy weight on my stomach. Why couldn't I roll over? My sleepy brain briefly considered following up this issue to find the cause of the weight, but I gave up and relaxed down where I was. No problem. I'd sleep on my back.

Digging my head deeper in the pillow, I sighed contentedly. Bliss. Pure bliss.

Ugh. Actually, no. Not bliss. The heavy weight now extending to my chest was starting to get quite uncomfortable. Peeling open my eyes to investigate, I found two blue pools twinkling down at me, and a lovely stubbly chin surrounding a stupendous grin. 'Good morning sleepyhead.'

A goofy smile immediately broke on my face as I instinctively reached up a hand and slid it in the soft hair at the nape of Sean's neck. It had been a month since his appearance on my doorstep after my girl's night out, but even now I could still barely believe he was really here.

'Morning,' I whispered. Now *this* was the icing on the cake; it was the weekend, and as well as being warm and cosy, I also had my gorgeous man propped over me with a wicked twinkle in his eye.

This pinned position was pretty much how I'd woken up for the past four weeks. Well, every day when he'd stayed over, anyway. All in all, the previous four and a bit weeks had been simply glorious. Working around both of our job commitments we'd managed to spend at least four nights a week together, and the evenings and weekends had basically blurred into one long superb shag fest. Sean's bedroom skills really knew no bounds.

Our lovemaking had, of course, been interspersed with talking, getting to know each other, and a few other boringly mundane activities, like actually having to leave the house to go to work, but overall the month had certainly been great. I'm not sure if the kids in my class noticed the difference in me, but my colleagues certainly did, with several of them commenting on my 'happy glow'.

Sean and I had decided to keep our relationship quiet while we really got to know each other, so I was thankful when my colleagues assumed it was excitement about my upcoming finishing date and travelling plans that had me in a bit of a tizzy, allowing me to stay quiet about the Hollywood star currently residing in my house and throwing my life, and heart, into complete chaos.

As it turned out, Sean was always rather intent on a morning snuggle before I left for work, so I was now almost used to being woken up exactly twenty minutes before my alarm. Not that I complained. It didn't necessarily involve sex. Often he just contented himself with an extended snuggle, although from the brooding look in his eyes this morning, I was fairly certain that sexy time was on the cards. Oh goody.

'Sleep well?' I asked huskily.

Nodding thoughtfully, he began to nudge his thighs in between mine, which as well as spreading me open for him, also removed some of the weight from my chest and stomach and allowing me to draw in a deeper breath. 'Very. I always sleep well with you in my arms.' His over the top declarations hadn't lessened in the last four weeks either, making me feel spoilt for attention and well and truly worshipped.

Smiling like a person crazy in love – which was exactly what I was – I slid both hands to his neck and pulled him down for a kiss. I had only meant it to be a chaste good morning kiss, but as soon as our lips met Sean had moaned into my mouth, plunged his tongue in to twist with mine and ignited into a man well and truly on a mission.

Crikey. What a wake-up call.

Suddenly, his hands and lips were everywhere; tracing along my neck, licking across my collarbone, pinching at my nipples and extending them, tickling down my sides, smoothing across my stomach, and finally, thankfully, cupping between my legs where I was now burning for him. Sean wasted no time sliding a finger into me, before groaning appreciatively and immediately adding a second digit and scissoring them to stretch me for him.

'Oh God, Sean ...' I murmured, as I absorbed the pleasure of his touch and set about my own morning exploration, taking in the broad expanse of his back and the lovely toned muscles of his arms before landing on his firm, delicious arse where I gave a hard squeeze to each cheek, which caused him to thrust his rock solid erection into my thigh.

'You've certainly woken up horny,' I murmured breathily, prompting Sean to suck my nipple into his mouth so hard that I yelped in surprise at the sting, before his head rose from my breast. Instead of seeing the cheeky expression I had expected, however, his brows were drawn into a frown, and he was now pursing his lips. Confused, I felt my gaze settle on the action of his mouth. He only did that when he was thinking or worried, so what on earth did he have on his mind now, midway through foreplay?

'Last day,' he murmured darkly, before his head plunged into the crook of my neck, where he gave a hard suck before resuming his furious kissing and nibbling again and causing me to buck and writhe beneath him.

Last day? Last day of what? But then, like a punch to the gut, it hit me. Last day ... It was our last day together; his filming started in LA next week and he had to fly out this afternoon. Shit. I'd been so drowsy that it hadn't even occurred to me that the date I'd been dreading for so long was actually here. We would be apart for over two months now, until my school term finished in April, and that thought made me tense, my body now stuck in a confusing mix of lusty neediness and sadness as I struggled to wake up and absorb it all.

'Don't,' he growled into my neck, 'Focus on me. Here. Now.' With that he thrust himself up into me so hard that I was jerked up the bed with a scream and left with very little chance to think about anything other than the huge cock now pulsing inside me and the hot, hard man arched over me. God. That felt even better than usual. I had adjusted to him over the weeks we'd been together, but nothing would ever quite prepare me for the delicious stretch when Sean thrust into me with that much vigour.

'So fucking good ...' he murmured, his body stilling as he paused to make sure I was all right – something he still did every single time – his eyes intent and staring straight at me as I panted and clung to his damp shoulders. This always amused me, because he could remove the need to check on me if he just reduced the vigour of his initial thrust, but that ability and control always seemed to escape him in the heat of the moment.

'Don't stop,' I begged, giving a circle of my hips. That was all the invitation Sean needed, because no sooner had I spoken he had pulled his length out right to the tip, where he hovered for several frustrating seconds and building my anticipation to almost painful levels as he held my wiggling hips immobile. I loved it when he was like this, so wild and determined. He could be rough when he was in this type of mood, but I loved that side of him. I needed it just as much as I needed tender Sean. It did, however, require me to fully relax so I could absorb the onslaught of hard, wonderful thrusts that I knew were about to come my way.

Sweat was building on Sean's forehead, and I could see his muscles bunching and twitching as he held himself back. 'Love you, so fucking much,' he grated, before bucking his hips down and crashing into me.

'Fuck!' Instead of returning his sentiment and telling him how much I also loved him, I had yelled. How very nice of me. But there was no time for apologies now; Sean's hips were clashing against mine relentlessly, the sound of groans and skin slapping together filling the air and I actually had to dig my nails into his back and wrap my legs around his waist to try and help me stay attached to him and not get thrust off the side of the bed from his frantic onslaught.

My head fell back, hanging off the side of the mattress, as I rolled my hips in time with his powerful moves, gasps and moans of pleasure escaping my lips as he hit against me in all the right places with each thrust of his talented hips. His lips dived to my neck again, sucking and kissing and licking as he continued to pound into me and drive me on toward a fast-approaching orgasm.

Supporting his weight on one hand, Sean propped himself above me, examining me intently with desire-filled eyes. His chest was heaving with laboured breathing as he continued to drive into me with long, deep lunges as he proceeded to play with one of my nipples, tweaking and rolling it until I was a mass of gasping, pleading flesh below him poised right on the edge of something that felt like it would be distinctly potent.

Giving one final hard twist to my nipple, he buried himself inside me so deeply that I was catapulted over the edge of my climax, stars flying before my eyes as I screamed my release, grasping desperately at his back to try and keep myself from passing out from the pleasure. Holy shit. I felt like I was coming apart from the inside out as my body kept on convulsing tightly around him in wave after wave of blissful pleasure. Barking his appreciation, Sean kicked his hips even deeper within me and came, his cock jerking and jumping within me as I felt his heat searing my insides.

Collapsing onto me, we both lay in a heap of tangled limbs and blankets, panting erratically and clinging to each other as we gradually came down from what had been an exceptionally explosive coupling. Had I said potent? Better upgrade that to earth-shattering, because holy shit, that had been incredible. Sex like I'd never experienced before. Not even with Sean.

After several minutes of silence, I felt Sean shift slightly on top of me. His glorious cock was still nestled inside of me, and to be honest, I could have quite happily stayed here all day. My eyes were still closed, but I knew he was looking at me.

Pulling in a satisfied breath I smiled lazily and opened my eyes to be met by his gaze. Instead of smiling like me, Sean's eyes were regretful, and his lips were once again pursed.

Assuming he was concerned by how rough he'd been, I rubbed at his sweaty back in reassurance and smiled. 'You didn't hurt me, Sean, I'm fine. I loved it. That was incredible.' It really had been. Even with our desperation, it had somehow all seemed so much more intimate than usual.

Blinking several long, slow flutters of his eyelashes, he sighed. 'I'm glad, but that wasn't what I was thinking about.' Concern settled in my stomach as I watched his face twist. He looked so distressed now that I really began to panic. Thinking about it, that sex really had been unlike anything we'd shared before, fraught and full of emotion and I suddenly began to wonder if I had just received a goodbye fuck? Was Sean going to finish with me now that he had to head back to his star studded life?

'Then what's the matter?' I asked timidly, my voice barely more than a whisper.

'I'm so sorry, Allie,' he murmured, wincing, and making me tense all around him. 'I ... I got so carried away that I ... I didn't use a condom.' As much as I should have been stressing out about that, I instantly felt my body relax because at this particular moment in time, him going bare inside me seemed a far more preferable option to being dumped. Shifting myself slightly, I could feel the wetness inside me and realised that this explained the extra intimacy I had felt, and was why I had been able to feel his heat exploding inside me so strongly.

'Oh,' I replied lamely, not entirely sure what else to say.

'Say something. Are you mad at me?' he urged, still looking worried.

What did you say to a question like that? 'Um. No, I'm not mad.' How could I be? It was just as much my responsibility to think about these things as it was his, and I'd also been way too caught up in the moment to even consider it for a second. 'Are you, you know ... clean?' I asked in embarrassment, realising now that this really was a question I should have asked him a long while ago. Like before I'd allowed him to plough himself inside me on his desk, perhaps. Or maybe before he'd bent me over the kitchen counter … hmm, maybe not. Things with Sean had been impulsive from the start. They still were, and as reckless as it was, discussions of sexual health had never really come to my mind.

'I am.' He nodded. I noticed he didn't bother to check about my state of health, not that he needed to. I was definitely clean. 'Are you on the pill?' he asked, his eyes suddenly narrowing as his lips went back to being tortured between his damn teeth. It was a wonder they weren't permanently swollen from the amount of abuse they took.

Was I on the pill? Oh, God. Swallowing hard, I drew in a deep breath. 'No.' I licked my dry lips, watching his reaction and waiting for him to explode with anger. But he didn't, he didn't look distressed by that news at all. In fact, he almost looked … excited. The thought of having children with Sean was actually a very appealing one, but not yet. Crikey, I was twenty-six and we'd only been together for a few months. It was *way* too early for that. 'I got the implant a few years ago, but I'm not sure when it runs out.'

He frowned at this news. 'What do you mean you don't know when it runs out?'

Flushing with embarrassment, I shrugged self-consciously. 'I got it done when I was first teaching, just in case I started dating anyone … but that was a few years back, and then I was too busy with work to bother. I've never had it changed because I wasn't dating, and since things happened with you, well, it all happened so fast that I didn't really think about it.' *Stupid, stupid girl.* I couldn't believe I'd been so reckless with my own body. How long did those bloody things last? Four years? Three? Shorter? I really had no idea, but I must have had it implanted at least four years ago now, so the chances of me being unprotected were surely quite high. Bugger it.

We both lay there, just staring at each other for several long, silent minutes. To my surprise, I felt Sean hardening slightly inside me again, causing me to briefly wonder if he actually liked the idea of me getting pregnant with his baby. I obviously didn't object as much as I had thought earlier either, because I was hardly rushing to get up and try to get his sperm out of myself, was I?

'I can go to the doctors, get it checked, and um … sort it out.' That would be a fun trip to Dr Massey tomorrow. She was one of my mother's best friends. Oh, the joy of living in a small village. Best hope her patient confidentiality skills were firmly in place, because if my mum found out I was requesting the morning after pill, she'd go ballistic at me for being so careless. To be honest, I was quite surprised that Sean wasn't going ballistic at me. He was just staring at me, his eyes impossible to read and his erection now fully hardened and twitching inside of me.

'Will you be OK? Do we need to go to the doctors now?'

Shaking my head, I bit my lip. 'I'll be fine. The doctors are closed today, I'll go tomorrow.'

We lay there in silence again, still with Sean inside me pulsing away distractingly. 'I love being inside you with no barriers,' he murmured suddenly, and I nodded in reply with a small smile – it did feel incredible.

This was all getting very deep though, so before he could say something crazy like "let's have kids," I decided to try to change the subject away from the possibility that right this very second, some of his little swimmers might be crusading their way up my unprotected tubes.

'When I saw you looking so worried, I thought you were going to finish with me,' I murmured quietly, lowering my eyes in embarrassment.

Gripping my chin, he pulled my gaze to his wild, blue eyes. 'Why would I do that?' he demanded harshly, causing me to shrug self-consciously. Pinning me with his intense gaze for a few more seconds, he then clicked his tongue in annoyance. 'Daft girl,' he murmured with an impatient shake of his head. 'You're mine now. No-one is dumping anyone.'

I was his now. Those words made my heart swell with love and relief. Although truthfully, I'd been his from the moment I'd allowed him to take me on his office desk. Even at that early stage I'd known then that I felt more for him than I had with any other man. Biting my lower lip in relief, and to conceal my amusement at just how serious he looked, I nodded solemnly before he placed a loving kiss on my brow and gingerly pulled out of me with a wince before standing up.

I lay there looking up at him, feeling both empty and full at the same time. I couldn't quite get my head around all this. Holding out a hand, I couldn't help but glance down at his erection. It was reddened from our round of sex and glistening with my juices, making it an incredibly erotic sight.

As crazy it seemed after the battering I had just taken, I found that I was more than ready to go again too. Sean however, had other ideas, and after pulling me to a sitting position, swept me into his arms and carried me towards the bathroom. 'Thought I was going to finish with her,' he muttered under his breath, finally causing my smile to escape as I rested my head on his shoulder and let him carry me. I'd given up arguing about how I was perfectly capable of doing this, because it was clear from his dismissive grunts that Sean was not going to be diverted from his routine.

Placing me gently on my feet in front of the sink, he sorted through my bathroom cupboard, looking for something. My gaze drifted towards the mirror, and as I stared at my reflection, I gasped. Love bites. I had reddening patches of skin that looked like they were threatening to bruise on several places across my body; my neck, my shoulder and most shockingly, my breast. My entire right nipple was now surrounded by a ring of red flesh that looked distinctly like teeth marks and I instantly remembered the moment that he had thrust into me and bitten down on my boob. God, it was like some bizarre tribal tattoo.

Choking on a breath that was half laugh, and half disbelief, I stumbled forwards to further examine it as Sean stood up behind me with a bottle of bath foam in his hand. Seeing the direction of my gaze I watched him in the mirror as his eyes dropped to my reflection and his cheeks reddened.

'You've marked me!' I sputtered, gently fingering my nipple and finding that as red as it was, it wasn't actually too sore. Yet.

'Sorry. The thought of leaving you freaked me out a bit.' Sean reached up and rubbed nervously at the back of his neck in agitation, causing me to look across at him in surprise. 'I might have gotten a bit carried away.' I felt my own cheeks redden as I looked at him. Oh God, I'd marked him too. What the hell was wrong with us? My eyes widened as I took in the big scratch marks on the left side of his chest. Oops. Reaching out my hand I traced the marks and grimaced. 'It looks like I did too, sorry.'

Turning to the mirror Sean looked at his chest, tipped his head thoughtfully as he examined my gouge marks, and then used his own hand to press mine flat against his pec right above his heart. 'It's OK. It'll remind me of you. The producer might not be too thrilled though,' he commented mildly, immediately reminding me that next week he's be in front of a camera and occasionally having to film topless scenes. The idea of the female members of the crew drooling all over him made me feel sick to my stomach, but then I chuckled – at least with these claw marks they might realise he was unavailable.

Wow. I was marking my territory, how very possessive of me.

Swivelling towards the bath, Sean bent to turn on the taps and I winced when I saw another set of angry-looking scratch marks on his right shoulder. Sheesh. I really needed to cut my nails. Or perhaps he just needed to tone down the ferocity with which he banged me so I didn't have to grip on so tightly. Ha, who was I kidding? I had loved the forceful way he'd taken me, and so with a roll my eyes I made a mental note to trim my nails after we'd soaked in the tub.

Once the bath was full and bubbly Sean climbed in and wafted his hand to indicate that I should get in and sit between his legs. As I sunk down into the relaxing water, Sean pulled me backwards so I was rested on his chest with my hands laid on his strong thighs, and his arms around my waist.

'Is the water OK? Not too hot?' he murmured by my ear, and I nodded. It was perfect, and I could immediately feel my earlier anxiety about his imminent departure seeping away.

We'd be fine. Of course we would. It was only a few months that we'd be apart.

We soaked for half an hour in companionable silence before Sean encouraged me to sit forwards so he could begin washing my hair for me. I smiled to myself as he began his quiet task, humming to himself happily as he trailed his fingers through my hair repeatedly to lather it up, rinse it, and apply a conditioner. This was still a regular occurrence when Sean was here. He'd insist on washing and drying both my body and hair at every opportunity that he got. At this rate, after another month I'd have completely forgotten how to clean myself.

If Sean had his way I'd never be allowed to wash or brush my own hair, because he really was quite obsessed with it. Especially when it was super long, like it was at the moment. He loved to burrow his face into my neck and inhale, and I frequently woke up to find him stroking it reverently. On more than one occasion he had also twisted great swathes of it around his fists whilst we were making love, which I had to say was incredibly erotic.

Earlier this week, I had finally won one small battle, and I now got to return the bathing favour by loading up Sean's sponge and scrubbing him down, a task I had thoroughly enjoyed. I did the same today, once he had finished tending to me I turned and straddled his lap, taking his sponge and starting to wash across the flat planes of his chest. To be honest, when he lay here willingly for me like this, looking completely content and watching my every move with a small smile, I could totally see why he enjoyed doing it to me, because the satisfaction I gained from such a simple task was immense.

Once we were both squeaky clean and Sean had dried me off thoroughly, we wandered back into the bedroom and began to dress, both of us selecting clothes from the hangers in my wardrobe where Sean now had a section to one side.

Our relationship might still be ridiculously new, but Sean had practically moved himself into my house over the last few weeks. Initially when we'd reunited and knew we would have at least five weeks together before he flew off, Sean had tried to persuade me to stay with him, which I would have loved to, of course, because his house was beautiful, but it was too far for me to travel to school every day. Once I'd told him that I'd only be able to visit him at weekends he had mumbled about it being "completely unacceptable" and had disappeared off in his car, only to arrive back a few hours later with several bags of clothes and belongings from his house. Just like that, he'd moved in. I hadn't really had much say in the matter, not that I had minded.

Once we were dressed, Sean looked at me unhappily and pulled out one of his holdalls with a sad smile. 'I guess I better pack some of this stuff to take with me. Can I leave a few things here?'

'Of course.' My voice was squeaky, my throat already closing up at the thought of him going. I was going to miss him so much. Watching as he folded his smarter clothes to pack, I saw him leave a pile of T-shirts and some jeans in the cupboard. Amongst the clothes being left behind was his favourite "round the house" T-shirt – a slightly faded but much loved Pearl Jam shirt – and I immediately knew that I would be wearing to in bed tonight to help ease the loss of him.

'I'm actually going to have to get going pretty soon, babe, because I need to pop across to my house to pack the rest of my things and get to the airport for four.' He sounded casual and unperturbed by this statement, but I was already missing him, and he hadn't even left yet. Was he not upset by the prospect of two months apart?

'OK.' Once again, my voice was tight with emotion, but this time Sean must have noticed because he turned to me, his own eyes looking a bit glassy, then dropped the holdall from his hand and dragged me into his arms. Ah, this was better. A proper emotional goodbye so I knew I wasn't the only one with wildly out of control feelings. My arms looped tightly around his waist as his face descended into my hair, drawing in a long, deep inhale, before his lips claimed mine in a fiercely hungry kiss that instantly had me melting against him and groaning loudly.

His tongue swept around my mouth with its usual lazy skill, exploring, teasing, and dancing with mine as if he was making sure to get a thorough final touch to remember me by. After well and truly claiming my mouth, Sean leant back and rubbed the tips of our noses together, but I noticed that his eyes were squeezed shut. Perhaps the thought of his imminent departure *was* upsetting him just as much as me.

'God, Allie, I'm going to miss you so fucking much.' His eyes popped open, and seeing his beautiful blues combined with the raw emotion in his voice finally tipped me over the edge as my eyes brimmed over and several tears rolled down my cheeks. Lifting a hand, Sean gently wiped them away with his thumb, a sad smile gracing his lips. 'Hey, no tears, my gorgeous girl. You'll be busy with school, and I'll be hectic with work, so time will fly by. We'll be back together before you know it.'

I really hoped that was true, because he hadn't even left yet and I was already falling apart inside.

Chapter Seventeen
Sean

Forget any ideas of being the strong, confident male in our relationship, it was less than two minutes after leaving Allie's house and I was a complete mess. Banging a hand on the steering wheel in frustration, I winced as my knuckles hit awkwardly and began to throb straight away. At least I had managed to hold it together in front of her, I suppose. She was the one who mattered. She'd been brave about my departure, but seeing those few tears escape from her eyes had nearly killed me.

It was almost impossible for me to comprehend the strength of the bond between Allie and I. I'd never felt anything like it before. Of course I'd experienced attraction, lust, and desire over the years, but this thing with Allie was ... simply all-consuming. A connection so intoxicating that it made me feel and act in ways I never had before. I felt like I was discovering a whole new side to myself, and I was loving every minute of it.

The primal need to care for her and protect her, however, was driving me crazy and starting to make me totally irrational. How could I keep her safe when I was on a whole other continent? I felt my breathing quicken just at the thought, as panic began to seep into my system. Deep down I knew she didn't need me to keep her safe; Allie was an independent, feisty, sensible girl, but there was some deeply ingrained part of me that felt the overwhelming need to do it. Maybe it was lingering thoughts of Elena's accident causing these feelings in me. Or perhaps the age gap making me feel so protective over her?

The stressful thought of being apart from her for so long was almost enough to make me consider hiring someone to keep an eye on her for me ... but Allie would no doubt go ballistic if I did that. It would certainly put my mind at ease, though, so I didn't discount the idea entirely.

Clenching my jaw, I resisted the urge to turn the car around and go back to her, but the further I drove from her house, the more I could feel panic rising inside me, smothering my sensibilities and clouding my vision. Classic panic attack symptoms. Fuck. I hated how feeble I felt when I had these attacks, but I seemed to have no control over them since Allie had walked into my life. No amount of muscles or brawn could cover the fact that I had this incredible weakness where she was concerned.

Pulling the car over to the edge of the road, I flung my head back on the headrest and drew in several deep, long breaths as my fingers rhythmically clenched and unclenched on the steering wheel. I couldn't believe I wouldn't see her again for over two months. That was an absolute eternity. Fuck. I needed to get some control over the way I felt about her, and quick, otherwise I was going to have a complete meltdown at the side of the road and do something insane.

Like quit my job.

My eye brows rose at that thought. It wasn't like I needed the money. The series of action films I'd done over the last five years had made me enough money to easily live on for the rest of my life. I could quit now and never have another financial worry ever again. With the way I felt right now, it was a seriously tempting notion. I wasn't entirely convinced that Allie would be thrilled at having my neurotic arse at her side twenty-four seven though. In fact, I was so completely infatuated by her that I'd probably end up pushing her away with the overwhelming strength of my feelings.

When I looked at it that way, perhaps it was best if I went back to work. I was so out of my depth with regards to how strongly I felt for her that actually, the distance could work in my favour and help me normalise my emotions a bit, level off the way I acted so possessively around her, and set us up for a more stable long-term relationship.

Long-term was good, that was what I wanted. And needed, with Allie.

Nodding my head decisively, I rubbed at my sore knuckles and then rolled my neck to relax the tense muscles bunching there. OK. I could do this, I could leave her in the UK and head off back to America and back to work. It was the right thing to do. Besides, it was only temporary.

As I focused on slowing my breathing I winced as I thought again about the way I had taken her this morning so roughly, and not even with protection. I felt like an utter shit, because truthfully, I had remembered my lack of a condom just before I came, but some crazy, primitive part of me had wanted, no, *needed*, to somehow mark Allie as mine before I left, so I hadn't pulled out. That made me a prize bastard, didn't it? It was fucking crazy the way she made me act. *I* was fucking crazy. God, Allie deserved so much better than me.

Had I wanted to get her pregnant? Wincing, I shook my head and ran a hand through my hair. Maybe. Who knew? I barely felt like my head was screwed on straight anymore. Huffing out a sharp breath, I shook my head, hoping to shake some sense back into me. From her statement of "I'll get it sorted" I assumed she meant the morning after pill, so pregnancy didn't look like it would be a probability. As crazy as it seemed, I couldn't decide how I felt about that.

As much as I wanted to hide away and try to clear my head where Allie was concerned, I couldn't. In fact, if I sat here at the side of the road for much longer, then I'd be in serious danger of missing my flight this afternoon.

Reluctantly starting the car again I pulled out into traffic, still with my mind stuffy and full of images and feelings relating to my girl, but suddenly a scowl fell onto my brows as I thought about my impending trip. First a flight to London where I would kill a few hours and then fourteen plus hours cramped on a fucking plane back to the sun and supposed glitz of LA.

In my early career, I had loved the excitement of days like this; packing up my suitcase and flying off to the glamour and easy living lifestyle that America offered to young actors like me. I literally wanted for nothing when I was there, whatever I requested would be promptly delivered; speciality food, specific made to order, drinks, women … you name it. I could get it if I wanted it. Not that I took advantage of these perks of my job – not anymore, anyway.

As well as flying back to America, I would be travelling back to Savannah Hilton. My co-star, and one of the most demanding women I had ever met in the business. I had no doubt that she frequently took advantage of her famous status, as she was prone to throwing tantrums at the drop of a hat whenever she didn't get her own way.

Seeing as she was also on a constant quest to get me to sleep with her I'm sure she'd be just thrilled to hear that I now had a girlfriend. Sighing, I shook my head and tried to focus on the road ahead. That would be an interesting conversation; that was for sure.

Chapter Eighteen
Allie

I stared at the dark curtains of my bedroom, wondering how long it would be until I could see any faint tinges of morning light seeping through them. Hours probably. I daren't even look at the clock yet. It was probably only one or two o'clock in the morning, which would mean a depressingly long time until I needed to get up. Releasing a long, weary breath, I ran a hand over my face, trying to push away the feeling of exhaustion clinging to my skin.

After Sean had left yesterday I had kept myself busy planning some of my modules for school and had ended up staying up late in the hope that exhaustion might help me sleep. It hadn't. I'd barely slept a wink and was already awake again.

After spending huge amounts of time with Sean over the past four and a bit weeks, I'd quickly become accustomed to his presence in my house, and as a result, yesterday afternoon and evening had seemed eerily quiet, not to mention depressingly snuggle-free. He might be a little over the top with his constant contact and caring, but I already dreadfully missed the attention from Sean. And now, there would be no being woken up twenty minutes before the alarm for a cuddle or sexy time either. All in all my life had gotten rather boring, rather quickly.

Even wearing Sean's T-shirt all afternoon hadn't really helped much, apart from to distract me from work because I kept sniffing at the fabric like some weird scent-obsessed stalker. In bed, I'd continued the trend and buried my face in the pillow he'd used, inhaling the lovely, spicy, smoky smell that remained, but instead of helping me get to sleep it just seemed to remind me of his absence.

Blurgh. This was rubbish. Flopping onto my back I wondered if Sean was having any of the same withdrawal symptoms. Probably not, he was no doubt too busy sliding back into his star-studded lifestyle of cameras, screaming fans, and sunshine. Although, actually, given how long the flight time was, he was probably still on the plane. Sighing, I sat up, finally giving up all attempts at work and decided to get a coffee to drink in bed.

This morning was so early that it really called for an extra pick-me-up, so I opted to grind some fresh beans for my coffee to make it a little more special. Poking my nose into the bag of Columbian beans, I pulled in a deep breath, the familiar smell immediately making me smile. These were the same brand that Sean used, purchased by him last week when my supply had dwindled from the presence of two coffee junkies co-habiting in my little house. As it was Sean's favourite, I knew that it was also going to be the brand I bought from now on.

Once I had brewed and poured my morning coffee kick I climbed back upstairs, snuggled myself against the head board, cradled my mug in my hands, and finally risked a look at the clock.

Five in the morning. Ugh. And it was February half-term this week too, so I didn't even need to get up for work, which was just typical. Unfortunately, it wasn't just missing Sean that was keeping me awake, because although he might be far away for the time being, he had left me with one thing to remind me of him, hadn't he? Which unfortunately meant a very embarrassing trip to the doctors was on the cards for me today.

Grimacing, I sipped my coffee and tried to slow my nervous heartbeat. I couldn't believe that I was going to have to go and get the morning after pill. Just the thought of having to say it out loud to Dr. Massey filled me with dread and made my stomach churn. I'd never needed one in the past, and the thought of having to go today just made me feel careless, stupid, and juvenile. Wasn't this what uneducated drunken teenagers did?

I was getting myself too worked up about it, and could really do with a supportive voice to help calm me, but Sean was on a plane, Cait was back in America, and Sarah probably wasn't even up yet. Doing a brief count I realised that, actually, with the time difference it was only nine at night in LA, so chances were that Cait would still be up.

Grabbing my iPad, I loaded Skype and saw the small green circle next to Cait's name, indicating that she was indeed online. I'm not sure I've ever been so pleased to see a green blob in my life, and wasted no time in pressing the button for video call and shuffling myself more upright.

After an impatient wait while the call tried to connect I finally saw the screen flicker to life as Cait's jerky image appeared on screen, her chestnut hair looking like a wild mass around her face until the screen settled and she came properly into focus.

'Howdy, stranger!' she greeted with a grin that immediately made me feel a bit better. 'I didn't think we were set for a Skype today, but I'll never turn down a chance to chat to my favourite bestie.'

'Hi, babes, no, we weren't, but I've gotten myself in a bit of a pickle and wanted some reassurance.'

Cait frowned, tucked her hair behind her ears, and nodded. 'Hang on, I'm in the communal lounge, let me move somewhere a bit quieter.'

I watched as the video bounced around as Cait and her phone obviously walked somewhere else, before the screen righted itself and I saw her now sat in front of a large bookcase, a look of concern on her pretty face. 'What's up?'

Oh God. Now it had actually come to the point where I had to say it out loud, this call suddenly didn't seem like such a good idea. Maybe I should have used the simple call option, then at least Cait wouldn't have been able to see the flush of mortification now spreading on my cheeks.

'I, um … well … what do you know about the morning after pill?' I blurted.

Watching Cait's eyebrows rising in surprise, I cringed, fully expecting to see a judgemental look on my friend's face, but was almost immediately surprised when she burst out laughing instead. 'Seriously? You're asking *me* this question? The girl who doesn't date?' Joining her in a small smile I immediately realised my mistake. As my best friend, Cait could give me fantastic reassurance and support, but since her experience with Greg the twat she had lived a completely celibate lifestyle, so she was hardly the most knowledgeable when it came to issues relating to sex. To be honest, I'd been so desperate for a friendly face that it hadn't even occurred to me.

'I'm hardly the best person to give advice on contraception, am I?' Cait chuckled, seemingly unfazed by the conversation. Bless her. I totally understood her caginess about dating again, but I also knew that I would hate to live an eternal life of spinsterhood like she was. I was independent and loved my life, but the excitement that meeting Sean had brought to it was indescribable. It made me sad to think that my friend would never allow herself to risk experiencing those types of feelings again.

I also noticed that she didn't dig for any details about why or how I had come to need the morning after pill, which was the typically sweet type of thing that Cait would do. 'What about Sarah? Is she around?'

Absently twirling some hair around my finger, I shrugged. 'I don't know, it's only ten past five here, so I doubt it.' I'd phoned Cait first because even though all three of us were besties, Cait and I had an especially close bond. But she was right, if anyone could give me advice on this subject, it was probably Sarah – she'd been a bit of a wild child as a teenager – so I'd probably have to wait a couple of hours and then give her a call.

Nodding, I watched as Cait narrowed her eyes and shook her head, 'No … wait, it's Monday with you already, isn't it? She had that early contract at the school for half-term so she should be up and at work already. Hang on, let me try adding her to the call.' I watched as Cait's finger appeared in the video feed as she tapped a few buttons on her phone.

'I didn't even know you could have more than one person on a call,' I murmured in surprise.

'Yep, it's like a conference call … I'm just not sure if I can do it while I'm mid call to you. Oh, wait, I think it's working.' Sure enough, a few seconds later my screen split in half, with Cait now on one side and the other half black.

There was a moment of silence, then a ringing tone and a loud huffing noise as Sarah answered, looking decidedly flustered and a little pink in the cheeks. 'Morning. You two are up early.'

'Hi, Sarah. It's evening here, so technically I haven't been to bed yet,' Cait explained with a smile. 'Our bestie has gotten herself into a bit of a pickle and we need your expertise.'

'Oh?' This seemed to get Sarah's attention, and she rapidly seemed to stop whatever she was doing, push some wild strands of hair from her face, and stare into the screen at me expectantly.

'Yeah, I … um … I need to get the morning after pill, but I'm freaking out about it. Can I just go to my regular GP or do I need a family planning clinic?' I blurted. As I expected, Sarah's eyes suddenly twinkled as she grinned at me, her interest in juicy gossip well and truly piqued by my confession.

'What happened? A vigorous rumpy-pumpy with Sean split the condom, did it?' I winced, mortified that I couldn't even use that as the excuse.

'Um … no, Sean was leaving to fly back to America yesterday and we sort of, uh, got a bit carried away with our goodbye.'

'You didn't even use a condom?' Sarah's eyes were wide, and I could tell she was bouncing up and down on her heels as she spoke – the gossip was out, and Sarah was clearly in her element. 'Alexis Shaw, is this where I need to give you the talk about the birds and bees?' she asked gleefully, causing me to glower at her. I hated when she used my full name.

'Shut up, Sarah. I know I was stupid. I just got caught up in the moment.'

Tilting her head, she pursed her lips thoughtfully. 'If I was banging a Hollywood superstar I think I'd probably get caught up in the moment too,' Sarah agreed, nodding sagely, her face completely stoic and serious, causing both myself, and Cait, to splutter out a giggle almost hysterically. I might be laughing, but she was spot on the money. Where it came to Sean, I had absolutely no self-control.

Blowing out a breath, I shrugged. 'I've never had to get the morning after pill before. It's embarrassing, I feel like some cheap slapper.' I whined, sipping at my coffee to try and cover some of my mortification.

'Are you saying I'm a cheap slapper then?' Sarah asked in mock horror. 'Because I've needed it twice in the past.'

Oops. I pursed my lips in a typical Sean gesture and winced – my words had probably come out wrong, but luckily I knew Sarah well enough to know she wouldn't take offence. 'You know that's not what I meant.'

'It's fine. To be honest, I probably *was* a bit of a slapper back then,' Sarah said with a wink. 'Anyway, I need to get back to work. You can usually just get it from the chemist if you have a quick consultation with the pharmacist, or your GP, they'll both be able to sort you out, and don't panic, it happens all the time.'

Don't panic? That was easier said than done, wasn't it? I was a supposedly responsible woman, but had happily allowed my unprotected body to be impaled by my virile whirlwind of a man as he once again swept me up and consumed me before dumping a lovely hot load of sperm inside me. I gave myself a mental slap on the forehead before rolling my eyes. It certainly wouldn't be happening again, that was for sure. Well, it might. I'd rather liked the feel of him skin on skin inside me, but I'd be protected next time because I planned on getting a new implant fitted pronto.

'I'll go the GP then, that way I can book to have my implant renewed.'

'Good idea. You could lie and say you were using a condom but it split,' Cait added helpfully, I could tell from her smile that she was joking, but actually, it wasn't a bad idea. It was certainly preferable to telling Dr Massey the embarrassing truth.

Four hours later and I was sat in the small waiting room of my little doctor's practice. It was times like this when I wished I lived down the road in Buxton, or was at least registered at one of the larger practices there, because explaining this situation to a stranger would be so much easier.

My eyes flicked around the room nervously as I chewed on the inside of my lip, once again cursing myself for my stupidity. Bloody men. They really got an easy ride in life, didn't they? Apart from a few embarrassing erections during their teenage years, what did they really have to deal with later on? Nothing. That's what. Whereas we woman had the joy of periods, the threat of pregnancy, embarrassing doctors' visits when we had been a little careless in bed, and then nine months of being fat and swollen if we did actually decide to have babies. Not to mention giving birth, which looked like an absolute nightmare of stomach splitting gore and pain.

Wasn't I in a fabulous mood today! An ironic chuckle left my lips at my internal feminist rantings and I picked up a magazine to pass the time until my name was called, which as it turned out, was only a few minutes.

Walking into Dr Massey's room I saw her sat at her desk smiling at me, and nervously propped myself on the edge of the seat before returning her smile with a limp one of my own. Dr Massey was in her late fifties, with greying blonde, shoulder length hair, glasses, and a kind, reassuring look that immediately made me want to weep and apologise for my stupidly reckless behaviour.

'Allie, how lovely to see you. It's been quite a while, hasn't it? How are you?'

'Oh, I'm fine, how are you?' *I'm fine?* Where had that come from? I was in the doctor's surgery, speaking to the flipping doctor, of course I wasn't fine. Idiot. I was so nervous I was spouting off random crap again.

'Very well, thank you, pottering along as always,' she replied cheerfully. 'Now, I see you requested an emergency appointment this morning, so what can I help you with?'

Right, small talk was over. Time to get down to the gritty details. Wincing, I just couldn't find the words to request the morning after pill, so instead I chickened out and went down a different route, even though I suspected that I knew the answer I'd get. 'Um, I was wondering when my, uh, my … implant ran out?' God, I couldn't even bring myself to say the word "contraceptive". I was such a chicken.

'You have a contraceptive one?' she asked with a mild frown as she turned to her computer screen.

'Hmmm. Yes.' I was now officially redder than I had ever been in my entire life.

'Well, let's have a look …' clicking her mouse a few times she then raised her eyebrows and looked at me with a surprised expression that I was fully expecting. 'You had it done a little over four years ago, Allie, so you won't have been covered for at least a year. Are you concerned you might be pregnant?'

'God no!' I replied instinctively before realising that, really, she wasn't that far off the mark. 'I mean, I don't think I'm pregnant, I've been using contraception …' Well, that was nearly the truth. *I* hadn't been using contraception, but thankfully, Sean had been on the ball enough to remember it each time. Until yesterday of course.

'… but I did, uh … well, we, I mean …' My tongue was well and truly getting itself twisted now, so with a grimace I gave in and told a little white lie. 'We had a bit of an accident yesterday …'

'I see. Condom split?' she asked knowingly, and like the complete lying wimp that I was, I simply nodded in reply.

'It happens. Don't look so mortified, Allie,' she said with a smile as she tapped a few keys on her computer. 'I assume you're here to get it sorted with the morning after pill? Or are you wanting to discuss your options? Perhaps motherhood is calling?' Motherhood? Options? As in taking my chances and seeing if I was pregnant? *Babies?* Now? God no. Not yet.

'The first one, I'd like the morning after pill,' I blurted, the words suddenly seeming far easier to say. 'It's still quite a new relationship and I don't think either of us are ready to be parents just yet.' Although Sean hadn't looked nearly as petrified at the thought as I'd expected.

'No problem. I'll sort you out a prescription,' she replied, tapping on her keyboard again. 'I didn't know you had a boyfriend,' she mused. Neither did my mother, so I really hope Dr Massey didn't let anything slip at their next dinner party. With Sean and I keeping things on the quiet to avoid media attention at this early stage I hadn't really told anyone except for Sarah and Cait, and they were sworn to secrecy on threat of death if they even so much as opened their mouths on the subject.

'No ... we've only been seeing each other since Christmas, so it's still all quite new,' I whispered, realising just how contradictory my words sounded – it was new, but clearly not new enough that I hadn't let him poke his bits around inside of me on a regular basis.

'My lips are sealed,' Dr Massey said, turning to me with a wink as if she had just read my mind. The relief was immediate and my shoulders slumped slightly as I let out a loud, long exhale. 'Thanks. It's just that it's all quite new and you know what my mum's like; she'll get all excited and start planning a wedding if I so much as mention that I'm a relationship.' She would as well. In fact, I'm fairly sure she's already bought a hat for the occasion, even though I've never had a long enough relationship to warrant it.

Dr Massey actually chuckled. 'Your mother can be a tad keen, yes,' she agreed with a nod and a knowing smile. Lots of mothers dread being a young grandparent, don't they? By my mum is fifty-one and can't wait for me to start sprouting offspring. She's told me numerous times that she wants to be surrounded by grandchildren in her older years, and even went through a hideous *Bridget Jones* style period of trying to set me up on blind dates. I'm only twenty-six, for goodness sake, I'm hardly past it just yet. And as for the hordes of grandkids?

She'll have to reign herself in a bit, because I am certainly not ready for that, as clearly proven by this trip to the doctor.

'Now, if you are in a relationship but not wanting children, may I suggest that you get the implant done again, or perhaps consider a different form of contraception like the pill?'

That sounded a very sensible idea. Nodding my head keenly, I smiled. 'Yes, please, that would be great.'

'OK then.' Fishing around in her desk drawer, Dr Massey pulled out a leaflet and spread it out before me. 'So, do you have any preference?' Scanning my eyes across the page I looked at the options. The pill would be OK, but I wasn't the world's most organised person, so I might forget to take it. I could get another implant, but what if I suddenly did want to have a baby before three years was up? Reading the information I immediately found my answer, as the leaflet stated that my menstrual cycle would return to normal if I chose to have the implant removed at any point. Not that I was considering babies with Sean in the upcoming future, but it was always best to check these things out, wasn't it?

Given the awkwardness of my current situation I was quite surprised when I found myself smiling. The cause of my amusement was the last line in the paragraph about the implant which stated: "The main benefit to the contraceptive implant is that it doesn't require a daily dose and in no way interrupts sex. You can be as spontaneous as you like, with no awkward pauses and fumbling for a condom." Remembering back to Sean's words yesterday as he'd laid there buried deep within me and whispered "I love being bare inside you," I flushed, Sean would absolutely love this method, then. Not to mention that he liked to jump me any place any time, so this would remove the need for him to carry condoms around with him. Yep, this was definitely the perfect option for us.

With a deep breath I looked up at Dr Massey. 'I'll go for the implant again.'

'Spontaneous fella, is he?' she asked with a secret smile that made me splutter and choke out a laugh at just how accurate she was.

'You have no idea,' I replied, as a matching smirk broke on my lips.

'Right then, well, let's sort you out with a prescription for the morning after pill.' After tapping away on the computer for a few seconds, my prescription popped out of the printer and Dr Massey signed it and held it out to me. 'It's best not to get the new implant on the same day as taking this, so take this today and come back in later this week or next week for the new one to be fitted.'

Nodding my agreement, I took the paper from her hand. Seeing as it was my half term I may as well get it done at the end of this week. 'Thank you, I'll make an appointment for Friday, would that be long enough?'

'That would be fine. Let me see if Nurse Sheila is available today to remove the old implant.' She paused to check the diary then looked across at me again. 'OK once you leave me you can pop straight next door and Sheila can whip that old one out for you in a jiffy. Ask her to book you in for Friday.' I stood to leave, but before I had even turned for the door Dr Massey stopped me again. 'Oh, and you'll need to use condoms in the meantime.'

'It's OK, he's away with work for a while now so I won't be seeing him for a bit.' Stupidly, as I said the words my mind latched onto images of Sean and just how much I was going to miss him, and I felt a sudden rush of emotions sweep over me, making my eyes sting and my throat tight. Swallowing hard, I tried my best attempt at a smile. 'Thanks for all your help, Dr Massey. Bye.'

With that, I left to get my old implant removed, which would involve having to get over my irrational dislike for needles, but perhaps would at least focus my mind away from wandering and depressing thoughts about Sean.

Chapter Nineteen
Allie

I was in the kitchen making my first coffee of the day. Probably the first of many, judging from the huge list of jobs I had to get through before school started back. Rays of sun were beginning to stream through the window, highlighting the specks of dust dancing in the air, and would soon be helping my aging central heating to take the chill from the early morning.

Cocking my head to the side, I listened for sound. Any sound. It was too quiet. I'd still not gotten used to Sean being gone, his size alone filled my small rooms, making the place seem busier, and he would sometimes hum when he was feeling particularly content – although when I commented on it he had looked embarrassed and denied it, so it was obviously a subconscious action. I wouldn't mind hearing some of that humming this morning, because it was now day two and I was definitely having some serious withdrawal symptoms.

Yesterday's mortifying trip to the doctor meant that I had now taken the morning after pill – thankfully with no nasty side-effects – and in addition, was also booked in to have a shiny new implant buried in my arm on Friday morning. It was quite ironic, really. Soon I'd be able to have sex and not worry about the risk of pregnancy, but my boyfriend was over six thousand miles away and on a whole other continent. How frustratingly depressing.

As I waited for the percolator to finish with its bubbling and steaming, I thought over my first task of the day – lesson planning for the following week. I normally dreaded my planning days; they tended to be rather tedious and more for the benefit of the government than my actual students, but my

Year Three class had recently started their new topic of the Roman invasion, a subject I also loved, so I was actually looking forward to sorting out the lessons.

I had just topped my large mug of coffee off with milk when I heard a strange warbling noise coming from the lounge – the sound of an incoming Skype call. There were only a handful of people who Skyped me; Cait, Sarah, and now Sean, so with an excited squeal I grabbed my cup and dashed through to the dining table and my laptop, thanking whatever forces had made me turn it on so early this morning.

The screen was flashing with a blue box and eight simple words: 'Video call from Sean Phillips – accept or decline?' which caused me to let out a delighted yelp. As if I would *ever* decline a call from Sean, I thought with a scoffed laugh as I settled on the dining chair, smoothed my wayward bed-hair and clicked 'accept'.

A large black box filled my screen, but disappointingly there was no video feed yet. I could hear shuffling noises, though so I leant closer and cocked my head, 'Sean?'

'Allie, there you are, my gorgeous girl.' He sounded relieved, and I smiled, still amused at how protective he was. When he'd left for LA on Sunday we'd agreed to call or text daily, and Skype once a week on a Saturday as it was convenient for both of us. Seeing as it was Tuesday, he was breaking his own rules already. Not that I was complaining. Although actually, he had probably only just arrived, because in total his travel time had been nearly twenty three hours, including a brief stopover in London.

'I couldn't see you for a second, but it's working now,' he murmured, the low rasp of his voice making my stomach churn with excitement and longing. He really did have the sexiest voice; masculine and gravelly and a huge turn on. Absorbing his fond diminutive, I smiled at how much it warmed me to hear such an intimate name roll from his tongue. Hearing his low tones still made my skin prickle with excitement and I rubbed at my arms with a smile. I hoped he would always have this effect on me. 'Video isn't working on my end yet,' I grumbled. 'Have you just arrived?'

232

'Yep, just got in from the airport. I'm shattered, but I needed to see your face before I went to bed.' *Needed*. I grinned, my chest suddenly feeling warm as his words sunk in – it was such a small thing, but I loved the fact that he had said *needed* instead of *wanted*.

Hearing Sean's voice brought home just how much I already missed him. Depressingly, I knew that his job meant I was going to have to get used to us being apart like this, but seeing as the alternative of not being with him at all was too horrific to even consider, it was an issue I would simply have to get used to. It was crazy, but being apart from him almost seemed to physically pain me if I let myself dwell on it. Which, unfortunately, I had done frequently in the past twenty-four or so hours.

Sighing heavily, I stared at the blank screen, willing it to flicker to life and show me his face. I really shouldn't be missing him this much already – it was less than two days ago that I'd seen him, but I suppose being in the throes of new love could do that to you. But now he was going to be living it up in the sunshine as he prepared for the start of another season filming *LA Blue* whereas I was sat in a typically cold UK February morning. Ugh. I was craving him in my bed again already too, like he really was some kind of drug to me.

'I can hear you, but I still can't see you,' I murmured huffily, staring intently at the endlessly black screen.

A chuckle resonated through the computer, 'I love that little frown you get when you're impatient,' Sean commented; a smile obvious in his tone, but infuriatingly not visible for me to see. Just as I was about to suggest restarting the call to see if it helped the connection, the black box on my screen sputtered to life and Sean's glorious features filled my screen.

A happy sigh slipped from my lips as I greedily soaked up his handsomeness; tousled dark hair, twinkling blue eyes, and what looked like a day's worth of stubble gracing his angular chin.

'I can see you!' I yelped excitedly, immediately realising that I sounded like a hormonal teenager and not a woman in her mid-twenties.

'Hey, baby,' Sean murmured quietly, his eyes softening as he looked at me.

'Hey, you,' I replied huskily. Last night before bed I'd gotten the calendar up on my phone and worked out that in total Sean and I had only known each other for just over nine weeks. Such a short space of time, especially when I considered just how crazily in love with him I was.

It seemed so unfair that we were apart so soon. This should be the honeymoon period of our relationship, where we were both driven by restless excitement and overactive sex drives. Well, we *were* driven by those things, but for the next few months we'd have no outlet for them apart from the phone or Skype screen.

'You look muzzy and cute,' he commented, making my eyebrows rise.

'Muzzy?'

'Yeah. All ruffled and cuddly. I wish I could snuggle up with you now,' he murmured, his eyes narrowing and words making my pulse spike as desire settled in my belly. Thank goodness for Skype. I wasn't sure I could have coped with two months of not seeing his heavy-lidded, desire-filled eyes. The pull between us was just as strong now as it had been we'd met at Christmas. If anything, the searing chemistry between us was growing stronger by the day – we were still explosive in the sheets, our bond stretching way beyond the bedroom and drawing us to each other whenever we were near. In the past weeks that we'd spent together we'd been almost inseparable, a need that was probably fuelled by our knowledge that we would be frequently separated due to his busy work schedule.

I watched his gorgeous face as he recalled the details of his long flight to me. I was just so attracted to him it was almost incomprehensible. Maybe Sean possessed the bad boy gene that women seemed to find so alluring. That might explain it, because he hadn't exactly made the best first impression, had he? Stuck in his snow-bound house he'd been glowering, moody, and hideously bad tempered. Not that that had stopped us being hopelessly attracted to each other.

It was odd to think that we might never have met if it hadn't been for that particularly bad snow storm. I guess fate works in mysterious ways, and seeing as we'd been stuck in his house it was almost inevitable that we would eventually end up in bed together. After we'd had sex on his desk, of course. Oh, and not forgetting the kitchen counter ... My cheeks flushed at the thought.

'How's LA?' I asked, a small pang of concern settling in my stomach as it frequently did when I thought about how far we were set to be for the coming months. Even with Sean's reassurance that I was the one he wanted, I still couldn't understand why he would choose me, not when he had so many more famous and beautiful options available to him on a daily basis. With him set to be flying back and forth between the UK and the US so regularly for work, it made me wonder just how long it would be until someone more exotic would catch his eye.

'Well, I only just arrived, so I haven't seen much apart from the inside of my cab, but it's certainly a fair bit warmer than the UK,' he joked, the corners of his eyes creasing as he broke into one of his gorgeous grins that I couldn't help but reflect. 'I need to get my head around these time differences, it's just gone half eleven at night here, what time is it with you?' he asked, studying his watch as he tried to work it out. I realised that I could see the Los Angeles skyline behind him, buildings illuminated by the twinkling lights from the multitude of windows all nestled before an inky black sky. He must be high up in a hotel, and from the glimpse I was getting now, I bet his view in the daytime was stunning.

Glancing at the corner of my laptop, I checked the clock, 'Half seven in the morning, it's bright, but it was bitterly cold out when I grabbed the post earlier.'

'Make sure you wrap up warm if you go out,' he instructed briskly, completely serious. Bossy boots. I merely rolled my eyes and agreed to his command with a nod and smile. 'I spent most of my flight looking up apartments. I think I found one, I've got an appointment to view it tomorrow.' Sean informed me. *LA Blue* was in its second season, and had become a success almost overnight. Before leaving, Sean had mentioned that instead of living out of a suitcase in a hotel every time he travelled over, he'd decided to invest in an apartment, which made sense especially as I was hoping to be working for myself soon, so I'd be flexible in where I was based and would be able to go and stay with him. God, I hope my writing did take off so I could work for myself. I wasn't sure I could bear the thought of going back to teaching.

'If it turns out to be as perfect as it looks then I'll sign for it immediately. It's got plenty of space, but isn't too big, and it's near enough to work but in a great neighbourhood. The pictures showed some beautiful views, too. If I go for it I'll send you the link so you can have a look. I think you'll love it, Allie. Hopefully I'll have it all sorted by the time you come over.'

He sounded excited, which made me happy, because he'd been really down and stressed when he'd had to leave on Sunday, as had I. He'd been trying to hide it because I'd been such a wreck, but I'd seen the tense, sad expression in his eyes as he'd waved to me from his car. Seeing Sean so insecure was always a surprise. Once he had explained his history with Elena I understood that her sudden death had left him reeling with misplaced guilt, but to see a man that was usually so confident and domineering reduced to a panicky, twitchy shell as he often was around me, was quite unnerving.

'It sounds perfect, Sean, text me and let me know how the viewing goes.' As I watched his handsome face I couldn't help but splurge out my feelings. 'I miss you,' I said in a slightly rushed, pathetic tone. Damn it, I'd been doing so well playing it cool until that point. In reply, Sean frowned and nodded as his lips suddenly took a battering between his teeth. Leaning closer, he raised a hand and I watched as he placed a fingertip on the screen. 'Me too. I wish I could touch you. You have no idea what I'd give to hold you right now, Allie,' he mumbled glumly, his tone matching mine and making me feel much better about the insane feelings I had for him.

I'd fallen fast for this man, and I'd fallen hard, but it seemed that so had Sean. I still couldn't believe he had declared that he loved me after just three weeks. This was certainly a whirlwind romance if ever there was one.

Lifting my own hand, I leaned forward and mirrored his move until our fingertips were lined up on the screen. He smiled fondly, before his eyes darkened and he licked on his lower lip. 'You little tease. You're not wearing a bra.'

Glancing down, I flushed, realising that in my baggy T-shirt I had pretty much just flashed my boobs at him when I'd leant forwards. 'Oops. It's early here, I only just got up.'

'I see that,' he commented, his tone suddenly sounding thick and lusty. 'I also recognise that T-shirt as one of mine,' he commented, making me blush at being caught wearing his clothes. 'Lean forwards again,' he demanded, his face taking on the commanding and intent expression that I loved. He was deadly serious too, I knew that, but there was still a slight twitch at the corners of his lips which gave away his amusement. He loved how I always melted when he used his raspy voice to its full effect.

Giggling at the sudden change in the conversation, I obediently played along and tried to put on my best flirtatious face as I leant forwards, giving my cleavage a helping hand by briefly squeezing my boobs together with my hands. His eyes darted between my face and my chest for several seconds as I watched a blush form on his cheeks. All in all, the effect was rather pleasing; Sean growled, narrowed his eyes, licked his lips, and shifted himself in his seat, apparently getting a little excitable as we shared a heated stare. 'The things I would do if I were there with you …' But his promise faded as his face became frustrated and he threw both hands up to grab at the back of his neck in agitation.

Licking his lips, Sean sighed heavily, an anxious frown landing on his brows and drawing them together. 'I hate being apart like this, Allie. And I don't just mean that I miss the sex. I miss *you*.' My stomach twisted painfully as I looked at his thoroughly dejected face, his blue eyes never leaving mine as they pinned me with an intense stare. 'I wish you were here already.' Running a hand through his hair, he left it spiky and messy, now looking thoroughly dishevelled and even more gorgeous.

'You won't forget to text me every night before you go to bed, will you?' As well as promising frequent texts and phone calls we had also agreed that I would message Sean every night before bed – this was one of his demands to help alleviate his stress over my well-being. 'No, I'll message every night, I promise.' No matter how many times we messaged or spoke though, I knew nothing would be the same as actually being with him.

I suddenly felt stupidly emotional, my eyes filling with tears and my throat tightening. All I wanted was his arms around me.

'Are you OK?' he asked, suddenly looking panicky and shifting in his seat. Nodding, I smiled, trying to reassure him, but I could see from the worry in his face that he'd picked up on my upset.

'Hey, it's all right, gorgeous girl, I'm here.' But that was just the problem wasn't it? He wasn't here. Not next to me where I wanted him to be. Looking uncomfortable, Sean cleared his throat. 'Did you go to the doctor's? Is that why you're upset?'

Pulling in a long, steady breath I composed myself, not wanting to make him feel any more stressed by our separation than he already was. 'I'm OK, really. Just tired. And yes, I did go. I'm all sorted now.'

'OK. I'm … I'm so sorry about Sunday, Allie. I lose my mind around you sometimes. I should have stopped but I couldn't help myself …' he mumbled, looking nervous, but I just gave a small chuckle as my mind flashed back to just how desperate we had both been.

'It's fine, Sean, the feeling was mutual, believe me. Besides, contraception is as much my responsibility as it is yours. When I was at the doctor's I arranged to have my implant replaced, so when we meet up we can …' I paused, suddenly embarrassed that I was about to suggest having sex without condoms. I'd never done that with any of my previous partners. Was it too soon? 'Well, we can, you know, skip the condoms. If you want to of course. But I mean either is fine by me … whatever.' I was babbling, a sure fire indication that I was nervous. Which I was. Incredibly so.

'Allie, calm down. I love that idea.' Glancing down, presumably at his groin, although my view through the screen didn't allow me to see that far down, he then looked at me again, his eyes now heavy-lidded with desire. 'I really love that idea. In fact, you've given me an instant stiffy,' he commented with a laugh, as his hand disappeared from the bottom of the screen as he seemed adjust himself.

'How long until you finish school and fly out?' he asked suddenly, the smile melting from his face and twisting into an impatient look that made me feel warm inside. These constant signs that he seemed to need me as much as I did him both thrilled and reassured me.

The distance and time apart were no doubt going to be both frustrating and exciting. It was horrible knowing we'd be separated, especially when things were still so new, but on the other hand it did keep things quite exhilarating, and I had no doubt that we did finally get back together we would really appreciate it.

And gosh, did being apart ramp up the sexual cravings. Absence certainly did make the heart grow fonder, and the body needier. Sex with Sean had been fiery from the start, but I seemed to be on a constant state of sexual frustration at the moment, desperate for him almost as soon as he'd left me on Sunday. I suspected that the next time we got together we'd barely make it through the front door before we were clawing at each other's clothes frantically. The thought made me warm just thinking about it.

It might only be one more term, but I was dreading every single day of it. 'Eight weeks,' I murmured, thinking miserably that right now, that sounded like an absolute eternity.

Epilogue
Sean

Shifting on the plush leather seat of the limo, I did up the buttons on my tux and sighed as we pulled up into the line of cars waiting outside the dazzling lights of the theatre. Looking out through the darkened windows, I scowled at the enormous crowd that had gathered on this warm evening to watch and cheer us on our arrival. For fuck's sake, it was like we were animals at the zoo or something. Didn't these people have better things to do with their lives than stand on street pavements gawking at us?

Running a hand over my face I tried to lighten up, but it was no good – I was in an absolutely foul mood.

Shaking my head, I knew I should be more appreciative of the fans and press gathered outside. After all, they were the reason that –*LA Blue* had been nominated for three awards tonight; best new drama, best director, and one final nomination for me as best actor. The screaming, clamouring mass of bodies waiting for us to emerge from the car were also responsible for me having the successful career that I did. If they didn't watch and support me, I'd be a nobody, out-of-work actor, this was a fact that I was very well aware of. Nodding decisively, I made a mental effort to smile on the red carpet tonight and sign plenty of autographs.

Even with my decision to be appreciative and receptive tonight there was no getting away from the fact that I disliked events like this immensely. Firstly, watching myself on the big screen seemed way to egotistical for my tastes, and secondly, the fact that I always had to accompany my co-stars to these bloody things really grated on me, especially now that I had Allie back in the UK to think of. No wonder she had been sceptical about my claims that I had been relatively well behaved during my recent career, because the press always had a field day about me and my supposed list of co-star conquests, making sure to snap plenty of pictures of me at these events with any female that I so much dared to speak to.

I'm sure tonight would be no different. Closing my eyes, I lay my head back on the seat and drew in a long breath as I prepared for the circus to begin. Our car shifted one slot closer and stopped again, giving me at least two more minutes of quiet time to prepare myself for the chaos of clamouring journalists and fans. What I wouldn't give to be back in England and snuggled up to my girl. A heavy sigh escaped my chest, and then the next second I felt a soft finger smooth down the line between my brows.

'That's a heavy frown, *darrrling*.'

Savannah Hilton's soft, purring voice broke me from my thoughts and had my eyes snapping open instantly. Blinking, I found her sat close beside me, leaning in and smiling at me flirtatiously as her strong, fragrant perfume filled the air.

Scowling harder, I knocked her hand away from where it was stroking my forehead and tried to shift myself away, which, in the close confines of the car was near impossible.

'Oh, don't be like that, darling. You know the press will want to see us looking loved up, so we may as well make a start now, hmm? We were so good together, weren't we? We could be like that again, Sean, you know we could,' she murmured invitingly.

Instead of rising to her bait, I sighed heavily and turned to look out of the car window again. Savannah and I had worked together for years now, on and off, and we did have some chemistry together, I'd give her that. Physically speaking, she was an attractive woman, any man could see that, but there had never really been enough beyond that to ever tempt me to go further.

Besides, I knew Savannah didn't really want me, not in a relationship sense anyway. She just wanted to sleep with me to add my name to the scores of others she had bedded in the past. Unfortunately, I'd made the mistake of messing around with her one night last year after a drunken awards party. It was long, long before I'd met Allie, and God did I regret that night. As drunken mistakes go, that was one that kept coming back to bite me in the arse. Thankfully, we hadn't actually gone the whole way because I'd been too plastered, but to be honest, if we had she would probably have lost her interest in me by now.

I might have had my time as a wild child where seemingly perfect women like Savannah would have been exactly my type, but my days of playing the field were long over. I knew for sure that Savannah's 'perfect' body and face were, in fact, the result of many small surgeries over the last few years, and I suspected the same was true of the tits that she now had pressed against my arm. She was the perfect woman in the eyes of many men, but not mine.

Lifting a hand, I placed it on her bare shoulder to stop any further advances, scowled, and turned my face away. 'Enough, Savannah. I told you, I have a girlfriend. What we have to do for the crowds is one thing, but what we do in private is completely separate.' I hated the fact that Savannah and I were supposed to put on a façade of closeness for the public. The director loved it, convinced that hints of a romance between his two lead co-stars was a massive boost to ratings, but to me it was just another tiresome side to Hollywood's supposed perfection. I'd prepared Allie as best I could, warning her what it would be like, but God knows what she would make of it all if when she saw the lengths we were supposed to go to.

I loved acting with a passion, but God, did I hate the shit that went along with it.

'It doesn't have to be,' Savannah pouted, her voice bringing me back. 'She'd never find out. England is a long way away, and I can be very discreet.'

Shaking my head in distaste, I was halted from saying any more as our car pulled up to the red carpet. Straightening my back, I smoothed down my suit and wished for the millionth time that Allie was here with me instead of Savannah, and then glanced across at her.

243

'Ready?' I asked briskly, and upon seeing Savannah's eager smile I shook my head warily and frowned at her. 'Behave tonight, Savannah, understand?'

Raising an eyebrow, she scoffed out a laugh. 'You're not the boss of me, Sean. Besides, surely you remember how naughty I could be in the bedroom, so why on earth would you expect me to behave now?' With that, she pushed open the door and slid out to the sound of the crowd erupting. Fucking hell, this woman was such a liability. If she wasn't such a good actress I would have demanded a re-cast and asked our director, Finlay Mark, to get rid of her.

Once Savannah was out of the car, I drew in a calming breath, wishing I could slam the door and instruct the driver to whisk me away. But I couldn't. As much as I wanted to escape, I was contractually obliged to attend these events, and so after attempting to paste a vague smile on my lips, I climbed from the car.

There were several seconds of fans erupting into a screaming cacophony of voices, and then I was temporarily blinded from the light of a multitude of cameras all going off. Gradually my ears and eyes adjusted, and I blinked to see Savannah waiting for me with an expectant look on her face and her hand held out to me.

Staring at her outstretched hand, I drew in a slow breath through my nose and lowered my eyes to pretend I was fiddling with the buttons of my suit. I was going to look unbelievably rude ignoring her gesture like this, but it was all I could think to do. Sidestepping her, I paused a little further down the red carpet and saw from the corner of my eye Savannah drop her hand on an irritated huff before she began to swagger her way towards me.

As much as I wanted to run, I couldn't, so I simply tensed my body and stared out at the crowds with a small, thin smile on my lips instead. I felt Savannah stopping by my side and continued to stare intently forwards, hoping she would follow my lead and give up on her quest to get me to touch her.

My eyes were forward, but I could see her gazing up at me. Predictably, I then felt one of her hands slide into the crook of my arm as she leant in close and lifted her face near my ear. Finally looking down at her, I found her in her element, smiling resplendently at the gathered journalists and waving with her free hand with gusto. Stiffening my arm, I discreetly attempted to disengage her hand but felt her grip tighten as she flashed me a narrow eyed smirk. She was doing this deliberately, just like the diva she was.

My body was rigid with annoyance and worry. If Allie saw pictures of me like this, she would go ballistic.

'You can't escape me forever, Sean,' Savannah murmured in my ear. Tensing my entire body, I endured a few minutes of pausing for some photographs and then went to shift myself away, only to find Savannah lifting her spare hand and placing in firmly on my chest, her fingers sliding underneath the lapel of my jacket out of view of the cameras and curling so they dug into my skin almost ferociously.

Anger ricocheted through me. What a fucking cunning bitch! We were supposed to pose for a few pictures together, and then could separately the rest of the way, but Savannah was gripping me so tightly now that the only way I could free myself would be to forcefully shove her away from me, no doubt causing a scene, which I was far too much of a gentleman to do. A fact that Savannah was no doubt fully aware of.

'Finlay will be very angry with you if you don't play along,' she murmured, referring to our the stupid clause our director had in our contracts – as much as I hated it, public shows of physical contact between Savannah and I were something else I was contractually obliged to do, a stupid scheme concocted only recently by Savannah and Finlay to keep the fans happy. Needless to say, it was a clause which made me decidedly *unhappy*.

Plastering a decidedly fake smile on my face, I was inwardly seething at her behaviour, while simultaneously panicking about what Allie would make of it if she saw any pictures on the internet or in gossip magazines next week. I'd have to call her tomorrow and explain, which seeing as she was already worried about my job and the differences in our lifestyles, wasn't a conversation I was particularly relishing.

'Smile, darling,' Savannah whispered as she slid her hand down to mine and interlocked our fingers as we began to trail up the red carpet. Flinching away from her breathy whisper, my scowl was well and truly in place as flashbulbs continued to pop around us and I began to practically drag her up the remainder of the carpet and towards the theatre doors. At least once we were inside away from the prying eyes of the fans and press I could stop this ridiculous pretence and get some space.

My eyes fell on a journalist to my left who was snapping pictures of us while his colleague furiously scribbled some notes on his pad and I shook my head, my heart sinking. No doubt the papers would be full of pictures of us hand in hand, followed by more regurgitated bullshit stories about me and my heartless conquests.

It hadn't always been like this. Back when I was a newbie, the papers had looked upon me in a much more favourable light. Then the stories had been about the handsome newcomer to Hollywood, the boyish chap who wooed interviewers with his easy banter and won over tough directors with his effortless skill and dedication to the job. But then the accident with Elena happened, and I withdrew into my shell, becoming snappy with journalists pushing for details and twitchy and irritable in front of crowds. Overnight, the press had gone from loving me to being out for my blood. That's how easy it was to lose favour in this town, and unfortunately for me, I'd never managed to win it back.

As I turned warily toward Savannah, I watched as her perfect face, perfect hair, and perfect mouth began moving towards mine as her warmth and perfume once again invaded my senses and my personal space. The crowd were chanting and cheering us, begging for a kiss, their voices drowning out practically every other sound around me. It would be easy enough to allow her to get her way … I was a hot blooded male, she was undeniably beautiful with a stunning body to match, and the producer would no doubt love the extra attention it would get the show.

As I considered this, Savannah's hand slid lower, her fingertips dipping just inside the belt at my waist and rubbing in a way that had my cock responding against my wishes as it gave a small twitch of interest. Christ, if she kept on like that I would be stood on the red carpet rocking a hard-on. Sliding her arm around my waist, Savannah leaned into me so her lips were hovering by my ear. 'Come on, Sean, just one quick kiss? For the cameras, hmm?'

Thank you for reading!

What will Sean do? Will his lifestyle pull him apart from Allie and their new found relationship? Or are they strong enough to survive the oppressive nature of Hollywood?

Find out in Unravelled, part two of the Revealed series, when Allie ventures across to America, due out February 2016 If you've read my previous series you will know I am a bit of a fan of a cliff hanger ending, but don't panic, I have worked hard with the publishers on this series to ensure there will only be minimal gaps between release dates.

I write for my readers, so I'd love to hear your thoughts, feel free get in touch with me:
E-mail: aliceraineauthor@gmail.com
Twitter: @AliceRaine1
Facebook: www.facebook.com/alice.raineauthor
Website: www.aliceraineauthor.com

When I write about my characters and scenes, I have certain images in my head. I've created a Pinterest page with these images in case you are curious. You can find it at http://www.pinterest.com/alice3083/

You will also find some teaser pics for upcoming books to whet your appetite!

Alice x

Cariad Titles

For more information about **Alice Raine**

and other **Accent Press** titles

please visit

www.accentpress.co.uk